THIEF OF SOULS

ORDER OF THE ELEMENTS: BOOK ONE

EMMA L. ADAMS

This book was written, produced and edited in the UK, where some spelling, grammar and word usage will vary from US English.

Copyright © 2020 Emma L. Adams
All rights reserved.

To be notified when Emma L. Adams's next novel is released and get a free prequel short story, sign up to her author newsletter.

PREFACE

The magically gifted have always lived among us.

After centuries of living in hiding, a group of mages banded together and created their own parallel world to the everyday one, a paradise designed as a home for the magically inclined. Mages, vampires, elves, shapeshifters and many others flocked there, and for centuries, they flourished, ruled over by the Council of the Elements.

Then, several decades ago, the spirit mages turned on their fellow Elements and slaughtered them. The resulting war brought an end to the old Council of the Elements and left the magical world in ruins.

Since then, it has remained fractured. Clans of shapeshifters, vampires, and others rule the cities, while the Court of the Dead dominates the areas even the bravest fear to tread. It may be a paradise no longer, but to many of the magically inclined, it's still home.

Welcome to the Parallel.

1

———

If there was one guarantee in my life, it was that I'd always end up visiting the swamplands of the dead the day after I'd bought new shoes. I wouldn't say there was ever a *good* time to set foot in a place where magic had scorched away all life and left only the dead behind, but the swampy water surged up to my ankles within two steps and drenched my new boots in the smell of death. Silently mourning my last payment bonus, I sidestepped the skeletal remains of some poor creature which had breathed its last here and continued north into the Death King's domain.

Over one shoulder, I carried the backpack I always took with me on missions to the Parallel, which contained a few snack bars, a bottle of water, a change of clothes, a first-aid kit, a couple of spare cantrips, and my bag of dice. Not only were they useful as a diversion, they made good weapons, too, mostly because of the element of surprise. Nobody expects to get knocked out cold by a D20.

I also carried several cantrips inside the pouch at my waist, coin-shaped magical constructs designed for paralysing foes or otherwise incapacitating them, and one for water-breathing in case I ended up having to go for a swim in the swamp. There's positive thinking and there's practical thinking, and I prefer to bet on the latter.

The swamplands had never looked appealing even at the height of the Elements' power. Small wonder, really, considering they surrounded the Death King's home, and nobody in their right mind would build their house on the doorstep of the most infamous lich around. Skeletal trees rose from the murky ground, their branches twisting up to the pale grey sky, while the only other signs of life were poisonous flowers and twisting vines that choked the life from any living creature foolish enough to stray too close.

Each step heightened the risk of meeting the same fate myself, but if I didn't find this thief, I'd fall one rung down the ladder of the Order of the Elements' retrieval unit and find it twice as hard to claw my way back up again. Truth be told, I wasn't so much on the career ladder as in the career basement, but I was decent at my job, and with any luck, a better thief than the dude I'd been sent to steal from. I kept both eyes open as I trekked across the marshy ground, searching for any signs of a hidden sanctuary amid the gloomy surroundings.

"Don't go that way," said Dex. "If you take one more step, you'll end up elbows-deep in swamp water."

"And you'd know?"

Dex was a fire sprite—a spirit with no substantial form —which made him lucky enough to be able to fly over the swamp rather than trekking through it. These days, elemental sprites were even rarer than their human counterparts, but I'd rescued him from the cage of an unscrupulous trader a few years back, and he'd repaid me by annoying the shit out of me and saving my life in equal measures.

My feet sank into deeper water, which surged right up to my knees and into my boots. My durable coat might be waterproof, but the clothes underneath weren't water-resistant. *Great.*

"Told you so." Dex hummed around my head, a cloud of fiery magic forming the vague shape of a person.

I rolled my eyes at him, withdrawing my soaked leg from the swamp. "Why don't you make yourself useful and scout ahead to find our thief's hideout?"

"There's no hideouts in here," he said. "This place is murkier than an Element's morals."

"Ha." I prodded the ground with my toe to find a steadier route to cross the swamp, and then trod forward. "I'm assuming even thieves with a death wish would need a roof over their heads while they count their treasures."

Why anyone would choose to hide out in a place like this was beyond me, but the Order's report claimed the guy had been seen fleeing the Death King's guards and disappearing somewhere in the lands surrounding his territory. By all accounts, he hadn't been seen to reach the city, which meant he must still be hiding out here in the swampland with his hoard.

"Swamp, swamp and more swamp." Dex used his fingers to mimic a pair of binoculars, peering around us. "If you ask me, the poor soul got himself torn to shreds by a pack of wights."

"If he had, the Order wouldn't have bothered sending me to chase him."

Cold air blew across the swampland, bringing the scent of decay and the reminder of the array of deathless monsters living out here. How the Death King could stand it, I hadn't a clue, but then again, he was rumoured to be worse than all the other monsters put together. *And here I am, walking up to his doorstep.*

Not to the castle itself, of course. In the distance, the dark shape of the Death King's home stood etched against the grey-white sky, a veritable fortress even without the undead army guarding its walls. Immortal death lords enjoyed a different existence to the rest of us, to say the least.

I halted on a rise slightly above the rest of the swamp. "He's got to be somewhere on the outskirts. No way is he within sniffing distance of the liches."

Like their king, liches were created by removing a soul from a person's body and storing it inside an object—which as far as I was concerned was glaring example of a fate worse than death. The rumours said that a fair proportion of his army had been turned into liches as a punishment from the Death King for straying too close to his territory, which was a fair reason to call it quits and return to searching the city.

My skin prickled as I passed close to a node at the crest of a hill, one of the natural wellsprings of magical energy that linked the Parallel to the ordinary world from whence it had sprung. Almost invisible to the non-magical, the node glimmered like a beacon of shimmering light, surging up to the sky. The temptation seized me to jump through the node back to the world on the other side—the world of central heating and D&D campaigns, not swampland and soul-eating phantoms—but the Order would tear me a new one if they found out I'd shirked my duty. Besides, I couldn't afford to skip out on the substantial bonus I'd get for returning the thief's haul to the Order's office.

I sidestepped the node, and a different glimmer entirely caught my eye. If I tilted my head to the side, the outline of a hut appeared on an island in the middle of the swamp, as faint as a mirage. "I think I found our thief."

He'd used an illusion cantrip to hide it—a good one, too—turning the hut entirely invisible to the naked eye. Either a chameleon charm or a straight-up reflective spell, I'd reckon. Devon would know.

Most practitioners could have seen through the illusion, even the likes of me, so it must have been placed there to drive off the dead. Smart play, considering the only living people for miles were the Death King's four personal Elemental Soldiers, and they rarely left his castle except on serious business. A petty thief hiding in the swamp wasn't worth their consideration.

I scanned the hut, looking out for traps. If any spell lay over the hut which couldn't be countered by any of the cantrips I had on me, I'd end up in a bind, but at least I knew where the thief was hiding.

"What're you waiting for?" asked Dex.

"Checking our thief hasn't booby trapped the place." I stepped forward. "We can't all be bodiless spirits, you know."

Dex frequently boasted that he was indestructible, but I wasn't clear on whether he'd ever been alive to begin with. Even the Order didn't know much about sprites. Unlike phantoms, he had a personality. More so than the liches, from what I'd seen, though it didn't help that they all *looked* the same. My heart jumped into my throat when a large shadow passed over the swampland behind the hut, but it was just a cloud of insects, not a lich.

"You worry too much."

"I have good reason to." I was well aware of my limitations, but the Order had insisted I come here alone, and refusing the Order was more foolish than stealing from the dead. I already had one permanent black mark on my record. "Okay. I'm going in."

I trod closer, fingering my bag of lucky dice, and pulled out a D20. Then I flicked it at the door. A pinging noise sounded, and the hut appeared from nowhere, a dilapidated shed with a sloping roof. Stooping low, I retrieved the die and returned it to my pouch.

"Roll for initiative..."

I peered through the single murky window to see who lurked within. Nobody, by the looks of things. I sidestepped and found the wooden door closed, but not locked. I pushed it inwards, halting on the threshold.

"Perception check," I muttered. "What's lurking in there?"

"Your eyesight is shit," Dex said.

He was dead right on that one. At the moment, my contacts were enhanced by a cantrip that gave me better eyesight than I had back in the regular world, but the hut was pitch-dark.

I stepped forward into the gloom, my shoulders tensed. The general musty scent of the swampland masked all magical signatures, which was probably why the thief had escaped notice, yet it struck me suspicious that I hadn't triggered any traps yet.

My gaze pinpointed a mud-coloured disc inside a square-shaped frame on the carpet, a thin chain looped through a hole drilled into its edge. That was more like it. I eased a thin bone-coloured wire from my belt and gently poked it into the square. One of Devon's creations, the wire could bypass most magical fields, but it took several attempts to hook the end of the wire around the hole in the tip of the amulet and lift it into the air. If the thief interrupted me now, I wouldn't be amused, but where'd he disappeared to, foraging for mushrooms? This wasn't exactly a practical hideout unless one already had supplies. Nothing much lived in the waters. The swamp-lands of death weren't designed to support the living.

On the other hand, the amulet looked valuable. If he'd stayed in the city, he'd have likely had the thing snatched off him the instant he set foot there. This place deterred trespassers by reputation alone.

I lifted the wire out of the circle and my hand closed around the disc, my fingers skimming its cold metal exterior. Lightweight as a cantrip, it sure didn't look worth risking the wrath of the Death King.

A faint breeze whispered against my neck as the hut door opened with a distinct wooden creak. Then a skeletal hand reached over my head, latching onto the end of the amulet. I tugged, hard, and a bony fist hit me in the face, sending me stumbling back a step.

And our intrepid adventurer rolls a critical failure and gets clubbed in the face. Wincing, I tugged back at the amulet, locking my free hand around the creature's wasted wrist. A wight. I was losing a tug-of-war with a skull-faced beast with the strength of a gnat. If Devon found out, I would never live this down.

Dex laughed in my ear. "Want me to help?"

"Spare my dignity." I gave one firm tug and managed to wrench the amulet from the skeletal beast's grip. "Let's get outta here."

You can't kill what's already dead, so running was my only option. Luckily, I'm a better runner than a fighter. I looped the amulet's chain around my neck and ran, swamp water splashing into my boots. My feet pounded on the ground, while I tucked the amulet into the neckline of my coat and skidded to a halt at the sight of a tall, heavyset male figure ahead of me.

So much for getting out of here without a major confrontation.

The thief wore a long durable coat and boots. His pockmarked face bore the scars of someone who'd lived in the Parallel long enough for the magical charge in the air to leave its permanent marks on him. Most people here had fallen on hard times since the war.

I folded my arms across my chest, one hand easing open the pouch at my belt. "Move or regret it. Your choice."

The swamp water stirred beneath my feet, swirling in circles. *Oh damn.* He wasn't a practitioner, but a full-blown mage. Muddy water surged to the surface around his boots, swirling in dark circles. If I wasn't careful, I'd need that water-breathing cantrip after all.

With swift fingers, I eased one of the coin-shaped discs from my pouch and flicked it at him. Then I ran like hell as the paralysing cantrip's blast went off, sending swamp water spraying in all directions. The thief shouted in fury, but I didn't look back to see if I'd hit my target accurately. My feet splashed in the water, then my right heel caught on something solid and hard. I caught my balance against a frail tree trunk and launched into a run again. I had to get out of—oh, *shit.*

The sharp points of a tall pair of obsidian gates loomed overhead. Somehow—no doubt via a confusion cantrip hidden beneath my feet—the swamp had turned me around, sending me running *towards* the Death King's castle instead of away from it. I should have guessed the thief would have hidden a few more traps around his hideout, and now, the dark shape of the Death King's castle stood closer than I'd ever seen before. It was pure luck that I hadn't run into any guards. There wasn't *exactly* a sign on the gates saying 'Trespassers will be stripped of their souls', but it was implied. To escape, I needed to get around my pursuer... who I'd just blown up with a cantrip. Great one, Liv.

The gates creaked inward, and I flung myself into the bushes, crouching low. Not a moment too soon. Two figures rode out into the swamp, their horses black and skeletal. Dead steeds for dead riders. *Now* I was screwed. Not only did the Death King have a castle, he also held an army to defend it. Two more figures followed the first pair, equally imposing and wearing armour straight out of a fantasy movie. As they drew closer to my hiding place, I glimpsed the insignia on each soldier's coat: a coat of arms signalling all four types of magic: fire, water, earth and air. The skull in the centre of the symbol represented the Death King himself. A little on the nose, but subtlety was not in the guy's forte. One of the soldiers gave a restless glance around, their eyes visible through a slit in their helmet. Human eyes.

Oh, damn. The four Elemental Soldiers themselves were out on patrol.

I remained still, my heart thudding, unable to believe my monumentally shitty luck. If the Elemental Soldiers were after the thief, then I was in real trouble if they figured out that I'd swiped his hoard. *They can't be. Surely.* I'd genuinely thought the Death King would have zero interest in petty thieves hiding in his swamp. Why send all four of his best soldiers to fight against a single thief, anyway?

The little magic I had was useless in this situation, and I had nothing more than the few cantrips in the pouch at my waist. There was no escaping this without a miracle. I sent a silent curse to Dirk Alban, wherever he'd ended up after his death. If he hadn't sought me out as a naïve student and taught me forbidden magic, I wouldn't have a black mark on my record, and I certainly wouldn't be staring down my own death beneath the skeletal hooves of the Death King's soldiers. Let's just say my old mentor's decision had backfired on him in a very literal sense, but I'd lived to reap the consequences of his actions. He hadn't.

The gates shuddered to a halt. The four figures rode past the bushes without looking at my hiding place, but before I could release the breath trapped in my chest, a fifth figure joined the others. Like them, the soldier rode a skeletal horse, and wore a long hooded dark cloak in the same style as the others. My gaze panned from the newcomer to the other four Elemental Soldiers, wondering who the fifth rider was. Their hooded cloaks were well-made, the insides dyed with their designated colour. Red for fire, green for air, blue for water, brown for earth. And black for—fuck my life. Was that the *Death King* himself on patrol with his soldiers?

Most people said he never left his castle, but the moment he rode past the bush, I knew my guess was right. Nobody else wore that armour, dark and moulded to his form as though made of living shadow, along with a black mask that obscured his features. Rumour told that nobody had ever seen his real face, but most of us suspected nothing lay beneath the mask at all. As the king of the liches, he hadn't been alive in a very long time.

The King of the Dead himself was inches away from me, riding a skeletal horse that hardly seemed to touch the swampy ground. A chill wind followed in his wake, sweeping through the gates and rendering my body frozen. I couldn't have moved if I wanted to—and I most definitely did not want to. *I'm dead. I'm so dead.*

Yet the soldiers were passing without slowing, without stopping, without looking back. I hardly dared breathe, my knees screaming with the pain of my hunched position. When the five of them were far enough away for me to risk breathing, I whispered, "Dex."

The fire sprite stirred at my side. "Yes?"

"I need your help." My heart hammered a wild beat against my ribcage, and if the rumours were true that the Death King could sense life and snuff it out, I was doomed. But there was one more target in the area. "Can you throw some sparks around over by our thieving friend? If you keep their attention over there until I can slip around them and get to the node, I might get out of this alive."

The other node lay within sight, but in an area of unbroken swampland. If I went that way, the five riders would spot me in an instant. I'd need to create a massive diversion to stand a chance of getting out of here as it was. The good news was, being a nuisance and a distraction was Dex's speciality.

Dex flitted out of sight, and a few tense seconds later, lights sparked above the thief's hut. The Death King's soldiers veered that way, and I eased a cantrip into my hand, counting down the seconds.

At the unmistakeable sound of the water mage's frantic scream, I ran out across the swamp. Vulnerability scraped me to the bone as I ran; no landmarks tall enough to hide me stood between me and the horsemen. They said the Death King could remove a man's soul from his body with a touch. Not a fate I'd wish on anyone, but rather the thief than me.

I ran, flat-out, my feet tearing at the swampy earth. The thief's screams rang out behind me, but I didn't look back. A tugging sensation propelled me towards the node. I was damned close. *I have to make it.*

A familiar tree drew my sight, and I halted with a gasp. *Here it is.* I'd made it to the crossing-over point, the node through which I'd entered the Parallel to begin with. I ran up to the tree and removed my weapons. Knives, cantrips — I thrust them into the hole in the side of the hollow tree so nobody would steal them when I was gone. Carrying any kind of weapons, magical or otherwise, wasn't allowed on the other side of the node. Cantrips weren't banned, per se, but I lived in perpetual fear of the Order showing up on Devon's doorstep and shutting down her business. Best to leave all evidence of her experimental magic behind. As for the amulet, my permit ought to be enough to cover anything I'd taken from the thief.

I reached the spot where the node rose to the sky like a fountain from the core of the earth. My heart surged against my ribs like a tidal wave, my blood thundering in my veins. Showing up at the Order covered in mud would not be wise, so I'd need to head home first, which was miles from the spot where this node overlapped with the real world. In theory, though, any node in the Parallel could connect with any on the other side. If you knew where they were.

"Come on." I tensed, feeling the buzz in my fingertips from the node, and pictured the image of my home as clearly as I could. "I'd like to go home at some point this century, please."

Magic roared through my veins. Then the node caught me, and I was gone.

2

When the elemental war came to a close, the Order of the Elements had held a vote on whether to open up access to the Parallel from Earth, or leave the paths closed forever. They compensated by making it legal to cross only if one carried a permit. Without one, you'd run the risk of ending up with half the Order's forces on your tail the instant you landed on Earth.

As for crossing the other way around... if you rejected the Order, you were welcome to go and put your talents to use in the Parallel, as long as you didn't come back.

No matter how many times I made the crossing, it never ceased to be terrifying beyond measure, exhilarating beyond comparison, and when you experienced it once, you never wanted it to end. The air rushed through my lungs, my hair streamed behind me, and my body soared through nothingness as though free falling from a ten-thousand-feet height.

Then the fall came to an end, and I landed on soft carpet in the back room behind Devon's shop.

"Holy shit, Liv." My best friend stood before me, her jeans and checked shirt drenched with the swamp water I'd unintentionally brought along with me. Her short punky hair was electric blue today, courtesy of one of the cantrips she wore on a string around her neck.

"Sorry." I squelched along the carpet, my once-pristine new boots trailing water and mud. "I had to run through the middle of the swamp. The Death King's people nearly rode me into the ground."

I shoved a handful of hair out of my eyes before any droplets got into my contacts. Like Devon, I kept it cut short, but ordinary brown instead of multi-coloured. With the amount of time I spent hunting thieves, it was better to be inconspicuous.

"I'd have more sympathy if you weren't dripping swamp water all over my floor," she said. "Did you at least get what you went for?"

"Yes." I removed the amulet from around my neck. "The Order had better give me my money for this thing on schedule."

"I hope so, considering I lost my keys again and you just wrecked my game board."

Oops. I'd interrupted her in the middle of preparing for a D&D session, and judging by the soggy cardboard covering the table, our intrepid party would be taking a detour through the swamp after all.

"Sorry." I shrugged out of my coat. "If I showed up at the Order's base dripping swamp water everywhere, they'd throw me out on my arse."

"And you're sure I won't do the same?" Her tone

carried a teasing hint. Devon wouldn't really throw me out. She just didn't handle surprise soakings particularly well.

The two of us had lived in the same shared house since we'd left the Order's academy, so six years was a long time to get used to one another's idiosyncrasies. I tolerated her hoarding habits and tendency to lose everything that wasn't glued down, while she bore my penchant for bringing weird shit back from missions. Luckily the swamp water had only hit the cardboard props and not the TV and games consoles. They might be second-hand, but we'd saved every penny for them.

"I hope not, or nobody would be able to find your keys." I crouched down, and sure enough, the keys lay under the armchair. I held them up and tossed them to Devon, who caught them in one hand. "There."

She shot a grin at me. "Just testing you."

"Uh-huh." I walked out of the back room and hung my coat up in the hallway to dry off. My new boots would need a wash before I could wear them again, so I left them in the hall before heading upstairs to change into clean clothes. I also switched my contacts for glasses, wishing I had time to shower. I'd have preferred to wait until tomorrow to hand over the amulet, too, but thieves and beggars can't be choosers.

If only the Order's ridiculous rules didn't prevent me from using the nodes to travel there via the Parallel instead of taking the bus. While I couldn't see the node connecting the two realms from this side, I'd be lying if I said it hadn't been a factor when we'd chosen to rent this house. Devon found it easier to make her cantrips on top of a node, too, but she also made her living selling charms to Order personnel, which made it doubly important that we stayed on their good side. Practitioners like her had to stay here and stick to the rules, or else go to the Parallel and stick to *their* rules. The Parallel came with magic, but the UK came with modern conveniences like transport and the NHS and no monsters in the basement. You know, the essentials.

When I got back downstairs, I found Devon had already cleaned up the swamp water. I updated her on the full story while I stuck my boots in the dryer and found some clean shoes. By the time I'd finished, she was shaking her head. "The Order might have warned you you'd be up against a full-on water mage."

"Since when did they give a shit?" I said. "The Death King, I didn't see coming. No clue what he was doing wandering about with his entire contingent of Elements like a bunch of Ringwraiths sniffing out nasty hobbitses."

"He wasn't looking for that thief, was he?" she asked.

"Petty thieves are beneath him," I said. "But I made it his problem when I sent the thief running in his direction. Only way I could get him off my back, but damn if I don't feel kinda sorry for the guy."

She grimaced. "How rare is this amulet?"

"Rare enough that the thief thought he'd be safer hiding out on the Death King's doorstep than the alternative." An effective strategy… until the man himself had left his castle, that is. It'd struck me as weird that he'd take the risk, but what did the King of the Dead have to fear from a single rogue mage? Liches like him gained their immortality by using magic off-limits to the rest of us, and he didn't need to fear anyone invading his territory or stealing his castle.

He didn't need to worry about the Order's hands whisking the memories from his head if he overstepped his mark.

"INCOMING!" roared the doorbell, making both of us jump. Since Devon had a tendency to get so wrapped up in her work that she sometimes didn't even notice customers come in, we'd installed a custom doorbell that was guaranteed to catch her attention, but at times like this, I wished she'd picked something quieter. "Expecting someone?"

Devon groaned. "Why are they always *early?*"

"Who…" I trailed off. "It's D&D night."

And I had to go to the bloody Order. They'd find me if I didn't, especially as half our group was in their employment. Resigned, I headed through the door leading into the shop which formed the other half of our livelihood. Cantrips filled most of the shelves, each made of a rare metal found only in the Parallel and inscribed with symbols by one of the pointed instruments lying on the desk. I yanked open the door and found myself face to face with my ex-boyfriend—Brant, the fire mage.

He hadn't changed much during our time apart. Clearing six feet tall, he filled out his dark coat, dark stubble dotted his square jaw, while his blue eyes held the same intensity as ever. I stared open-mouthed for a very long two seconds, and then slammed the door in his face. Then I rotated to face Devon. "You invited *him* to our D&D night?"

"Yeah, why? We're open to newbies."

"I thought I said no elemental mages," I said. "Don't you remember the incident with the water mage who rolled a natural one, got killed by a giant, and wrecked the plumbing in protest?"

Devon rolled her eyes. "Yeah, yeah."

"We were dealing with flooding and busted pipes for a solid month afterwards," I reminded her. "No mages."

"I couldn't just throw him out. He wants to talk to you."

"He made his feelings clear last time we spoke. Since when was he even back in town? Also, since when did he play?"

Most of our group consisted of regular old practitioners, like Devon. Those who lived in the Parallel were too busy playing with literal fire to be bothered with us mere mortals. Brant must have a permit from the Order to be here and I'd bet it didn't cover gaming night, but that didn't make me happy to see him again.

Devon nudged me. "Liv, I'll have to open the door when the other players show up. I'm guessing he'll stick around until I let him in?"

"Probably." Brant was as stubborn as a wight when he was on a mission. "Fine, but I'm gonna have to run. I need to get this amulet to the Order before it gets dark outside."

Devon leaned past me and opened the door. "Hey, Brant. You're early."

What the hell is going on? Devon let anyone come to our D&D nights, true, but the guy had screwed me over, as she knew well. He gave me an apologetic look as he entered, but I side-stepped him without catching his gaze, despite the tugging sensation in the pit of my stomach.

"I'm off to the Order," I told him. "Mission to report on, rare magical artefact to get off my hands. Have fun."

Then I ducked out into the cold evening. I heard him calling my name, but I was already striding to the bus stop.

You'd think a magical organisation would have an easier way to get there without having to use public transport, but it was that or drive through rush-hour traffic. Weirdos always sat next to me on the bus or train, perhaps sensing a kindred spirit. I had to listen to an old lady telling me all about her family's medical issues for a solid twenty minutes while a teen's phone blared nightclub music from the back row.

My relief at getting off the bus faded at the sight of the office block which housed Birmingham's branch of the Order. Most people thought it belonged to an exclusive club, thanks to the security guards on duty 24/7. The Order pulled all kinds of tricks to make ordinary people overlook their magical neighbours, but if anyone noticed the stream of odd people walking in and out of the place, they didn't comment. Most mages and practitioners could only make real use of their powers in the Parallel, and with magic dampened on this side of the nodes, nobody would have a clue of our real nature.

The security guard at the doors scanned my ID and took a moment to linger on the visible black mark imprinted on the edge. Since I'd been underage when my mentor and I had been caught practising spirit magic, I'd been stripped of just my memories, not my magic, but the Order didn't screw around. Three strikes and you were out. Thankfully, the guard moved aside to let me through the double doors into the reception area without further comment.

Order employees milled around the lobby, some

wearing ordinary work clothes, others dressed in the more durable attire suited for the Parallel's unpredictable climate. Two carried a large cage between them which emitted a series of bizarre cawing noises, while a small group of shapeshifters conversed in hushed whispers as they made for the corridor at the far end. As a low-grade employee, I hadn't ever set eyes on the upper floors, and the retrieval unit was practically in the basement. I had zero desire to get stuck in one of the notoriously temperamental elevators, so I took the stairs instead.

My footsteps echoed on the concrete steps, my old boots pinching my feet. I didn't know why I thought spending my payment bonus on new shoes doomed to be ruined on the first day wouldn't backfire on me. I might as well have just bought a new anime figurine from eBay instead. Silence filled the cold basement aside from the occasional clicking sound from where a kid with greasy red hair sat behind the computer, a bored expression on his face. Only a broke student trying to earn some extra cash would be here on a Friday evening.

"Hey there," I said to him. "Got an artefact for you. An amulet."

He tapped some keys on the computer, squinting at the screen. "There's no amulet on today's list."

"It's under 'Cartwright'." The kid must be new. He'd hear about me soon enough, no doubt—if not at the academy, then as soon as he graduated and joined the Order full-time. The joys of being a walking cautionary tale.

"Olivia Cartwright." He looked from me to the screen with his brow furrowed. "Is it true that you killed an Order employee?"

"No, it isn't, but that's irrelevant." I held out the amulet by its chain. "Found it?"

"No… there's nothing on here about an amulet," he said, not sounding like he cared either way. "You're on the rota for a retrieval job today."

"Yes, and this is what I found." I dropped the amulet on the desk. "Believe me, I wouldn't have set foot in the swamplands on a lark."

"The swamplands?" He dragged his gaze from the computer screen, his eyes going wide. "You went *there?* Did you meet the Death King?"

Yes. Kind of. He almost trampled me to death, actually.

"Of course not. I was chasing a thief who set up a safe house there with his hoard."

"I'll take your word for it." He regarded the amulet with an expression of reverence. "Nobody in their right mind would ever set foot near *his* place. You're brave."

"I didn't have a choice." I didn't particularly want to chat about it with a kid who'd probably never even set foot in the Parallel yet. They didn't start on that in the academy until after graduation to avoid calls from concerned parents, which would explain what he was doing slumming here in the basement to earn cash. Being one of the Order's retrievers was the lowest possible place for an academy graduate to end up.

"Is it a punishment?" Now the kid sounded frightened. "For lawbreaking?"

"No, it isn't." My punishment had ended when they took my memories, in theory. "It's because I'm unqualified for a higher job. Look up my exam results and you'll see why. So, if you ever wanted an incentive to study…"

The colour drained from his face. "Oh."

As it turned out, having one's short-term memory

temporarily rendered useless does not help with retaining information, and the resulting chain reaction had ricocheted all the way through my entire school experience. Whole chunks were just… gone. I hadn't been able to relearn years of education in mere weeks, and it took four years for my memory to return to functioning normally. By then, I'd had to drop out and take a cleaning job at the Order's HQ, which involved vacuuming up far more werewolf hair than I'd have liked. Eventually, they'd decided they could make use of my thieving skills, and to be perfectly honest, I wasn't sure I'd picked the better option.

"I'm sure you'll do fine." I pushed the amulet across the desk. "Anyway, this is all I got from the thief."

"Is that a skull on it?" He held up the amulet under the light to examine the surface.

"Looks that way," I said. "It's always skulls or occult symbols. Really, you'd think someone would try carving unicorns or flowers onto their amulets for a little variety."

He gave an uncertain laugh, his fingers clutching the amulet. "I'll put this away."

As I left the room, I heard a mouse clicking and his attention became more focused on the screen. Probably watching porn or something. Whatever. We all did what we could to get through the day.

Is it true that you killed an Order employee? That was a new one, and I thought I'd heard them all by now. The rumour mill spun on, even all these years later, and I could count on one hand the number of people who'd cared to hear my side of the story. My parents were not among them, though it wasn't really their fault. Like anyone born into a non-magical family, I was only allowed to share certain details, and mentioning the Parallel to the non-magical was as frowned upon as shapeshifting in public. Dad thought I worked in an office and certainly didn't know I stole from criminals more often than I saw a computer screen, and since he lived in Manchester, it was easier to keep up the ruse. Mum knew a little more, but she'd just got engaged to Elise when everything had blown up and I didn't want to crash their wedding plans by casually bringing up the fact that I might have permanent brain damage from having two years of memories yanked out of me by the Order.

In the end, the damage hadn't been permanent. The after-effects were a different story.

Once again, I climbed the stairs into the Order's lobby. The two guys carrying the cage had gone, while Mrs Carlisle, head of the retrieval unit, stood in conversation with a harried-looking receptionist. I strode to the doors to avoid catching her gaze and walked out into the street.

"Hey, Cartwright," a voice called from behind me.

I wheeled around. "Name's Liv. Nobody calls one another by their last names anymore."

That habit alone told me he was one of my peers from the academy. He was tall, dark-haired, and decently good-looking, and I had absolutely no idea who he was. I prodded my memory to see if I could dredge up his face from the years I was missing, but I drew a blank.

"I wondered if you wanted to head out and get a drink," he said. "My shift just finished, and I'm guessing yours did, too."

"I'm a retriever." Might as well get one of my shameful secrets out of the way early on.

"I know," he said. "I know you probably don't

remember me, but we knew one another at the academy. Wanna catch up?"

On the one hand, I hated missing D&D night. On the other, I'd happily take another stint in the swamp to avoid talking to Brant again. The guy was cute. Why not go for it?

One of these days I'll learn to listen to my instincts.

———

"Why," I said, "do my dates always turn out to be trying to fuck around with my missing memories?"

"Because you attract weirdos?" Devon hunched over the keyboard of her gaming PC, hammering away at the keys.

"Thanks." I sighed, kicking off my shoes and sinking my sore feet into the carpet.

And it'd started so well, considering my low expectations. At least until I'd tried asking a few questions about how we'd known one another at the academy, which sparked a memory of him ambushing me a week after the mind-wipe and trying to convince me that we were dating. It might have been convincing if a dozen guys hadn't tried the exact same thing. I couldn't look him in the eye after I remembered, so I'd made my excuses and left for home.

By now, the rest of our D&D group had departed, leaving a sea of takeout containers and crumbs behind. I'd missed all the fun, but I'd also missed another painful trip down memory lane with Brant, so I had that going for me.

"There's always Craig," said Devon. "He was asking after you."

I rolled my eyes. "You could replace me with a pair of boobs on a stick and he'd still flirt with it."

She cracked up laughing. "You're not wrong. So, who'd you meet?"

"Someone from the academy." I pulled a face. "Took me too long to remember he was one of the dickheads who claimed we were dating after... you know."

"Dickhead," she said. "Don't let the bastards get you down."

"No, but I really didn't need the reminder." Following the mind-wipe, I'd spent so much time dodging guys out to take advantage of my vulnerable state that I'd eventually started dating one of them just to shut the rumours up. But if anything, capitulating had only encouraged the others. Nowadays, being a nerd was cool, at least in certain circles, and being quirky and different didn't result in being treated like a pariah. Unless, that is, you crossed an invisible line and ended up in the category of 'just plain weird', as Devon put it, and to most people, magically induced amnesia was one of those lines.

"Could be worse," she said. "Carter asked me out."

"Carter?" I said. "He knows you're not into romance, right?"

Devon rarely noticed when people hit on her, but the last time a guy called her 'quirky', she'd hit him with a cantrip that made him smell of a sewer for a week. She'd once described her sexuality as "slightly less interested than in watching paint dry" and ranked romance even lower. She didn't mind helping other people with their relationship drama, though, and if I ever needed a bucket of common sense in the face, I'd ask her opinion.

"Supposedly." She pulled a face. "He tried to do it *in*

character. Like, his super suave dragonborn guy wanted to bone my sexy elf lady. Anyway, I told him no."

"Ugh. So is he out of the group?" I said. "If we're restructuring, I'm all for giving Brant a lifelong ban as well."

"He didn't even do anything," she said. "And he's not a regular member. He's out of the Parallel on business with an Order-recognised permit. Just in case you were wondering if he's here legally."

"What did he want with me, then?" I asked. "Did he say?"

"He wanted to know what you stole for the Order today, for a start."

I sprawled on the sofa and put my feet up on the footrest. "I didn't steal the amulet, I liberated it from the previous thief. The Order didn't tell me who it used to belong to, so as far as I'm concerned, it's off my hands."

"Did they give you another mission?" she queried.

"No, thankfully." I needed a weekend off for once. "I think it'll be good for my health to avoid the swamp while the Death King's people are riding around looking for trouble."

Despite my lucky escape, the presence of the four Elemental Soldiers and their leader had unnerved me, to say the least. Walking legends didn't cross my path every day.

"No kidding," said Devon. "You saw all of them? All four?"

"And their leader." Most mages were loners by nature, but the Death King always hired one highly gifted elemental mage of each class to join his army, perhaps so nobody would accuse him of favouritism. I imagined he paid them well, since they were willing to ignore the fact that their employer was an undead despot. Despite its title, the Order of the Elements didn't have many mages among its full-time staff, partly due to their disdain for authority, and partly due to the fact that to get proper training in magic, the Parallel was the place to go. After all, they could openly use their talents on the other side, even if they had to fight tooth and nail to stay alive on a daily basis.

It was why I could understand why Brant had left, even if he'd screwed me over in the process. The Order acted surprised when most people with any real skill cut them loose and moved into the Parallel, but not everyone was cut out to comply with their rules. Devon could just about tolerate making custom spells for the Order's employees, but the little power I had was locked out of my memories. I was lucky to still be able to use the nodes at all.

Devon pushed away from the computer. "I'm gonna work on my new cantrip design. If you like, I can make one to give Brant itchy balls."

"Nah, he's not worth wasting a perfectly good cantrip on." I shifted into an upright position on the sofa as she crossed the room to the door leading into the shop at the front. Dark shadows streamed through the crack in the door, and a muffled thump sounded from behind it.

Did someone break into our shop?

The two of us exchanged glances. Then Devon reached into her pocket and snatched up a cantrip, while I rose to my feet and crept over to the door. Beyond, darkness flooded the shop. Even with my glasses, I couldn't see anyone in the gloom ahead, but I wasn't taking any chances. I let Devon take the lead and grabbed my coat from the hook, pulling a cantrip out of the pocket.

Devon kicked the door open and strode into the shop. "Whoever's in here, you have three seconds to speak up before I blow your face off."

My gaze skimmed the shadows at the room's edges, catching sight of a flickering that shouldn't be there.

Phantom.

I nudged Devon, indicating the shimmering patch of air in the corner. As insubstantial as dust, it was hard to spot with my poor eyesight, but the intruder definitely wasn't human. Devon grabbed a tool from the desk and flung it at the intruder, but it sailed right through the beast's transparent form.

"Devon, you know they're ghosts, right?" I flicked on my cantrip and light bloomed in my hands, illuminating the phantom's shadowy outline.

"It was a reflex." She grabbed another tool as the phantom surged upright, bringing a rush of icy air that rattled the shelves. Cold tendrils of shadow oozed across the floor, but it cringed away from the light blooming from my hand.

Nobody knew if phantoms had ever been human, but they were said to be remnants of the dark magic the spirit mages had unleashed during the elemental war. It shouldn't be here, in a world where magic was barely existent. If not for the node on top of the shop, it would have disintegrated on the spot the instant it'd tried to cross over.

Who sent that thing after us? Most likely, it'd hitched a ride when I'd hopped into the living room. No weapon could harm a spirit, nor any cantrips, but I'd prefer not to sign up a permanent third housemate, especially one who couldn't pay rent. Not to mention if the Order caught us, we'd be the ones to face the backlash.

I kept the light spell in front of my face, forcing the phantom back. Out of the corner of my eye, I spotted Devon sneaking past carrying an empty jar as though we were evacuating a spider, not a ghostly monster from the Death King's own territory. Not ideal, but capturing the intruder was our only option if we didn't want to let it wreak havoc around the shop all night.

The phantom must have sensed Devon's nerves, because it whooshed at her the instant the jar appeared, causing her to drop it. The jar clattered to a halt on the floor, and I scooped it up in my hands. "I'll get it."

I held the jar in one hand, using the other to toss the light cantrip to Devon. She held the light out, driving the phantom backwards. As it came within range, I pounced. The jar slammed over the phantom's ghostly form, which filled the glass like smoke or liquid. Devon thrust the lid into my hands, and I flipped the jar over and slammed the lid on, screwing it tight. Sorted.

"Evil little shit," I said. "Since when do those things know how to travel through the nodes?"

I hadn't thought using the node to transport myself directly into the shop would have side effects, but next time, I was sorely tempted to go straight into the Order's headquarters, swamp water or none. If anyone deserved a phantom infestation, it was them.

"What are you going to do with it?" asked Devon. "I'm not sleeping with that thing in my room."

I laid the jar down on a shelf near the back of the shop. "I'll take it with me on my next trip to the other side."

3

The following day, I woke early, half convinced the draught streaming through the door was the phantom, come to strangle me in my sleep. Then I woke up a little more and realised I'd left the window open. If not for Devon's witnessing yesterday's attack, I might have been convinced I'd dreamt it. Phantoms didn't fit into this everyday world, where sleeping in a comfy bed and taking a warm shower weren't rarer than gold.

Silence filled the house. No phantoms—and no Brant, either. Devon wasn't up yet, so I busied myself tidying the shop downstairs. I also stowed the phantom jar in the back room, making a mental note to take it back into the Parallel before Devon forgot it was occupied and tried to use it to store her dice in. It was the sort of thing she'd do. I vacuumed up the remnants of last night's D&D game, silently mourning my absurd decision to go out drinking with a former classmate. I chalked that up to a temporary blip following the shock of seeing Brant on my doorstep.

The guy had never paid social calls while we were dating, let alone showed up for gaming night. I was usually the one chasing him. Hence, our problem.

As I was sweeping the shop floor, I caught sight of someone outside. Before I could figure out who, the person knocked on the door, then rang the doorbell. Twice. The twin yells of *INCOMING* woke up Devon— and probably our neighbours, too—so I had no excuse not to wrench open the door.

Instead of Brant, I found myself facing Judith French, one of my peers from the Order. What was she doing here?

"Oh, hello, Olivia," she said.

I plastered on a false smile. "You're aware we're not open until ten on weekends?"

"I'm not here to buy anything," she said. "May I come in?"

"We already did the numbers this month." I stepped aside to let her enter before she started reciting the Order's rulebook at me. The Order required all kinds of paperwork for us to operate as we did, especially as Devon used so many restricted substances from the Parallel to make her cantrips. Every month, Devon and I had to hand in reports on exactly what she'd done with each of them. Filling out forms wasn't her forte, so my main role was to double-check the figures before she turned them in.

"That's not what I'm here for." She peered at the row of coins on the nearest shelf. "Illusion charms? Interesting. Shame she can't make a memory spell, isn't it?"

Ha-bloody-ha. She knew perfectly well that when someone's memories had been stripped by the Order, it'd take more than a cantrip to get them back. But that was Judith for you. She'd been the same way at the academy, and people like her could only remain civil for so long before the claws came out. Luckily, when you go from model student to full-time amnesiac while having the misfortune to still be stuck at school, you learn some coping mechanisms for dealing with the shitty bullies.

"Isn't it?" I said. "Shame they can't change someone's personality, either, but I guess some things are unfixable."

"The Order wants to see you," she said, not noting my comment. "At their office. Two hours ago, in fact."

"What do they want now?" I asked. "I already handed over the amulet they sent me to retrieve."

"You weren't sent to retrieve an amulet," she said.

"I'm sorry, what?"

She repeated the words, slower, while I entertained the idea of 'accidentally' opening the phantom jar into her face. "That's not what you were sent to find."

"How many thieves hiding in the wastelands are there?" I responded. "I didn't know there was a contingent."

"Yes, you never were the sharpest knife in the drawer," she said.

Hilarious. "Oh, I don't keep sharp knives in the drawer. I keep them in the back room with my machetes and tasers. Want to see?"

I flashed her a smile, all teeth, and she paled a little. "The Order does want to see you. If I were you, I'd hurry up."

She turned around and left the shop, the door swinging shut behind her. She had to be joking. The Order wanted me to give the amulet *back* to the thieving bastard who'd stolen it? With the Death King and his soldiers on the prowl? In her dreams.

Devon entered the shop behind me, wearing a Totoro onesie, with her hair standing up in all directions. "What was Judith Stick-Up-Her-Arse doing here?"

"Telling me to go to the Order," I said. "Apparently, I stole from the wrong thief. Or she's screwing with me. One or the other."

"Hey, you might get another free trip into the Parallel," she said.

"I'd rather swim in the swamp than deal with *more* Order bullshit." But what the hell. I'd already missed D&D night. It wasn't as though my week could get any worse.

Way to tempt fate there, Liv.

I switched my glasses for contacts, grabbed my backpack, and for the second time in two days, I caught the bus to the Order's headquarters. Since it was a weekend, the bus was packed and running at the speed of a legless wight, so it took me a full three-quarters of an hour to reach town.

The instant I stepped off the bus, a blast of smoke hit me in the face, and my vision blurred, my eyes tearing up. At once, the humans around me erupted into panic, yelling and rubbing their eyes. They were under the impression someone had unleashed tear gas into the air, but I knew better.

Someone had set off a cantrip. Someone who was willing to use magic in daylight, with human witnesses, no less. I'd scanned my fellow passengers on the bus, and none were magically inclined except for me. That made me the most likely target, but thanks to the smoke, I could hardly see where I was going, let alone who'd set off the cantrip. I felt my way forward with one hand outstretched, my instincts driving me to take this as far away from the bus stop as possible before I got yet another black mark on my record for making a scene in front of a bunch of ordinary humans.

With my other hand, I reached into my pocket for a cantrip of my own. I couldn't use anything overtly flashy for the sake of my human audience, but I could at least get my eyesight back before I walked into traffic.

The instant I turned on the cantrip, a rush of sensation hit me. My sight returned to almost normal, while my sense of hearing and smell went into overdrive. The rumble of traffic rose to a roar like an oncoming truck, the wind became a storm, and the echoing sound of the attacker's departure pounded against my ears.

I pelted after the culprit down a street where the scent of traffic mingled with an unmistakeable tang of magic. I stood as good a chance of being hit by a passing car as I did by the attacker, but I was gaining on him. I dug into my bag for my umbrella, the closest thing to a weapon I was allowed to carry on this side, and gave it a swing, but it passed through empty air. A rush of energy tingling in my fingertips told me a node had switched on—and the thief had vanished from sight.

I blinked hard, the glint of the node resolving into a steady stream of energy. I hadn't even known there was a node in here, but the attacker would be running for freedom through the Parallel by now. Crap on toast.

Footsteps came from behind me. I spun around and swung the umbrella with all my might. There came a crunch and a yelp, and my ex-boyfriend staggered away from me with one hand pressed to his face. Oops.

Brant spat out curses. "Ow! What the hell, Liv?"

"Sorry, couldn't see you." He was lucky I hadn't carried anything stronger. Of course, knives and guns weren't allowed, because of the ordinary humans. Which, fair enough. Most of us aren't attacked by magically gifted rogues twice in two days. "I was chasing someone."

"In public?" He moved his hand to his nose as though checking if it was broken.

"They attacked a bunch of ordinary humans in broad daylight." I blinked, trying to clear the remainder of the smoke from my eyes. "What the hell are you doing here? Checking in with the Order?"

"What else would I be doing?" He rubbed his cheek, where a livid bruise was beginning to form. "I saw you running, and I came to help you."

"Yeah, you got here too late," I told him. "The person who set off the cantrip hopped through the node to the other side."

My eyes stung and burned as the effects of the sense-enhancing cantrip faded and the pain of the attacker's spell returned. Nasty piece of work, that.

"Who was it, a practitioner?" he asked.

"I assume so. I'm also guessing the dude bought it from the market on the other side, unless it was a custom job." I shoved my umbrella back into my bag. "What the hell did anyone have to gain by targeting human bystanders?"

"I don't know. Hang on a second." He turned on his heel and headed towards the crowd dispersing around the bus stop.

"Hey!" I followed after him, the weak daylight making the stinging sensation in my eyes worse. "What are you doing?"

"Looking for any traces of the attacker."

"There won't be any." Cantrips were made of a magical substance set to disintegrate within seconds of activation—a practice invented by rogues to prevent anyone tracking a spell back to its user. It also proved a handy way to hide the evidence from the ordinary humans, too, but today, it'd worked against us in a major way. "Does it matter if there is?"

He turned back to me, his form blurring before my eyes. "I wanted to make sure you wouldn't be blamed for it."

"If you go over there and start acting suspiciously, they'll blame you instead." I blinked hard, willing my eyes to stop stinging. "Leave it alone."

He was silent for an instant. "I think we need to talk."

"That's not what you said a year ago. I thought we were done talking."

He winced. "Look, there's something major going on. And it's not about us. Though if you'd like to talk about that, too, we can go ahead, but—"

"I have to go to the Order," I told him. "I can report the attack while I'm at it. Someone might have seen the chaos from over there."

"You can't tell them!" His alarmed expression prompted me to look around to see if there were any Order employees within earshot, but there weren't any. That cemented my suspicion that I'd been the target. If the attacker had been aiming for the Order, he'd have gone closer to their doors.

"Why not? They're more likely to help me than you are." I drew in a breath. "You ditched me for the Parallel without so much as a goodbye. Now you have the nerve to show up here on what is shaping up to be the shittiest week of my life and butt into my business? Forget it."

I walked past him, resisting the impulse to rub the stinging from my eyes—it'd only make the pain worse. Like talking to Brant, pretty much. No matter how many times I'd rehearsed what I'd say if he showed up on my doorstep again, I hadn't accounted for the universe's habit of throwing plot twists in my path.

Brant watched me walk. Then he said, "If you change your mind, you have my number."

If I did, it was on my old phone, buried in my junk drawer. I was late enough checking into the retrieval unit as it was, so I put that out of mind and walked towards the Order.

As I neared the glass doors, doubts set in. Unwelcome as his presence might be, Brant might know something about who was targeting me. Besides, the Order hadn't witnessed the attack. Telling them might well paint a target on my own head, especially with no proof. Would it really be worth the risk of another black mark on my record? The odds were slim, but for all I knew, the attacker had been aiming for someone else, someone with clout within the Order. Besides, now he was the Parallel's problem, not mine.

I made for the retrieval unit downstairs, where I found Mrs Carlisle, the department head, arranging a stack of boxes behind the desk where the kid had been sitting yesterday evening.

"Mrs Carlisle," I said. "I heard you wanted to talk to me. What's the issue?"

"Mr Cobb wants to see you," she said shortly.

"He does?" Why would a supervisor from another

division want to talk to the likes of me? I ranked some-where between pond scum and dirt in his eyes, and the only time we'd spoken was for him to yell at me for treading mud in the lobby. "Is it true what Judith said— that the amulet's the wrong one? Because I think there's been a mistake."

"Take it up with him," she said, without lifting her head.

I debated telling her a practitioner had attacked me in front of ordinary human witnesses, but as the head of the lowest branch of the Order, Mrs Carlisle had little more authority than I did.

Instead, I climbed the stairs and made for the corridor of offices containing the supervisors for this Order branch. Mr Cobb oversaw finance or something equally inscrutable, so it was anyone's guess what he wanted with me. I'd almost achieved a negative score in my statistics exam. He must be important if he had his own name on his office door, so I dragged a hand through my hair to tidy it and hoped my eyes weren't too red and teary from the cantrip blast.

I rapped on the door with my knuckles, and a voice barked out, "Come in."

Drawing in a steadying breath, I entered. Mr Cobb sat at a desk in the office, wearing a tie so tight it was a wonder he could breathe, and a matching iron-grey suit. His dark hair was streaked with grey, too, his milky blue eyes too large for his pallid face. He held the amulet in one wrinkled hand, which banished all my hopes that the whole thing had been a mistake.

"What is the issue?" I closed the door behind me. "I followed the orders to the letter. I was told to find a thief and retrieve his haul, and that amulet was all I found in his hideout."

"Forgive me if I don't take your word for it, given your track record," he said, in cold tones.

So that's what this is about. I'd always suspected he was one of the supervisors involved in passing the sentence on me, and that he'd argued for me to lose more than my memories. His contempt for me made little sense otherwise. On the other hand, why make such a fuss over a simple amulet?

"What do you want me to do?" I asked. "I brought everything I found inside the thief's hideout—who was a water mage, by the way. *That* part wasn't in the job description. But there were no other practitioners hiding in the Death King's territory. I assumed that amulet was valuable, since it was hidden within a magical ward."

"You were mistaken," he said. "This isn't what we were looking for."

"It's not the amulet you were looking for?" From his blank expression, it seemed he couldn't appreciate a good Star Wars reference. "It was literally the only thing of value the thief had on him, as far as I'm aware."

How many amulets carved with decorative skulls were typically found lying around the swamp? Given that it was the Death King's territory... a lot, possibly. Didn't make his request to return it any less weird.

"This is what I've been told from the upper room," he said. "We can't store this amulet here with no paperwork for it. It has to go back to the Parallel."

"The thief who stole it is dead. Or worse." A shiver danced over my skin at the memory of his horrified screaming as the Death King and his four soldiers had cornered him. If he'd had anything else of value, they'd doubtless have taken it off him before they burned his corpse.

"That doesn't matter," he said. "The instructions from the upper room are clear. Take this amulet back with you and leave it where you found it."

"I reckon the Death King probably had his Fire Element burn the place to a crisp along with its owner."

His brow arched. "The Death King doesn't leave his territory."

"I was *on* his territory." I might as well have been addressing a brick wall. "That's why I had to cross the node into my house instead of outside the Order's head-quarters. The Death King's people were all riding in the swamp at once. They chased down the thief. It's not safe for me to return there now."

Surprise momentarily crossed his face, mingling with contempt. "You used a node to travel into your house?"

"Yeah, why?" I said. "I had a permit. It's not against the rules."

I'd have thought he'd be grateful that I'd avoided drip-ping swamp water all over the lobby. Not to mention, if I'd used the node to hop into the Order's headquarters, the phantom would have followed me here instead of home. The brief amusement wouldn't have made up for how much trouble I'd have been in.

He leaned forward in his seat. "No, but I'm surprised, given your… history, that you would use magic outside of the Order's jurisdiction."

"It's not magic." Not in the usual sense. Anyone could travel via a node if they knew how to, but the Order kept that information under wraps for a reason.

Couldn't have the general public getting dangerous ideas.

"Technicalities," he said. "In any case, there's no excuses. Take the amulet back to the swamplands and then come back here. Those are your orders."

Arse. "Can't another retriever take it with them? There's got to be at least one person in the building heading into the Parallel today."

"Certainly not," he responded. "This is your responsibility to handle, Olivia. Consider your record."

As if I could forget it. I debated mentioning the attack at the bus stop, but I had an inkling I'd be wasting my time trying to justify myself to this guy. If I pushed the wrong buttons, he'd raise hell among the upper room, and I'd find myself in deeper shit than ever. Nearly half the senior supervisors had argued against me being allowed to keep my magic, while others had claimed that I should have lost more than two years of memories.

I slid the amulet into my pocket with shaking hands, feeling Mr Cobb's stare on my back. Looking for signs of lawbreaking, I'd guess.

All right, then. I needed to take the amulet back to where I'd found it, and hope that this time, nothing followed me back home.

4

I was fifteen the first time I set eyes on Dirk Alban. At one time, I might have claimed I wasn't enamoured the instant I saw him, but that would be a lie. Everyone was. When our academy class took a trip to the Order's offices, he'd been the one to greet us, and he'd opened our eyes to the magical riches on the other side of the nodes. At the end of the day, he singled me out and gave me his contact details, telling me he could teach me magic.

I didn't know why I took him up on his offer. I only knew what the reports said, and by all accounts, he didn't lure me in by using a spell or coerce me in any other manner. If he had, the Order might not have been forced to put me on trial. Sometimes I still heard his voice in my dreams, but whenever I tried to probe further, all I recalled was my mind cracking in two, leaving nothing but dust and regret and the stench of magic gone bad.

In my first concrete memory after the incident, I'd come to, sitting on a steel-backed chair in one of the

Order's courtrooms. I'd been dizzy and disorientated, yet part of me knew I'd broken a deep, unforgivable rule, and that I was lucky to be alive.

The Order told me Dirk was dead. They told me they'd found me standing beside his body, and that we'd both been found guilty of practising spirit magic. Only the fact that I was underage kept them from sentencing me to death. Instead, they'd tried to strip away my memories of our lessons, but in the process, they'd taken much, much more.

Lost in sour thoughts, I walked straight past Brant on my way out of the Order.

"Hey," said Brant. "I'm sorry if I was too forward earlier."

"Uh-huh." Even without the stinging aftereffects of the spell in my eyes, I still didn't want to look directly at him. "I have to go back to the Parallel, so I won't be seeing you later."

"What for?" he pressed. "If it's a routine mission, I'm heading that way anyway. I did mean it when I said I owed you."

For an instant, I was tempted to take him up on the offer. "I was told to find an amulet yesterday. The Order then decided I brought them the wrong artefact, so I have to put it back in the middle of the swamp. If you really want to waste your time with *that,* then feel free."

His brows shot up. "Amulet, you say?"

"Yeah, why? I don't understand what the problem is."

The amulet didn't even feel magical, however creepy it looked. Perhaps that's why I wasn't supposed to have bothered with it, but the lengths the water mage had gone to keep it protected said otherwise.

"Nor me, if you don't tell me," he said. "Who stole it?"

"A water mage who's currently sleeping with the fishes," I responded. "I'm just gonna run this errand, and if you still want to talk to me, you can come and see me when the Order's supervisors aren't breathing down my neck."

"This is bullshit," he said. "Look, you could just hand that amulet to me instead. It's not like they're going to walk into the Parallel and check. It'll be stolen the instant you put it down, besides."

I know. That's why it's so weird for them to make such a fuss.

"Why are you offering me help?" Call me suspicious, but he hadn't walked back into my life for no reason. My thoughts might be clouded by the emotions brought on by our shared history, but I knew that much.

"Because..." He hesitated. "I know the Order stole your magic from you. What if I could get it back?"

I stared openly at him. "Are you out of your mind?"

"I know of someone who's researching memory spells," he said, speaking quickly. "I've met a lot of people in the last year who can do things with magic you've never seen before. In the Parallel, anything is possible."

No way. The Order had the monopoly on that kind of magic. If he'd found some dodgy experimental practitioner in the Parallel, who knew what the side effects would be? Besides, perhaps it was for the best that I didn't remember a single word of Dirk Alban's lessons. Ignorance meant the Order had no extra leverage to use against me.

"No, thanks," I said. "I'm good. But I really do need to get this amulet back where it came from."

"I'll come with you," he persisted.

I shook my head. "The Order will think we're working together."

"We're not breaking the law." He reached out a hand. "You're going to have to start trusting again, someday, Liv."

I forced a laugh. Today had brought a dozen reminders of why that was a bad idea already and it was barely mid-morning. "I just want to be left alone. Please."

Hurt flashed in his eyes, but he withdrew his hand. I felt like the biggest shithead in the world as I walked to the nearest node and rode the current over into the Parallel.

I landed at the edge of the Death King's swamp, energy coursing through my veins. Everyone said the nodes were the original source of the spirit mages' power, and even without magic, I could still feel the current humming inside me. Yet everyone knew most of the spirit mages had died in the war and the rest had been executed for war crimes, and if I went back down that road, I'd end up the same way. Brant's offer might be sincere, but it wasn't worth the risk.

I headed for the tree I'd used to store my spare cantrips in and retrieved them along with my weapons. As I took my first step onto the marshy ground, the shapes of several figures on horseback appeared in the mist.

Not the Death King again. I ducked behind the tree, my heart thudding. No fewer than seven figures rode skeletal steeds across the swamp. Judging by their identical appearances, they weren't the Death King's Elemental Soldiers, but his foot-soldiers instead. I remained still, hoping they were wights and not liches. Liches were rumoured to be able to sense the living even when they were hidden from sight, but wights were little more than cavalry. Regardless, the Lich King didn't typically send his army this close to the city.

Something's wrong. No shit, Liv. Surely it couldn't all be about the amulet. If they'd killed the thief, then the matter should have been taken care of. Unless the soldiers were fired up for some other reason. Had the Order sent me out here into their path on purpose? No way. They might not be my biggest fans, but bumping me off would create too much paperwork. Still, it couldn't be plainer there was something rotten in the state of Denmark, as Hamlet would say. For reasons I couldn't fathom, Shakespeare quotes were the only part of my education I remembered. I got an A on *that* exam. I just failed everything else.

I held my breath until the last of the horsemen had passed my hiding place. Then I ran across the swampland in search of the thief's hut.

As I'd feared, the place was gone. Burned to cinders. The Fire Element was rumoured to be the most violent of the Death King's chosen soldiers. Playing up to stereotypes, maybe. Brant wasn't that bad. Not to me, anyway. His offer to help me get my magic back was oddly heartfelt, even if it was misplaced.

Maybe I should have at least taken him up on his offer of help at the very least, but the idea of abandoning the amulet in the swamp struck me as a waste. Maybe I could sell it instead. It wasn't like the Order would check, and the thing was hand-carved, by the looks of things. There were plenty of people buying and selling artefacts at the market who might take it off my hands and give me some much-needed cash as a bonus.

Mind made up, I turned around and walked out of the swampland towards the outskirts of town. Like every-where on this side of the nodes, the city of Arcadia had been hit hard by the war. Roughly constructed stone houses filled the winding streets, while practitioners gath-ered around the ramshackle warehouses to sell their wares.

In the city's centre stood the Citadel of the Elements, where the elemental council had once held power before the spirit mages had killed off their brethren and then perished themselves. The towering spire looked as imposing as ever, but it had stood empty since the coun-cil's demise.

Nowadays, most elemental mages were to be found skulking in the city's crooked streets alongside shapeshifters, elves, vampires and others who found it preferable to struggle here rather than surviving under the Order's rules on the other side. The majority of prac-titioners had little talent worth a damn, and while the Parallel used to be self-sufficient before the war, it had grown dependent on supplies brought in from the other side.

I ducked into the warehouse marked with a sign desig-nating it as a trading area for magic, and a man with lizard-like features accosted me. "Can I interest you in a trinket or two?"

"No, thanks," I said. "I'm selling, in fact."

He extended a leathery hand. "Ooh, what d'you have?"

I held up the amulet. "Know what this is made of?"

The man recoiled with a gasp. "Death! Don't bring that in here. Are you out of your mind?"

I stiffened, then backed out into the street before his yells drew too much attention. A trickle of fear ran down my spine as I held the amulet up to the light and looked at it. *Really* looked at it.

Please tell me that's not what I think it is.

Spirit magic might be forbidden, but one individual lay outside of the Order's jurisdiction. The Death King—and by association, the Court of the Dead.

Some say the first liches made a deal with the devil, others say they were backed into a corner after the war. Whatever the reason, their souls and their bodies existed in separate vessels. Every soldier held a pendant which contained their soul, and as long as it existed, no matter how many times they were killed, they couldn't die.

Now I had one of those souls in my own hands. The person it belonged to was likely pissed as hell that someone had taken it, which explained why those foot-soldiers had been scouring the swampland. They'd figured out the thief had stolen a soul straight from the Death King's own territory, but when they'd caught him, he didn't have the soul on him… because *I'd* stolen it.

No wonder the Order wanted me to take it back to the swamp. Would have been nice if they'd told me in the first place, but soul amulets were probably classified information, and given my history, they wouldn't have wanted to risk telling someone who'd broken the law once already. Soul amulets were close enough to spirit magic to make most people uncomfortable.

Whose soul might it be? Was it possible for me to return it to its owner? It wasn't like I could ask one of the foot-soldiers. Wights weren't capable of listening to reason. They were the cavalry, nothing more. They'd cut me up without answering any questions. I needed to speak to an actual person and tell them there'd been a mistake.

The idea of striding right up to the gates of the Death King's castle and handing it back to him, however, was laughable. He'd assume I'd had a moment of guilty conscience and have his soldier incinerate me the same way he'd killed the unfortunate water mage. I'd have liked to ask *him* how he'd stolen it, come to that. It couldn't have been an easy job.

I peered into the fog, my shoulders stiffening. Armoured figures appeared in the gloom of the swamp, heading this way. Speak of the devil. If the guy at the market told the Death King's foot-soldiers that he'd seen me carrying an amulet around… I was screwed.

I needed to get out of here. Running for the node by the tree would put me in the soldiers' sight, so I had no option but to move deeper into the city's outskirts.

I ducked into the nearest alley and found a knife at my throat.

5

I kicked out, knocking my attacker backwards. In response, he dropped the knife, trod on the end of his own coat and would have fallen on his face if I hadn't caught his arm.

"Oh, it's you, Trix." I released him, my heart thumping. "What the hell are you doing?"

"You told me to practise my ambushes." The elf shuffled back. "How was that?"

"Except for the bit when you dropped your knife? Not bad."

"Good." He gave a wide smile. "I missed you at the game night."

"Something came up."

Trix was the only elf member of our D&D group. Pointed ears stuck up from his silky dark hair, while his luminescent skin glowed in the dim lighting. That was elves for you. Pretty, but lacking in the survival skills department. I figured that the only reason they'd survived the war in the Parallel was because there was so little that could actually kill them.

"What're they looking for?" he asked. "The Death King's people, I mean?"

Uh... I think they're looking for me. Catch me giving that away now I knew what I held... a soul amulet. Trix would probably blurt it out by accident to the first person who asked.

"No clue," I lied easily. "Is he around?"

"Who, the Death King?"

I winced. "Maybe don't talk so loudly when they can hear us?"

"Why do you want to know if he's here?" His brow furrowed in genuine confusion. He might be a little slow on the uptake, but he wouldn't turn me in.

"I'm in a spot of trouble." There was no point in underplaying it at this point. "I need to speak to a representative from the same place those walking skeletons came from."

"You want to talk to *them?*"

I rubbed my forehead. "No. I want to talk to someone from the Death Kingdom who has a brain. Or some approximation of one, anyway."

I didn't know the rules on metaphysics for death-cheating monsters, but even someone who could remove their soul and trap it in an object must still have something to think with. If I knew one thing, there was absolutely no way the Death King himself would ever listen to me when he likely assumed that I'd stolen from him. Instead, I needed to waylay one of his people and explain the situation. Someone who was willing to listen, if anyone in the Court of the Dead fitted that criteria.

The sound of hooves thudding on the muddy path sent a fresh wave of alarm blaring through me. *They came out of the swamp?* The Death King's people had entered the city itself?

"Please tell me there's a node near here," I said to Trix. "I need to get out."

"They *are* looking for you." He pulled out his knife again. "I'll scare them off."

"Trix, they're dead. A knife won't even tickle them." I backed down the alley as the hoofbeats grew louder. "I don't normally cross over here. Which way did you come in?"

"Underground. There's a node just west of here if you go under the street."

Wonderful. "Do you have somewhere safe to hide?"

"Of course," he said. "I promise, I won't breathe a word about you to anyone who asks."

"Thanks," I said. "Best to pretend you don't know me at all, for both our sakes."

I backed between the warehouses, cursing my luck. If a lone horseman had come here, I might have considered speaking to them, but it sounded like half the army was pounding down the streets and spreading throughout the city. Wherever Dex had disappeared to, I had no clue, but I wouldn't drag any more of my friends into this mess.

The nearest route into the city's underground lay down a rickety set of stairs at the alley's end. I climbed down into darkness, hoping I wouldn't run into worse than a wight there in the gloom. The labyrinthine passages beneath the city were mostly home to beings as friendly as the Death King's lot, but I was counting on the inhabitants being too distracted by the chaos aboveground to notice me sneaking into their midst.

The tunnel appeared empty at first, lit by the dim lights of old-fashioned lanterns. I shuffled across the damp floor, mentally mapping my surroundings to the streets aboveground. If Trix's geography was accurate, I needed to head west to find the way out.

A spark of light caught on my vision. Then a sharp pain stung my wrist. A pair of miniature flaming eyes stared accusingly at me. "What in blazes and tides are you doing here?"

"Dex?"

"You don't know any other fire sprites," he said. "You'd better not, anyway."

"Shh," I hissed. "I'm in hiding. Anyone in the tunnel?"

"Nope. They're all up there, looking to see what all the fuss is about."

"You mean the wights." I walked further into the gloom. "I wondered if they'd taken you."

"I've been hiding in a tree since those skeletal monsters started rampaging around," he said accusingly. "Nice of you to come looking for me."

"I'm in major trouble." I spoke in a low voice. "You know that amulet we found? It's a soul amulet. Someone must have swiped it from one of the Death King's own soldiers."

"Shit, Liv," he said in a low, awed voice.

"Yeah, exactly. I need to get to the node and get the fuck out of here." Never mind the Death King. I'd take the amulet back to the Order and tell them exactly what they'd planted on me and why it was a death sentence to send me to return it.

Dex flitted around my head. "Uh, slight issue. There *may* be someone else using the node."

I stopped walking. "You said there wasn't anyone down here."

"Not right here, no," he said. "But there's always things near the node. They feed on the magic."

"By 'things', you don't mean humans." Just perfect. Nodes, sources of magic, were also sources of nourishment to some of the Parallel's less than savoury beings. There wasn't another way out, so I'd have to risk it.

As we neared the corner, I sensed the node, its pulsing point like a beating heart deep in the darkness. Three creatures shaped like scrawny, hairless humans surrounded its flowing current. Revenants.

After the Elements fell, there weren't enough survivors to control the city, and others rushed in to fill the gap. Revenants—vampiric creatures which fed on the magic of the nodes—paled in comparison to their full-vampire counterparts, but the node was a feast they wouldn't abandon without a fight.

"Don't mind me," I said, when they all looked up at me with sightless eyes. "I just need to borrow your node."

A revenant hissed, lashing out with a bony hand. Coldness brushed against my skin, and the node's power rattled in my veins. Dammit. I couldn't take out all three of them at once without a struggle, and I didn't want to know what the Order would do if I brought three revenants with me into the middle of town. Lock me up for a decade, no doubt.

Dex flew in front of them, his transparent form blazing with orange light. They cringed away from the fire, hairless heads reflecting the gleaming light. I, meanwhile, backed around the corner and headed to the ladder leading aboveground. There'd better be another node in the city, or else I was in deeper shit than ever.

I climbed the ladder, my hands slipping on the rungs, and pushed my way into the alley. Trix had vanished, as I'd expected, but the hoofbeats sounded louder than ever. My nerves jangled, my hands shivering with the echo of the node. *Dammit. There's got to be another one somewhere.*

Instinct drove me around a corner, deeper into the warren of warehouses that formed the outskirts of the city. The liches wouldn't have the nerve to march right up to the ruling vampire council's doorstep, would they? If the amulet was that valuable, perhaps they would. I couldn't take the chance. My heart beat wildly against my ribs, and a current of magic drew me like the point of a compass. The node *did* come out aboveground—if I was willing to risk being spotted.

Screw it. I followed the tug of magic until I spotted the node gleaming ahead. Revenants didn't come to the surface in daylight, and the Death King had no reason to send his people into a realm where the magic keeping them intact no longer functioned. My path was clear. I'd have no better shot at escaping. *Here we go.*

I broke into a full-out sprint at the torrent of light. The node tugged at me, and I willingly fell into its embrace.

Just as the current caught me, a pair of grasping hands dug into my arm from behind, and I kicked out, trying to dislodge my attacker. With a jolt, I crashed through the node and skidded to a halt on the pavement.

A skeletal creature lay in a heap next to me, as out of place against the concrete backdrop as a unicorn on the high street. The wight had followed me home. *Oh, Elements.*

As it rose upright, I kicked out, feeling bone splinter beneath my heel. Wights were weaklings on this side, sapped of the power they gained from the Court of the Dead, but that didn't change the fact that it'd *followed me through.*

I gave another kick, breaking its leg. The wight fell into a heap, its bones already turning into dust without the magic of the node to sustain it.

I reached for a cantrip and crouched over the wight's body, but before I could move another inch, someone shouted, "Freeze!"

Judith French marched over to me, her expression livid. Oh, boy.

"What are you doing?" she demanded.

"This wight followed me." I indicated the monster's skeletal form, or what was left of it. "Through the node. Tried to kill me."

"You brought it with you," she said. "That's a violation of our rules."

"It tried to *kill* me," I repeated. "There's something really messed up going on over there—"

"Is there a problem?" said another, male voice.

Brant. I'd never thought I'd be glad to see him, but he'd come at the right moment to offer a diversion. He walked over, looking unexpectedly menacing in his long cloak, his messy dark hair blowing in the breeze.

"Who are you?" said Judith.

"None of your concern," he said. "If Liv says the wight tried to kill her, she's telling the truth."

"That may be," said Judith, "but this is a public location, and not an appropriate place to engage with a magical attacker."

"Is that why you're yelling at Liv about wights in front of everyone within hearing distance?" he said.

Judith flushed bright red. "There's nobody but you within hearing distance."

"Good job I'm not an ordinary human, then," he said. "That was careless. Worth reporting to your supervisor, even."

"Don't you threaten me, mage," said Judith.

"Not a threat," he said breezily. "A warning. I'll help Liv take care of this guy, and you'll leave her alone. Then nobody gets reported. Deal?"

Her furious gaze trailed over us, but apparently it wasn't worth risking a black mark on her own record over a decomposing wight. "Don't let it happen again."

Relief swept over me. Brant might be reckless some-times, but he could barbecue the Order's guards with his back turned. Judith knew better than to pick a fight at this point, even with backup around the corner.

"Thanks," I whispered to him.

"Anytime." Flames sparked between his hands, trans-ferring to the wight's remains. In a flash, they turned to ashes, drifting away on the chilly March breeze. "There. No harm done."

I released a slow, steady breath. "Not on this side, anyway. I'm in trouble."

He cut me a concerned look. "How bad?"

"Bad," I said. "I need to go to the Order."

He shook his head. "You got lucky this time, but if you go in there now, they'll want to know why you're already back without following their instructions."

I opened my mouth to argue, but he had a point. Brant might act like a hothead, but the guy was sharp.

"I know," I said, "but I have something I need to return to the Order if I want to stop everyone trying to kill me."

His brow cocked. "Care to tell me what it is?"

"As I told you earlier, the Order sent me on a mission to steal an amulet yesterday," I said. "Then they back-tracked and sent me to put it back where I found it. Turns out it's more than an amulet. It's someone's soul."

Brant's eyes widened. "A soul amulet?"

"You've got it." I checked it was still in my pocket. "I have to give it back to the Order, or else the Death King's people will find out I'm the one who has it. And then? I'll envy that decomposing skeleton, that's for sure."

"You can't," he said.

"What do you mean, I can't?" I said. "I can't keep it. And the Death King isn't exactly known for listening to reason. This is the Order's responsibility."

"I don't disagree, but they already told you to return it to the Parallel."

"There was nobody to return it to," I responded. "The place was overrun with wights. I guess the Death King found out about the theft, but his people didn't find the amulet because *I* had it. He's going to think it was me who stole it."

Which… I had. Accidentally, of course, but to the King of the Dead, I doubted it mattered.

His mouth flattened. "All right. I offered to help you before, and I meant it. Don't go back to the Order. They'll blame you, Liv. You know they will."

Damn him for speaking the truth. As a rogue, he wasn't beholden to the Order, and he'd shunned them for a reason. He also knew I was desperate. Desperate enough to consider taking him up on his offer.

"What is it you're offering me?" I asked. "Can these so-called contacts of yours help me with this situation?"

He glanced around. "Not here. We can talk somewhere else."

I shouldn't. And yet.

"All right."

6

———

Brant and I walked into a near-empty pub. He ordered a pint, while I ordered a diet coke. Alcohol made me sleepy, which was the last thing I needed at the moment. We took our drinks to a table in the far corner, and I checked to make sure nobody lurked nearby before I addressed Brant. "Tell me about these contacts of yours."

"First things first," he said. "That soul amulet. I heard rumours… but now you've confirmed how serious it is."

"Rumours of what?"

"A thief who trades in souls."

I stared at him for a second. "Since when was there trade in souls?"

"For years. Decades. At least as long as I've lived in the Parallel."

I raised a brow. "Seriously? What use is a soul without a body?"

"To some, it's as valuable as gold."

"You mean, to spirit mages," I said. "They're extinct."

"And Dirk Alban?"

A flinch travelled through my limbs. I gripped my glass. "He wasn't a spirit mage. Just a practitioner."

"Same difference," he said. "Yes, most of them died out in the war, but it's possible for any practitioner to learn basic spirit magic with the right teacher. You're proof of that."

My grip tightened. "You know how well it turned out for me. I stepped over a line and I'm still paying for it now."

The worst part? I didn't know what I'd done to draw the Order's attention on that fateful day. All I knew Dirk had lost his life, while I'd lost my memories.

"I'm not denying you have reason to turn your back on it," he said, "but trust me when I say the knowledge alone is valuable in the right hands, and the rumours say there's a thief out there looking for items exactly like that amulet."

I shook my head firmly. "Whatever you're twisted up in, I want no part in it."

"As long as you have that soul amulet, you're involved," he insisted. "I reckon you stole it from one of the soul thief's underlings who was instructed to bring it back to him."

"Then his underling shouldn't have left it unattended," I said. "Besides, the Death King's people blew the thief's hideout to pieces."

A moment passed. "That's not good. The Death King himself has his eye on the situation, and now you have the amulet—"

"He's going to think I'm allied with this so-called soul thief." My gut clenched. "Hence why I wanted it back in the Order's hands, so *they* can give it back to him. Unless they sent me after it on purpose, but that's paranoid even by my standards."

He shook his head. "I suspect they sent you after a thief without knowing exactly what he stole. They might have heard of a stolen amulet…"

"But not that it had someone's soul in it," I finished. "That doesn't mean I can't return it to the Order. Whether they knew they were dealing with it or not, they have enough clout behind them that the Death King won't slaughter them all on the spot."

He shifted in his seat. "I don't disagree, but there're rumours drifting around the Parallel about disputes within the Order's upper ranks. They won't help you."

"You seem confident of that."

"I know them, and I know you," he said in soft tones. "If the Order was fair, your punishment would have fit the crime. The way they treated you…"

I broke my gaze from his. Brant had always been intense, and one of the reasons he'd left for the Parallel was because he hadn't been able to handle working in close proximity to the Order. I hadn't realised that their treatment of me had struck him that deeply.

I turned my attention back to the matter at hand. "I should have dropped the damned soul amulet in the sewers."

"No way," he said. "Anyone might have found it, connected to the soul thief or otherwise, and then who knows what damage they might have caused?"

"I'd have returned it to the Death King himself if I didn't think it'd get me blasted to pieces like that water mage." I drank the rest of my diet coke and rose to my feet. "Look, I appreciate you looking out for me, but we're talking in circles. If the Order is out, then I need to cross over into the swamp and find someone who can give the amulet to the person it originally belonged to."

"Without witnesses," he added. "Those wights are as likely to lose the amulet again as not. And liches are basically ghosts. You need to speak to a person."

"Meaning one of the four Elemental Soldiers." I doubted I'd be lucky enough to find all four of them patrolling again, but if I got Devon to make me a cantrip for invisibility, maybe I'd stand a chance of slipping past the gates and planting the amulet on one of them without being seen. It was starting to seem like my only remaining option.

"Liv, don't go back there today," he insisted. "The Death King will be on high alert this soon after the theft. You were lucky only a wight jumped you."

"Yeah, I know." I wanted rid of the amulet, but now I had him here, I might as well give him a grilling. "And this memory spell? Were you ever going tell me there was a way to get my magic back?"

His mouth pressed into a line. "I didn't know. Not for a while. The Order has total control over spells of that nature, as well you know. But... I know people in the Parallel who are looking to change that."

"Are you recruiting me to join a group of illicit practitioners?" Even he must know my job revolved around arresting said crooks, not joining their ranks.

"No," he insisted. "I'm asking you to trust me. Have I

ever given you reason to think I wouldn't keep my word?"

"Ignoring the fact that you ditched me and ran off into Arcadia?" He could have come to see me any time I'd been in the Parallel, but he'd avoided it up until now. "What are you doing here, really?"

"Helping you," he said. "I swear I didn't know you were involved at first, but I worried you'd become a target."

It was classic Brant to shove his way into a case which had nothing to do with him when he got a hint of trouble pointing in my direction, but that didn't work quell the lingering suspicions in the back of my mind. He hated the Order. Always had. But ultimately, I'd refused his offer to join him as a rogue, so we'd agreed to go our separate ways and he hadn't contacted me since.

"Is that why you're here, then?" I said. "You *do* have a permit, don't you?"

"Of a sort."

A forgery. Just perfect. "You expect me to believe you risked the Order's wrath on a hunch that I might end up being targeted?"

"No, but I heard some odd reports from the Order's direction via my contacts."

"You still haven't told me who these contacts of yours are."

Brant had never exactly been on the straight and narrow. We'd met when I was fairly new to the Parallel, when I'd been on my first big mission to track down a rogue mage. His contacts in the city had saved my neck back then, but like all mages, he was willing to bend the rules at any time to further his own ends. When you could conjure up fire with a snap of your fingers, the Parallel seemed easy to navigate, and if I'd taken him up on his offer, I'd have spent my life hiding behind him. I hadn't wanted that, and I'd assumed he understood.

The door creaked open, and Brant's shoulders stiffened when someone walked in. Ordinary person or not, I couldn't see in the dim lighting. Brant rose to his feet, then relaxed. "Hey, Vaughn."

A skinny white guy with dark eyes and longish rocker-style hair sauntered over, looking me up and down. "This is she?"

"Hey," I said warily. "I'm Liv."

"I know." He gave Brant a concerned look. "Just so you know, there's a couple of Order employees putting out a warrant for a rogue someone spotted near their place. I think they may have seen through your fake permit."

Brant swore. "Busybodies. Liv, you should go. Before they realise we're together."

Damn. The rest of our discussion would have to wait. I gave his mate a suspicious look, which he returned with a smile, and slipped out into the street.

Brant's words hung over me like a raincloud as I headed home. The amulet's weight in my pocket seemed to double with each step, and it was only now the chaos had calmed down that it hit me I was carrying someone's life essence. Separating a soul from a body was impossible for anyone except for one of the Death King's best, so it must belong to someone important. Most of his foot soldiers were like those wights—unthinking, unfeeling, inhuman. His fellow liches weren't much better. Removing a soul had fairly intense side effects, most of which I'd have to ask the Death King himself about.

I entered the shop, finding Devon had closed up for lunch, and heard voices in the back. Mum and Elise. Oh, bugger. Why did my family have to be the sort of people who invited themselves over without being asked? In fairness, I wasn't set to be working this weekend, but heaven knew what story Devon had told them.

I entered the living room to find Mum sitting beside her wife on the sofa. Mum and I shared the same pale skin and dark curly hair, with a smattering of freckles which only appeared in summer. Elise was a pretty woman of Asian descent who gave me a friendly smile as I walked in. Mum was as tall as Elise was mousy and small, and the adoring way they looked at one another would have been mildly sickening if they hadn't been so bloody cute.

"How long have you been here?" I asked.

"Half an hour," said Mum. "Devon made us tea. Or, she tried to."

I bit back a laugh. Devon made tea about as well as I played hockey. "Which did she forget? The milk or the teabags?"

"To boil the kettle," Elise answered.

Devon shot me an irritated look. "In my defence, I expected you to be back by now."

"Me too." I wasn't about to tell them about my near-brush with death or three—not to mention the dead person's soul currently sitting in my pocket. Mum and Elise didn't need to be burdened with my shit show of a life. As far as they knew, I worked in the Order's office filing paperwork. "Want me to make some actual tea?"

"I handled it," said Mum. "How have you been? What's that on your coat?"

Swamp water. And essence of death. "Mud. Took a shortcut through the park on my way back from the shop."

Small talk was not my strong point, and while I could tell Mum almost anything, her wife knew next to nothing of the magical world. Dad knew even less. He and Mum had split when I was a toddler, and he'd moved up to Manchester before the Order had contacted me at eleven and inducted me into the magical world. It was easier that way.

"Shop?" asked Elise. "What'd you get? You don't have any shopping bags."

"That'd be because I forgot to take my list with me." And I needed to come up with better cover stories.

Mum cleared her throat. "I thought you might be handing out CVs."

That would have been a better excuse. "Mum, people don't do that anymore, not with online applications."

I'd told her I was applying for jobs last time she'd visited, just to get her off my back. It was difficult to explain that I had zero options outside of the Order short of a permanent move into the Parallel. For all my unpleasant history with magic, cutting it out of my life would be akin to chopping off a limb.

Mum cast her gaze around the living room, which was tidy for once, given the dusting I'd given it this morning. Like most non-nerds, both Mum and Elise found our choice of décor baffling to say the least, from the anime figurines to the life-sized poster of the TARDIS on the living room door and the expanse of monster-infested dungeons covering the dining table.

"What's that jar for?" She indicated the container where I'd trapped the phantom.

"There's a dead person trapped in there," said Devon.

I shot her a warning look. Elise blinked, confused,

while Mum laughed. "Right, of course there is. Gaming prop, is it?"

"More or less." Holding my tongue in front of Mum and Elise was an exercise in extreme self-control, sometimes, but in the long-term, it was better for them not to know that in my world, phantoms in jars were like fluffy bunny rabbits compared to some of the crap I'd seen in the Parallel. "So, how's work?"

Having successfully diverted their attention from the jar, I moved onto safer topics. Devon kept trying to catch my eye, but there was no way I'd so much as allude to my chat with Brant in front of either of them. Not least because it'd kick off a *why don't you have a boyfriend* conversation, which frankly I was in even less of a mood for than a chat about creepy phantoms in jars. Luckily, when Devon returned to the shop after her lunch break, the two of them took it as their cue to leave.

"We should be getting home," Elise said. "Before rush hour."

If you asked me, she was probably concerned that if she stayed too long, we'd rope her into a D&D game. "Sure. I'll see you in a bit, okay? You too, Mum. Maybe text me first?"

Mum pulled me into a hug. "See you soon, pumpkin."

I walked with them through the shop, where Devon sat fiddling with a cantrip behind the desk. There as a time when Mum would have been the first to know everything, but those days seemed as distant as my missing memories.

After the door closed behind them, Devon put down the cantrip. "Now you're going to tell me why you were late back, right? What did the Order want?"

Right. The Order. She thought I'd gone there, not into the Parallel again. "I need an invisibility cantrip."

"You want it by when?"

"Yesterday," I said. "I need to get that amulet back into the right hands without being seen. I had a lucky escape earlier."

"Back up a step," she said. "You're saying the amulet definitely isn't what the Order wanted you to take? They made a mistake?"

Her words struck a chord in my brain, and a suspicion rose to the forefront of my mind. "I think someone tried to kill me."

Devon stared at me for a moment. "You can't leave me hanging like that. Go on."

I told her everything, barely pausing for breath. When I got to the part about the soul amulet, she swore. "Why didn't I realise what it was?"

"Because I never showed you." I held out the amulet for her to look at. "I should have thought of it, too. But it's absurd. I mean, who'd steal a lich's soul?"

She took the amulet in both hands and held it up to the light, admiring the carved lines of the skull etched onto the surface. "So its owner is out to kill you."

"Them and the rest of the Court of the Dead, yeah," I said.

She let out a low whistle. "I can see why you'd need to be invisible. You want to get in and out of the Death King's territory without being detected."

"And put that amulet safely out of reach of any more potential thieves," I said. "Brant told me—"

"Brant told you?" she said. "You went back to him?"

"I ran into him outside the Order," I said. "He stopped

them from slapping me with a disciplinary warning when a wight followed me from the other side, too."

"So a wight attacked you, and you still want to go back?"

"Pretty sure I don't have a choice in the matter. The Order aren't going to help me."

"Did Brant himself tell you that, by any chance?" she said. "You know, he is a rogue. And now he shows up while all this is going on…"

"He's out to help me," I said. "I don't really have a choice but to trust him at this point."

"You do," she said. "Don't get me wrong, you two have a fair bit in common, but the trouble factor multiplies when you're around one another. If it's not one of you who's deep in crap, it's the other."

I shook my head. "I need allies. Even ones who attract as much trouble as I do. Anyway, I'm lying low until the Death King calls his soldiers off. Then I'll head back to the Parallel, but I need to be invisible when I do it."

She was silent for a moment. "I think I can pull it off overnight, but I'll need help."

"Whatever you need, I'll do it," I said. "I owe you—"

She held up a hand. "You've already saved me from being buried alive in paperwork fifty times over. But once that amulet is gone, I think you should stay out of Brant's business. Whoever's hunting down souls isn't someone you wanna tangle with."

"I have no idea who it even is," I said. "But the thief is probably looking for the amulet, too. After all, they presumably know the Death King's people don't have it, or else they wouldn't be tearing the place apart trying to find it."

She dropped the amulet onto the desk. "I think you should toss it out. Its owner was foolish enough to detach their soul, so it's their problem if it goes missing."

"Nice idea, but something tells me this thief won't stop with a single soul," I said. "Besides, Brant said he'd had an inkling I might be drawn into this before it all started, and there's something weird going on at the Order."

I might not know what exactly Dirk Alban and I had done which had ultimately left him dead and me with a black mark on my record, but if the spirit thief knew my history, I'd be drawn in whether I wanted to be or not.

Devon swore under her breath. "Get that amulet back where it belongs. Hear me? No getting distracted by side quests."

"Ha." I paused. "You should know... Brant also told me he knows someone who might be able to get my memories back."

Her mouth parted. "Legally?"

"Of course not," I said. "Reversing the Order's decrees is breaking the law in a major way, if it's even possible."

"Don't you even think about it," she said. "Getting those memories back won't solve any of your current problems."

"It'll stop me from getting taunted by every person I run into at the Order." I fiddled with a loose hangnail. "And it'll stop me second-guessing everything I did during that time."

"Is it worth getting shoved in jail?"

"I wouldn't *tell* the Order," I said. "They don't know how much I remember, besides."

"Then is it worth it?" Her concerned gaze washed over me. "Liv, I mean it. Forget those shitty guys from the academy. Not that I'm advising you to hook up with Brant now I know he's in as much trouble as you are, but he at least respects the person you are now."

"And who the hell even is that?" I said. "I have no idea who I was during that time."

I hadn't even started talking to Devon until we'd both been put on the list to retake our exams. Me because of the memory loss, Devon because of as-yet undiagnosed ADHD—neither of which were considered good excuses in the Order's eyes.

"Trust me, you don't need to know everything that happened in the interim," she said. "School was shit. We all know it."

"Devon, I could literally have ridden a unicorn to the prom with Gap-Toothed Dave and I would have no memory of it."

"Gap-Toothed Dave went to the prom with Judith. Anyway, if I could get your memories back with magic, I'd remember where I left my fucking keys."

"They're in the door," I said. "And I know it's not that simple. But those memories have some damned important stuff buried in them."

Maybe they would even tell me how to get into the Death King's lair and return his missing amulet. Yeah, right. But it was nice to imagine there was a solution buried somewhere in my subconscious. I doubted the Order had left one, and yes, I should be giving them a serious talking-to, but realistically, what could I do? I was nothing in their eyes except a troublemaker who'd already broken the law. While I was supposed to have two more chances, that wasn't how things worked in reality.

Devon was right on one count, though. If I didn't get

that amulet off my hands, I'd die before I ever got to the truth.

7

The invisibility cantrip was done by five in the morning, at which point Devon and I went to bed for a few hours of sleep. I set an early alarm, knowing I'd regret sleeping the day away. The sooner this sorry business was dealt with, the better. Not only did I still have that soul amulet, I also had a phantom in a jar which the Order might well use as an excuse to throw the book at us the next time they came here.

And to think I'd expected to take the weekend off.

After I'd taken a shower and dressed, I headed downstairs. The phantom jar wouldn't fit in my pocket, so I stashed it in my rucksack, hoping the lid was fastened securely enough that the ghost wouldn't burst out of my bag at an inopportune moment. The invisibility cantrip lay on the front desk, gleaming in the early morning light. I picked up the coin-shaped spell gingerly, grimacing at its sharp heat. Once activated, the invisibility effect would last only as long as I stood within the coin's proximity, so I wished we'd had time to devise a way to fix it to me so there was no danger of it falling out of my pocket and giving the game away.

In the end, I zipped the cantrip into the pocket of my coat, then I sent a text to Brant telling him I was heading to the Parallel. He'd be annoyed at best if I did this alone, and besides, he'd offered to help me. Despite my numerous misgivings about getting involved with him again, I'd be a fool to pass up his offer of help. It had nothing to do with our past relationship—or so I told myself, anyway.

He responded a moment later: *Thought you'd be asleep.*

No time, I replied. *Want to use the node in my living room to cross over?*

I didn't know there was a node in your house.

How else do you think Devon makes her cantrips? I sent back. *Best way not to get caught. I'm not going near Order HQ until this amulet is off my hands.*

I'll be over in five.

That must mean he was staying nearby, surely. He still hadn't told me the details on this 'permit' he'd acquired. Or why. As flattering as it might seem to imagine he'd done all this for my sake, Brant had had over a year to get in touch with me after he'd taken off, yet he'd chosen to wait until my name came up in connection with illegal soul trade. I didn't think he was plotting against me, but there were people in his contacts I didn't want to get involved with.

I had a more pressing matter at hand, however. Namely, getting rid of the amulet, and finding out why the Order had sent me on that bogus job to begin with. It was enough to make me suspect more than a simple mistake had been at work, but what did the Order have to gain by getting rid of me? Even if they'd voted to give me the boot, it didn't seem worth risking the life of whoever's soul was in the amulet, and as a consequence, incurring the wrath of the Death King. Even the Order knew better than to screw with the Court of the Dead.

It wasn't like there was anything I could do about it either way. The Order held the authority here, the Death King held it on the other side, and if anyone, even Brant, thought I possessed the power to get in their way, they were going to be sorely disappointed.

Brant knocked on the door, sparing the neighbours from another round of Devon's wailing doorbell. He'd always been an early riser, so he looked far more awake than I did, his hair curling across his forehead and his dark cloak making his blue eyes look deeper. He'd always dressed well, even in the Parallel.

"Hey," he said. "You've made a spell, then?"

"You bet." I held up the invisibility cantrip, careful not to flick the switch on the side of the coin that would activate it. "I'd test it now, but it has a time limit."

I'd never actually used a full-on invisibility cantrip myself, but I'd defused a fair few, including the one in the swamp the other day. I was relying on the hope that the Death King's people would be outside in daylight, and that the liches themselves didn't sense my presence even if I couldn't be seen. There were rumours of their abilities to detect living forms, but it wasn't like I'd ever had a conversation with one of them. Still, the four Elemental Soldiers were fully human, and they were my ideal targets. I just had to hope they were out and about and would overlook an invisible trespasser.

"Will the invisibility shield cover both of us?" Brant asked.

"If you're standing close enough." According to Devon, anyway. "I reckon we stand a better chance of getting the amulet into the right hands if we track down one of the Death King's four soldiers. They're human, without supernatural senses, and they also have a direct link to their boss. They'd want the amulet back in his hands."

"Doesn't mean it's worth the risk of showing our faces." He shot me a concerned look. "Where's the amulet?"

I tugged on the chain looped around my neck. "It's secured, don't worry."

He tilted his head. "It's inside your bra, isn't it?"

"As I said—secured." I was pretty sure the soul's owner wouldn't have a clue. At least, I hoped not. From his suggestive smile, Brant was recalling how his own fingers had explored my bare skin as we'd learned our way around one another's bodies, but I wasn't about to open that door when we had more important shit to deal with. "Weird how the amulet's hooked up to a flimsy chain, isn't it? You'd think the Death King would have used something more expensive."

"Hmm." He cast his gaze around the shop. "Where's this node?"

"In the back," I said. "I'll be honest, I'd rather know whereabouts the Death King's four soldiers hang out at this time of day before going in."

"We'll check the swampland first," he said. "If his people are still patrolling, an opportunity might present itself."

I didn't like going in without a secure plan, but as

every DM knows, no plan survives contact with the other players. I led the way into the living room, where Brant took in the cabinets of collectibles and the gaming board on the coffee table. It was weird for him to be here in my house—even when we'd been together, we'd mostly met at his place over in Arcadia.

"Devon's still asleep?" he asked.

"Yeah, we were up pretty late working on the cantrip." I found the centre of the node, intending not to disturb anything on this side when we crossed over. "Okay, I'm going in."

Together, Brant and I stepped into the node's path. The current caught me, and I let it carry me away, revelling in the rush of energy which thoroughly banished my tiredness. Who needed a caffeine high when you could hop between realms? I fixed the image of the warehouses in my mind and was rewarded when we landed in precisely the right spot, at a safe enough distance from the swamp that if the Death King's people had been rampaging around, they wouldn't see us before the invisibility spell kicked in.

"I left Dex near here last time." I scanned the deserted street. "Hope he's okay."

"You're still hanging out with that sprite?" he asked.

"Yeah, so?"

He shrugged. "I guess I didn't take sprites for the type who'd make good sidekicks."

"If anything, being incorporeal is an advantage when you hang out with me."

"Damn right," said a voice from behind Brant's shoulder. Dex appeared in a flash of light, his arms folded across his semi-transparent chest. "Thanks for the help, Dex, you're welcome."

"Sorry, Dex," I said. "I was running for my life earlier, as you may have gathered."

Brant's mouth pressed together in disapproval. "No invisibility spell will work on him."

"Like anyone's looking for me anyway." Dex snorted.

"They don't even know what *I* look like, let alone you," I said. "And I'd like to keep it that way. Hence the invisibility cantrip."

"You have a death wish," Dex said. "Those wights only cleared off when some of them got into a scuffle with the revenants and got themselves dismembered. His Deathly Highness is not going to be pleased."

I suppressed a shudder, recalling the wight that'd followed me home. "Yeah, I figured they'd have gone back to the swamp by now."

Dex flipped over in mid-air. "More like they went back to get reinforcements. Whatever your plan is, I'd like you to tell me so I can decide whether to ditch you or not."

"That's nice," I said. "Our plan is to get into the Court of the Dead and leave the amulet with someone who'll hand it to its rightful owner with minimal fuss."

"Meaning…?"

"One of the Elements, of course," I said. "Why?"

Dex wasn't generally one to question my plans. He grumbled—a lot—but he took my lead most of the time.

"Oh, nothing," he said. "I just find it suspect that someone with a castle as well-guarded as the Death King's abode managed to lose a valuable item to a single thief without anyone tracking him down."

I blinked. "What are you saying? One of his people helped the thief?"

Maybe they did. It went a long way to explaining how he'd overlooked the theft to begin with, but the Death King's disputes with his fellow undead were none of my business. I had quite enough adversaries of my own without being forced to take sides in a dispute in the Court of the Dead, thanks.

"Whatever the case, it doesn't matter," Brant interjected. "Once you get that thing off your hands, you've done your job, and everyone will leave you alone."

"Exactly." I held up the cantrip. "Wanna take this for a spin?"

"I'm ready." Brant stepped to my side.

I flicked the switch on the side of the cantrip, and in an instant, a rush of energy shot through my limbs. Then in a blur of smoke, Brant vanished. I looked straight through him, a peculiar feeling washing over me. The knowledge that he was there warred with the evidence of my own eyes. Looking down, the sight of nothing but emptiness where I knew my legs were made my head spin with vertigo.

Dex flew at the spot where we'd been standing, and Brant made a noise of annoyance. "You crashed into my face."

"Didn't see you there." Dex laughed hysterically at his own joke.

"Let's get this done," I said, before he could start needling Brant any further.

The three of us made an odd team as we walked towards the edges of the swampland, past the tree where I'd stashed my weapons. With any luck, I wouldn't need them—there wasn't much a knife could do against phantoms or wights, and I did not intend to wind up in a position where I'd have to stab any of the four Elemental Soldiers.

"Stealth check." I scanned the area. "Here's hoping for a natural twenty." As long as neither of us tripped over or sneezed, that is.

Dex flew in circles above our heads. "Being invisible won't stop you from making footprints in the mud."

"I know."

"Or being sniffed out."

I twisted to face the spot where I thought Brant was. "Is that possible?"

"Maybe." He sounded doubtful. "Not in this place, I wouldn't think. The swamp's smell would mask our traces. He's right about the footprints, but if we stick to the water, they should disappear."

"Yeah, got it. I'm not planning on hanging around here for too long, believe me." I walked on. Water splashed around my feet and ankles, but the marshy ground swallowed up my footprints as soon as they appeared. What with the imminent threat to my life, I'd forgotten my ruined new boots, but that hardly mattered now. I'd gladly swim through the heart of the swamp if it meant getting the amulet off my hands before the Death King realised I was the one who had it.

Low-level fog obscured our surroundings, including the dark shape of the castle in the distance beyond the gates, but not so much as a single wight appeared. Maybe we'd have to ride up to the Death King's gates to find someone to hand the amulet to. Or I could lob it over the fence, but Dex's comment about a potential traitor on the inside worried me more than I'd let on. What if I gave up the amulet only for it to fall into the wrong hands again?

A faint breeze blew from the direction of the castle, and with it came the sound of movement. I halted, squinting into the fog, as a shadowy figure approached us. *Dead or alive?* It was hard to tell at this distance, but the amulet around my neck seemed to grow heavier, colder, burning against my neck. I fought the urge to grab it. *Chill out, Liv. Whoever it is, they can't see you.*

Dex hissed out a warning. "Element."

"One of his?" I whispered.

No response came. The figure grew more distinct, resolving into the shape of a person wearing armour. A sword hung at their waist, while their helmet disguised their features. The shape of the Death King's coat of arms shimmered on the figure's coat. Although they weren't on a horse this time, I recognised the armoured gear and the swirling coat. One of the four soldiers had come out alone. The timing couldn't have been more perfect if I'd tried.

Now all I needed to do was to hand over the amulet.

I walked closer, my heart in my throat. This was one of the most powerful mages in the Parallel, hand-picked and given the title of Element by the Death King himself. Durable armour covered the soldier's entire body, making it hard to tell their gender or age, nor anything else about their appearance. The inside of the coat was dark green, marking them as the Air Element. Okay. I could deal with that.

I reached for the amulet around my neck, and the soldier's gaze snapped onto the spot where Brant and I stood. "Who's out there?"

The guard knew I was here, even though I was invisible. Did they sense the amulet? Maybe I shouldn't have touched it, but there was no other way for me to give it back. I was *so* close.

"Reveal yourself." The sound of metal rang as the soldier's blade appeared in their hand. "Or I'll run you through. I know you're there."

A cold breeze blasted into me, driving me backwards. I braced my feet on the ground, but the wind hit me like a solid barrier, preventing me from getting any closer. The Air Element's power held me pinned to the spot. *Dammit.*

I spoke in a whisper. "I'm not an enemy. I'm here to return something that was stolen from your master."

"Show your face."

No chance. I looped the amulet around my neck. "I don't have a quarrel with you—"

A current of air slammed into me, sending me flying back head over heels. The breath punched from my lungs, my body soaring through the air like a rag doll. I'd have grabbed onto the nearest target, but there wasn't one. Air buffeted me on all sides, and my mouth stretched open in a scream.

This is gonna hurt.

I slammed into the ground so hard that for a long moment, I couldn't move. My limbs twitched, cold as the grave, and a voice came from somewhere nearby.

"Liv. Liv, are you okay? Can you hear me?"

Who was that? Not Brant, though the voice was male. I'd heard it before...

"Who are you?" I tried to say, but it came out as a groan.

"Liv!" The voice was frantic. Familiar and yet unfamiliar. *"He's dead. She needs help."*

Dead? Who was dead? The image of a room flickered behind my eyes—an office with iron-grey walls painted with splatters of blood.

The real world swam back into focus. My eyes flickered open to a steel-grey sky, and something painfully sharp in my rucksack dug into my back and shoulders.

Brant was leaning over me, his face pale and his eyes wide. "Shit, Liv. Don't scare me like that."

I pushed upright, wheezing. "Didn't really have a choice."

"Are you all right?" He helped me to my feet, where I promptly fell against him. His hand trailed through my hair, touched the back of my head. "You're bleeding."

"Hit my head." I coughed. "Damn, the Death King's Elements are strong. Did you get hit, too?"

"No, you got the brunt of the attack," he said. "I'm sorry. Did you give the amulet to the guard?"

"What d'you think?" I searched around my neck. Then my pocket. "Dammit. I was holding it when I got sucker-punched across the swamp." I didn't even recognise the area I'd landed in, a patch of rain-soaked ground behind the warehouses where the city and the swampland met. Mud soaked through the legs of my jeans and the back of my coat, dampness creeping underneath to my bare skin.

I searched my other pocket, but my fingers closed on emptiness. The amulet was gone, and worse, the invisibility cantrip had worn off. Presumably because said cantrip had fallen out of my pocket, too. This just kept getting better and better.

I scanned my surroundings, cursing under my breath.

We were close to the place where I'd run into Trix last time, and I'd been lucky not to fall through a warehouse roof with the speed at which the Air Element had thrown me. The amulet might have landed anywhere, in the swamp or otherwise. Devon would be pissed at me for losing her cantrip, but that was the least of my problems.

"C'mon," said Brant. "You can't walk around bleeding like that."

"Says who?" I paced across the muddy ground. "I can't leave that thing lying around, even out here."

If a vampire found the lich's soul, for instance, it might well kick off a war with the Court of the Dead. And I didn't even want to know what that soul thief could do with a lich's soul at his disposal.

A nagging sensation in the back of my mind drew my attention like a hard-to-reach itch. I'd seen... something, when I'd hit the ground. A scene from my past, from among my lost memories. The echo of the coppery taste of blood lingered at the back of my throat, while my hands tingled as though I'd stepped headlong into a node. Spirit magic was linked to death—everyone knew that— and maybe hitting my head had knocked something loose, but not being able to identify the owner of the voice bothered me in a way I couldn't put my finger on. It wasn't Dirk Alban, because by then, he'd already been dead.

He's dead. She needs help...

Brant swore under his breath. "There's trouble."

I looked where he pointed. A tall pale figure stood in the mouth of an alley between warehouses, the skull amulet dangling from his hands. A smirk came to his mouth, from which a pair of gleaming fangs protruded. "Looking for this?"

8

The man was tall, thin, and wore a floor-length grey coat. His perfectly formed fangs and the intelligent gleam in his dark eyes gave him away as a vampire—not a revenant, but a blood-drinking, genuine vampire. Of all the people to get his paws on the amulet, it had to be one of the Death King's immortal enemies.

"Give that here," I warned.

"What's one of the Order's underlings doing with a soul amulet, I wonder?" The vampire smirked, showing his pointed teeth. "Interesting. Is this a valuable possession of the Death King's?"

"Give. That. Back." My head pounded with every word, and while part of me was tempted to let him take his prize and fuck off, I knew better than to think letting him steal the amulet would take any of the responsibility away from me. The vampires had been trying to get in on the Death King's territory ever since they'd taken power in Arcadia, and I wasn't about to let them start another war because the Death King's trigger-happy Elemental Soldier had decided to hit first and ask questions later.

"I'm not sure you know who you're dealing with, human." His fangs flashed. "If that amulet is not yours, it's forfeited to the first person to find it by default."

"Like *hell*." Now I recognised him. I'd had a run-in with him and a couple of his fellow vamps a few months back, and knew he made a habit of 'acquiring' things from unwitting humans in the city.

The slight problem? Vampires could move faster than an Olympic runner and had strength higher than a professional powerlifter. As I reached for the amulet, he sidestepped with lethal grace, his sharp fangs snagging my wrist.

"*Ow.*" Damn, that hurt. Blood trickled down my hand, and Brant's shout of rage reverberated in my ears.

Fire flashed from his hands, but hitting a vampire was like trying to catch smoke in a fishing net. The vamp's slim figure disappeared into the alley, and Brant ran after him. Flames flickered outwards and left burn marks on the wall, but in an enclosed space like this, he was as likely to hit me as the vampire.

Cursing myself for leaving most of my weapons in the tree, I reached for the amulet again and my fingers closed on nothing. Next thing I knew, the vampire had Brant in a headlock. "I wouldn't push your luck, mage. Be careful who you ally with."

"I'm with Liv," he said though gritted teeth. Flames burst from his hands, but the vampire released him before his attack made contact.

Cold hands closed around my own throat an instant later. I rammed my elbow backwards, and pain splintered up my arm. *Ow. Note to self: do not hit any more vampires.* It was like striking a boulder.

"Give me that amulet," I gasped, my eyes watering with pain.

"Why spoil the fun?" said another voice.

Two more vampires appeared in the alley's mouth. *Just great.* Vamps were known for playing with their food, and I should have figured the blood dripping from my hand would draw every bloodsucker in the vicinity. Fighting them all off at once would be out of the question. I squirmed in the vampire's grip, and my rucksack emitted an odd rattling sound. *Huh?*

Wait. The jar I'd trapped the phantom in. I was lucky I hadn't broken it when I'd fallen onto my back, but it sounded like the lid had come loose in the process. I'd bet that phantom wasn't happy in the slightest. *I can work with that.*

The other two vampires closed in, teeth bared, lusting for blood. I tried to catch Brant's eye, but his attention was on our foes, his hands alight with fire magic. The third vampire held me in his grip, his cold hands squeezing the life from me.

With all my strength, I threw myself backwards into his body with a crash which would have knocked me senseless if I hadn't put my rucksack in the way. As I'd hoped, the phantom shot out of my bag like the cork from a champagne bottle, straight into the vampire's face. He released me with a startled cry, giving Brant the opportunity to grab my arm and tug me out of the alleyway. I would have objected to being manhandled, but the blood pulsing from my wrist hadn't slowed, and my arm felt dislocated. *Definitely shouldn't have hit that vampire.*

Lightheaded and shaking, I ran after Brant through the alley and around a corner. Next thing I knew, Brant was opening a door and ushering me into a dark room. He closed the door, and a spark from his hand ignited an old-fashioned lantern.

"Where is this place?" I wheezed.

"A hideout of mine." He took my arm. "You're still bleeding. Your head, too."

"Shit." I touched the back of my head with my fingertips. "It's not deep."

"No, but we'll be lucky if the vampires don't follow us once they've shaken off our little friend." He released my hand. "I have a cantrip here that can stop the pain and another for bleeding."

I watched, bemused, as he reached for a set of wooden drawers and opened the topmost one. The room was around the size of a studio flat complete with a small kitchen and a sofa bed. This must be one of his bolt holes, albeit one I'd never seen before.

"I think my arm's either broken or dislocated," I added. "I left my cantrips in a tree, and there's an angry air mage and three vamps standing in the way."

"Let me see." He held up two coin-shaped cantrips and paced over to me, his fingers brushing my arm. Tingles of heat sparked in the pit of my stomach, despite the adrenaline surging through my veins. One cantrip stopped the pain shooting through my arm, back and shoulders, while a second stopped the blood flowing from my wrist and the back of my head. "That should do it."

"Thanks." I smiled at him with a rush of genuine gratitude. "It's appreciated. Did you buy those cantrips from here?"

"Yeah, I figure that you can never have too many healing cantrips," he said. "I keep them at most of my hideouts."

"I thought you used to live north of Arcadia," I said.

"I do, but this is a useful place to have a base." He headed into the kitchen area and I followed him. "Anyway, let's see that wrist of yours. Better clean off the blood."

"I'm not going to turn into a vampire." To do that, the vamp would have had to make me drink *his* blood. No, thanks.

Brant ran a cloth under the tap and dabbed at the blood on my wrist. "You've never met those vampires before, have you?"

"Yes," I said. "They were stealing from Order personnel a few months ago. I was sent to raid one of their hideouts. Reckon I pissed them off, too."

"You should have called me," he said.

"Excuse me?" I jerked my wrist away. "It was a job for the Order. I had no obligation to go chasing after you. I assumed you never wanted to see me again."

"That came out wrong," he said. "There's a rumour going around that some of the vampires are in league with the soul thief. Or at least they know he's here in the city and have no intention of stopping him."

"Not the council, surely." The vampires who ruled the city might be avaricious and greedy, but even they wouldn't be foolish enough to risk the ire of the Order *and* the Death King.

"Not that I'm aware of," he said, "but the vampires have been getting bolder in their attacks on mages lately. There's a rumour that some of them are intending to drive us out of the city altogether. They want to keep the regular practitioners around… a food source, you know."

"Got it." I took the cloth from him and dabbed at the back of my head before tossing it into the sink. "Is that why he bit me and not you?"

"No, he knew I'd torch his skin off if he got too close." He scowled. "Anyway, I'll send someone after those vampires, and they'll get your amulet back. You should go—"

"Home?" My hands clenched. "I might not have any magic to speak of, but that doesn't mean you get to tell me what to do. That's the Order's job."

He winced. "It's not that I don't want you around, but—"

There came a knocking at the door. Was it the vampires? I should have guessed they'd shake off the phantom and follow the scent of my blood, but then again, would they really take the trouble to knock? The legend about vampires having to be invited in wasn't based in reality, but perhaps these guys were more polite than your average thieves.

Or maybe it was someone from the Death King instead. Which would be worse, because I didn't have the amulet on me, and I had no way to prove my innocence.

The knocking came again, louder. Brant's mouth pressed together. Then he walked to the door and yanked it open. "Yes?"

"Hey," said a guy I recognised as the person who'd interrupted Brant and me when we'd been talking at the pub. "Thought I saw you sneaking around."

So much for the invisibility spell. "Yeah, we had a run-in with some vampires."

"We… right, your girlfriend's here." He gave me an appreciative look-over. "Liv, right?"

"Yes," I said. "Also, not his girlfriend. So you know the vampires?"

"You might say that," said Vaughn. "What did the vamps do, rough you up and run?"

"They took something of ours," Brant said, to my surprise. "I intend to get it back."

I shot him a sideways look, but he didn't catch my eye. Did this dude know about the soul amulet? Maybe Brant trusted him, but I'd seen no more reason to believe he wasn't out to get me than anyone else.

"No surprise there." Vaughn turned to me. "Brant's been looking for an excuse to get those rogue vamps ever since they started picking fights with the mages. He told you about the soul thief?"

"He did," I said. "So the vamps work for this soul thief, then?"

"They work for whoever pays them," Brant replied. "I think they deserve a good kicking, personally. Not least for what they did to you."

Heat prickled at my neck. "They do, but I'd like to be better prepared before we provoke them again."

"How'd you drive them off?" asked Vaughn.

"I threw a phantom at them," I told him.

He laughed. "Bet that ruined their day."

I didn't return his easy smile. Something about his knack for timing rubbed me up the wrong way.

"I assume he hasn't picked up the blood trail I left yet." I paced to the door.

"No, they're still running around in circles." Dex

appeared in a flash of light. "That phantom scared them silly."

Vaughn jumped at the sight of the fire sprite. "Who's that?"

"This is Dex," I said. "A fire sprite. This is Vaughn, a…?" I ended on a question.

"Earth mage," Brant said.

"Well, I'll be damned." Vaughn nodded to Brant. "She's the one, all right."

"What's that supposed to mean?" I looked between them, but Brant's gaze bypassed mine.

"It means Brant has some explaining to do," he said. "But I'd rather talk it over when vampires aren't hunting us down."

I agreed. Unfortunately. "I dropped my invisibility cantrip. If I had it, we'd be able to sneak past the vamps and corner them this time."

"Invisibility?" echoed Vaughn. "Made it yourself, did you?"

"Nah, a friend did." I wouldn't be able to pull the phantom trick off twice, so their distraction would be the one shot I had at getting the amulet back. "Dex, did you see where my cantrip landed? It fell out of my pocket when our armoured friend sucker-punched me."

"That's what fell? I thought it was the amulet you dropped." Dex flew over my head. "Oh. The vamps have it. *Oh.*"

"Exactly," I said. "Whereabouts did the cantrip land, did you see?"

"Somewhere near the warehouses," he said.

"Oh, right in front of the Air Element." Bloody perfect.

"Did you say the—" Vaughn looked at Brant in alarm. "You picked a fight with the Death King's soldiers?"

"Turns out they don't like invisible people trespassing on their territory," I said, wishing he'd go away. I'd barely begun to trust Brant again, let alone this stranger. "Tell you what, though, if we lure the vampires into the swamp, it'd be a good way to distract both of them for long enough to get the amulet back."

Vaughn glanced at Brant. "She has a point."

"Getting blasted by an Air Element would certainly get their circulation going again," put in Dex, snickering. "I don't want to miss this one."

"Rather them than me." I turned to the fire sprite. "Can you scout ahead and let us know if anyone's outside, vampire or otherwise?"

He vanished, while I returned my attention to Brant. "We need to get the cantrip. If we'd been invisible when the vamps showed up, they wouldn't have been able to corner us."

"True," Brant said. "They were toying with us, but even invisible, they'd be able to track us down."

"Which is why I think we should lure them into the swamp," I said. "I'm covered in mud and I smell like I've been for a swim in there anyway. Even if they do know we're there and they follow us into the swamp, the Air Element will target them and not us."

Though I'd prefer not to have another conflict with the Elemental Soldiers, I refused to let the vampires run off with the liches' amulet. I might not be worth much to them, dead or otherwise, but that didn't mean I wanted to be the accidental catalyst for another supernatural war. Even if the vampires weren't working for the soul thief, they could cause a lot of trouble with an artefact like that on their hands, depending on how valuable the soul's owner was to the Death King.

"I won't weep if there's three fewer vamps in the world," said Vaughn. "You want to get that cantrip of yours back first?"

"You've got it." I glanced at Brant. "I'll get the cantrip. You can create a diversion from afar, can't you?"

"Of course I can," said Brant.

Vaughn laughed. "He's been shooting fireballs for fun since before he could ride a bike."

So they'd known one another for a while. I filed that information away for future reference. "Can you help with the diversion?"

Translation: *please stay out of the way.* The more people were involved, the more likely it was that this would go sideways. Three of us wouldn't fare any better than two against the combined strength of a trio of full-grown vampires.

No, our best bet was to let the Air Element do the work. The vamps would take the fall for carrying the amulet, while it would end up back in the right hands where it belonged. Win/win.

"Clear." Dex appeared out of the air. "Be quick about it. Those vamps are still running in circles trying to shake that phantom off."

"Good." I made for the door, but Brant put a hand on my shoulder.

"Be careful," he said. "You're vulnerable with the scent of fresh blood on you. Other vamps might sniff it out."

"If I don't get that cantrip, they'll be able to see as well as smell me." I pulled away, angry with myself for getting bitten to begin with. And angrier still for knowing there was something Brant wasn't telling me. Vaugh too, but he was a relative stranger. *She's the one?* he'd asked Brant. I needed to have words with him, but not in front of his wisecracking friend with a group of vampires hunting us down.

I followed Dex's lead, treading through the back alley where we'd fled from the vampires and towards the area in front of the warehouses where the city merged with the swampland. Dex halted near the spot where I'd landed after the mage had thrown me out and pointed into a nearby gutter. "There's your cantrip."

"You know I can't reach that, don't you?" I craned my neck, standing on tiptoe to see onto the warehouse roof.

Brant stepped in. "I'll grab it."

As he did so, Vaughn caught my arm. "Don't think badly of him. He didn't expect you to wind up caught in our drama."

"*I* didn't expect me to get caught in your drama," I said evenly. "People lying to me is a sore point, just so you know."

"Brant would never do it to you on purpose," he said in a low voice. "He's never stopped talking about you since we met. Brant is willing to walk through fire for you, girl."

Dex snickered. "He's a fire mage. That's not noteworthy."

Vaughn burst into laughter. I glanced in Brant's direction, feeling slightly guilty, but he didn't seem to have heard. He lowered his hand, holding the invisibility cantrip, and headed back to us.

"Thanks." I took the cantrip from him, turning it over in my hand. "Dex, which way are the vampires?"

He pointed among the warehouses. "Want me to drive them this way? Into the line of fire, so to speak?"

"Perfect." I turned to Brant. "You go with Dex. Vaughn… you can join them, or you can hang back here, whichever you want. I'll head into the swamp ready to ambush the vampires."

Brant opened his mouth to argue, but the sound of snarls and crashes erupted from the nearest alley. At once, I flicked the cantrip's switch, and vanished. So did Brant, though his hands were solid as he took my arm, leaning closer to me. "Please be careful."

I didn't respond, not that he'd have heard me with the racket coming from the alley. Dex zipped out, and two of the vampires pelted after him, pursued by the furious phantom. Damn, that thing was persistent.

"Vampires hate phantoms," Brant said in my ear. "And the phantom blames them for its capture. I thought that's why you set it loose."

"Nope, I forgot I had the jar in my bag," I whispered back. "I'm guessing it's trying to get back home to the swamp."

Dex's laugh sounded as he flew overhead, drawing the vampires along with him. Brant's retreating footsteps sounded, and he appeared with a popping sound behind the vampires.

"It's him!" one of them crowed, dodging the phantom's outstretched hands.

I made a mental note to bring a whole collection of trapped phantoms the next time I went into a vampire's lair and resumed my retreat into the swampland. The vampires followed. There wasn't anywhere else to go, with Dex and Brant shooting fireballs at them from above and the phantom's relentless pursuit. Their shouts mingled with the crackling of flames and the distant sound of clopping hooves—

Oh, bugger.

The air split down the middle, and a torrent of wind slammed into the vampires like a physical force. I flung myself to the side just in time, as the air current sent the vampires flying backwards. The amulet flew loose, arcing though the air over the warehouses. Cursing inwardly, I took off after it, still invisible. The hoofbeats grew louder. The Air Element wasn't riding a horse, so they must have brought reinforcements.

The amulet hit the warehouse roof, clattering to a halt. I swore quietly and ran around the side, seeking a way to climb up and retrieve it. The sagging walls were made of some kind of corrugated metal, which creaked alarmingly when I dug my hands into the side and attempted to climb. It took three flying leaps before I got a substantial grip on the edge.

My hands slipped and slid as I pulled myself upward. The amulet protruded over the ledge. Almost there—

The pale, livid face of a vampire appeared opposite me, peering over the roof's edge. "I smell a rat."

"Dammit." I grabbed for the amulet, but the vampire's swift hand knocked mine aside. The warehouse gave an alarming shake under the vampire's overwhelming physical strength, and the amulet slid in my direction. I grinned up at the vampire. "Bad idea, that."

The roof split down the middle, and the vampire snarled with rage as the crumpled metal collapsed on top of him. As for me, I let go, dropping to the ground along with the amulet. Scooping up the chain with my fingertips, I gave the vampire the finger and backed away from the warehouse.

"Whoever you are, you're more trouble than you're worth," I told the skull on the amulet.

Then I looped the chain around my neck and ran like hell.

9

As I ran, I shoved the amulet into my cleavage and tucked the chain beneath my collar. The other two vampires had vanished somewhere in the swampland along with Brant, Vaughn, and the Air Element. I didn't know where Dex had disappeared to, either, but perhaps even a fire sprite wasn't immune to the sheer power of the Air Element.

So much for returning the amulet to its owner. I slowed as I reached the stretch of open ground behind the warehouses. The vampire might not be able to see me, but the cantrip wouldn't last forever, and without my allies, I was at a disadvantage. I needed to find a node and get the hell out, but I wouldn't leave Brant to the vamps' mercy.

Footsteps sounded. The vampire walked unsteadily towards me, his pupils dilated, his lips peeled back from his teeth to display sharp canines.

"I smell you," he hissed. "I smell a spirit mage. I know you're here."

What?

I remained still, trying to breathe as quietly as possible. If I could get the jump on him before he realised how close I was, I might stand a shot of bringing him down, but his words sent a cold chill through my veins. *Spirit mage.* They were extinct, no matter what Dirk Alban might have claimed. I was pretty sure even I would remember if anyone had found evidence otherwise.

Slowly, I reached into my pocket for another cantrip, hoping I'd picked the right one. That was the downside to being invisible—too much guesswork. The vampire staggered towards me, limping a little, and I turned the cantrip on.

A blaze of light sent the vampire cringing backwards. Seizing my chance, I snatched up a sharp-looking branch and swung wildly at the vampire. The improvised stake struck the vampire in the neck, sending blood pouring down his front.

As he crumpled, I lowered the stick, breathing hard. A howl sounded from the swamp ahead, and the second vampire ran at me, releasing a snarl. "You'll pay for that, bitch."

"No, she won't."

The vampire burst into flames. He didn't even have the chance to cry out before Brant's fire ripped open his skin and disintegrated the undead flesh beneath. Brant hurried over to me, brushing the vampire's ashes off his hands. The invisibility cantrip had worn off again. Checking my pocket confirmed my suspicion that I'd run through the time limit. With one vamp still alive and the amulet still in my hands.

"Thanks," I said. "Where's your friend?"

"Chasing the third guy." He took my arm, concern brimming in his eyes. "You're not hurt?"

"Not at all," I said. "I got the amulet back, but I'm guessing the Air Element still isn't playing nice."

"The Air Element isn't alone," he said in grim tones. "The liches are out. Shelter first. Questions later."

I didn't argue. Standing beside the remains of two dead vampires with a group of liches on patrol seemed too much like tempting fate.

He led the way back to the street where his hideout lay and opened the door. I checked in my pockets to see which cantrips I still had on me. "I'll need to take some of those cantrips, if it's okay. I doubt I'll be able to get to my hiding place anytime soon."

I'd been stashing my weapons in that tree for years, relying on most people's avoidance of the swamp to keep them safe from being stolen, and now it seemed everyone was using that place as their stomping ground. It pissed me off.

"Take whatever you like," Brant said easily. "Nice job staking that vampire."

"Nothing like the element of surprise," I said. "Almost the only Element I'm a fan of."

A smile flickered on his mouth. "Except for me?"

I didn't return his smile. "Brant, that vampire said something weird. He said—he could smell that I'm a spirit mage. Which is absurd, but he didn't sound like he was joking."

His expression turned serious. "I was afraid of this."

"Not helping my trust levels, Brant."

He took in a breath. "Spirit magic isn't something that goes away on its own, despite what the Order might want to pretend. They took your memories, but not your magic."

My throat went dry. "Doesn't make me a real mage."

"Vampires have strong senses," he added. "They can tell if someone's a mage or a regular practitioner. They can also sniff out our gifts."

"Not a gift." A cold hand clenched inside my chest. I'd thought I'd closed the door on that part of my past. Wanting my memories back didn't make me want the mistakes that came with them, mistakes which had led to me winding up in a room with a dead body and my mentor's blood all over my hands.

"Regardless, their vampire senses registered you as a spirit mage," he said. "Not a good or a bad thing, it just is."

"Is that what Vaughn meant when he said, 'she's the one'?" I swallowed hard. "What are you hiding from me?"

"Vaughn…" He paused. "It's complicated. I did say your name came up—*not* from me, Liv, I promise. But your case was pretty well-known."

"Yeah, you might say that." A bitter laugh escaped. "If this spirit thief thinks I might be a worthy adversary, he'll be disappointed."

"I won't let him get to you," Brant said firmly. "I hoped you'd escape his attention, but when you were handed the soul amulet…"

"You mean, when I stole it from a thief."

He shook his head. "No. The Order as good as placed it in your hands. They wanted you to fall into the line of fire."

"I thought—" I broke off. His claim sounded utterly absurd, and yet… and yet I hadn't seen anything to contradict his word. "I thought you said the soul thief was allied with the vampires against the mages. Spirit mages don't count. We barely exist."

"No, but a spirit mage would prove a serious obstacle to a thief of souls," he said.

"I wasn't in his way," I insisted. "Not until the Order sent me here."

Then it hit me. Who outside of the Order even knew I'd been involved in spirit magic? Not many people. Even Brant hadn't known until I'd let it slip one day when I'd been injured and half delirious. I'd been afraid he'd ditch me, and when he'd left, part of me had wondered if that hadn't played a part in his choice. Now, though…

Someone at the Order wants me dead.

Was this all because of Dirk Alban? If so, it was hardly fair. I didn't remember a word of our lessons. The Order had done their job well. But if I was still registering as a spirit mage as far as vampires' enhanced senses were concerned, then perhaps they'd ruled that it was safer for me to be gone.

Brant's gaze was full of sadness. "I'm sorry. I wish I knew who it was, but I'm operating on mostly rumour here, and I don't know the Order's personnel. But I don't think it's coincidental that the Order sent you after the thief. There's no way the person who ordered the mission didn't know what it was they were dealing with."

"If they sent me after the thief, why did they then order me to take it back into the Parallel once I had the amulet?" That part, I didn't get. Was there a genuine mistake at work, or were parts of the Order at cross-purposes? "Was the thief supposed to kill me, or the Death King?"

That, I suspected, depended on whether they thought

I'd team up with the soul thief or not. Perhaps they wanted me taken down before I had the chance to break the rules again. But that was as much of a guess as the notion of a faceless soul thief lurking in the city's shadows, sending vampires out to do his bidding.

Brant released a breath. "I don't know. I also have no idea what the Death King's relationship is with the Order. If I did, I'd feel safer leaving the amulet in their hands."

"Yeah, that plan went up in smoke the instant they brought out the threats." Anger clenched inside me. "I don't even know any bloody spirit magic. The Order *knows* that."

He put an arm around my shoulder and gave a reassuring squeeze. "And so do I. Once the amulet is out of your hands, your part in this will be over."

"Not if I want to keep working in the Parallel," I said. "Also, I doubt this is going to die down overnight. Phantoms and wights have followed me to the other side before, and I still don't know what the hell that other dude was playing at, hitting human witnesses with a cantrip. Besides, I don't think handing you the amulet and going into hiding will increase anyone's survival rate."

"She's got you there," Dex said. "Nice job on that vampire, by the way. Somewhere between crispy and well done."

"Ha." I turned back to Brant. "Seriously. If you have anything else to tell me about how *you* ended up involved in this case, it'll help me decide whether to trust you. I'll freely admit I don't trust your friend."

Dex cleared his throat. "I'll leave you two alone for a while."

He vanished, and Brant sighed. "You'd like Vaughn, if you'd met under different circumstances."

"I doubt it. He's a mage." Brant was one of the few elemental mages who didn't make me want to throw things at him every time he opened his mouth. "I notice he didn't step in to risk his neck against the vampires."

"They took us both by surprise," he said. "He's fighting on our side, trust me. He knows what's at stake."

"Which is…?" I prompted. "Why are you here? Don't lie. There's something in it for you, too. You're not just chasing this soul thief down for my sake. It's not all about the Order, either. Why'd you come back? What's at stake for you?"

"My soul."

"Excuse me?"

His mouth pinched. "A few months ago, the vampires tried to set up a trade deal with the surviving mages. You know how it is, we can't work in the same areas without someone starting a fight. I hoped a proper formal agreement with the vampires' council would change that."

"I take it that didn't quite work out, then?" I said.

"We showed up at this vampire's fancy old house on the other side of the city," he said. "The council members weren't there, but I didn't think anything of it. There was music and entertainment, and gatherings of practitioners. I'd never been invited to an event among the vampires which was open to mages. Vaughn hadn't, either. That's where I first heard the soul thief mentioned."

"By the vampires?"

"By their lackeys," he said. "There were… contests, among the guests. I may have got cocky and staked rather more money than I had on me on a game with a vampire. Vaughn did, too."

"Oh, boy." I could see where this was going.

"We lost," he said. "Badly. And since we couldn't pay up, the vampire was going to slit our throats and drink every drop of our blood. But he claimed that he'd spare us if we pledged to hand over our souls to their benefactor."

I gaped at him. "You're still living and breathing and walking around. You aren't a lich."

"I never said they took my soul... yet." He grimaced. "But the soul thief has me on a list, as the vampires make a point of reminding me every time we run into one another. The vamp's exact words were, *he will claim your soul when the war is won*. I assumed he meant the vamps were going to start a scuffle with the local mages and that his threat would disappear when we won, but so far, there's been nothing."

"If he's collecting mages' souls, then why take one from the Death King?" I asked.

"I don't know," he said. "That one took me by surprise. Vaughn and I were only two of the victims... there was a water mage who lost a game to the vampires when we were there, too."

I clapped my hands to my mouth. "The one who stole the amulet and hid in the swamp."

"Yeah," he said. "Perhaps he hoped doing the soul thief's bidding would make him spare his life."

"Got himself burned to a crisp instead," I said. "Too bad for him. Why does this soul thief need the souls of elemental mages, then?"

"To use in a spell, I think," he responded. "The rumours say that if one gains possession of a mage's soul and conducts a certain ritual, they can take our magic for their own."

A chill raised goose-bumps on my arms. His words sounded vaguely familiar, as though I'd heard them before. "But… it's not like a regular practitioner can actually remove someone's soul like the Death King can."

"We're not talking a regular practitioner." He released a breath. "Look, Liv, I've already told you too much. Just believe me when I say I'm on your side and I'll do my best to keep you out of this."

"This coming from someone who gambled away his own soul by accident." The guy was even worse than me, and that was saying a lot.

Dex zipped into the room. "The Death King's folks are out on the streets again."

"Bugger." Had the Air Element finally snapped? "Are the soldiers out?"

"No, just the liches," he responded. "Something about an escaped prisoner. Wouldn't know anything about that, would you?"

I blinked. "Don't look at me. I'm not a prisoner. They didn't even know I was there."

"They didn't," said Brant. "Who are they looking for?"

"A thief who was found on their territory, apparently," Dex said.

"Wait, you mean they're after the water mage?" I asked. "I didn't know they left him alive."

I'd seen the scorched ruins of his hut… but not a body.

Wait. The water mage knew where the amulet had come from. If I found him before the Death King did, I might be able to salvage this situation before anyone else got hurt.

"Want me to find him?" Dex said. "I can throw up some sparks where he's hiding."

"I doubt that'll endear us to him."

"Coming from the person who blew him up."

He had a point there. "Look, that guy knows how to get into the Death King's home. He sneaked in once already. If I corner him and get him to tell me—without letting on that I'm carrying the amulet—I might be able to return the damned thing after all."

"Assuming you don't get caught on the way," said Brant. "I don't know…"

"Got any better ideas?" I tensed at the sound of pounding hooves from outside. "You know, they never did see my face. Not even the Air Element. I'm going out."

Ignoring Brant's shout of protest, I wrenched the door open and ran into the street. Thundering hoofbeats reverberated in the dusty air, but I forced myself to walk at a normal pace, as though I was nothing more than a curious onlooker.

Brant caught me up. "Liv."

"Don't you start," I hissed. "I need to find a node anyway. You can't argue with that."

He couldn't. We moved casually through the alleys, glimpsing black-clad figures riding past and peering into doorways. Chill winds accompanied them, as though the breeze of death had crept among us with their presence. Creepy bastards. Without their souls, the liches had turned into something between spirit and human, their bodies fading into identical cloaked figures with shadowy faces.

A gasping figure pelted along the alley, in the direction of the node. *Not* a lich, but a human—wide-eyed, panicking, and running as though the hounds of hell were on his tail.

"Ooh, there he is," said Dex. "If I didn't know better, I'd say he was…"

Crossing over.

The water mage ran straight into the node. At once, a current of energy soared, and he vanished.

I didn't think. I ran after him. Brant shouted my name, but I was already in the path of the node. The surge of energy slammed into me, pouring through my veins, filling my body and spirit with exhilarating energy.

My knees slammed into hard concrete. An unfamiliar street surrounded me, terraced houses and cold grey sky —and no sign of the water mage.

Curses exploded from my mouth. I'd lost him. He must have hopped out somewhere else, and now I'd landed in some unknown location.

Brant appeared behind me, breathless. "Shit, Liv. You had me worried there."

"He's gone." I pushed to my feet, my knees stinging. "The bastard legged it. He must have come out somewhere else." I hadn't thought to fix a clear image in my head. I'd been focused on following him, and now I'd wound up lost.

"You're bleeding again."

So I was. My jeans were torn at the knees, while gravel studded the holes ripped into my legs. *Ow.* I rotated on my heel. "Any idea how to get to my house from here?"

"You aren't far." He pointed ahead and to the right. "The water mage won't resurface, in all likelihood. He was running for his life."

"He's as likely to get caught by the Order as not." I took

a painful step forward. "They're always on the lookout for rogues."

"Yeah, well, people do unwise things in order to survive," he said.

"Like wager their souls in poker games." My knees gave another throb. "Or jump through nodes illegally, multiple times in one day. Better hope the Order doesn't send another assassin after me, because I'm not winning any races in this state."

"Don't joke about that, Liv," he said. "Someone wants you dead."

"I know. Unfortunately." I heaved out a breath. "All right. Once I've cleaned up, I'm going directly to the Order. I think the only way to find out what's going on is to head there, not the Parallel."

My thoughts spun in circles as I walked. Someone who worked for the *Order* wanted me dead. I'd never thought of myself as particularly valuable or dangerous to them, but there must be a good reason one of them wanted me out of the picture. And I'd bet it had to do with the spirit magic buried in my memories.

———

After Brant and I parted ways, I entered the shop to find Devon sitting at the desk, idly playing with a couple of orc miniatures. "You look like you tore your way out of a dragon's mouth."

"Nah, I'd have fewer limbs left if I had," I replied. "Still, I've had one hell of a day."

"Please tell me you got rid of that amulet," she said.

"Judith showed up asking about you again. I told her you were still in the Parallel."

"Judith," I muttered. "Was it her who put them up to this?"

"Er, what?" she said. "Look, sit down. You're not doing yourself any favours by walking around with blood pouring down your legs."

I staggered into the back room, collapsed onto the sofa, and told her just how much trouble I was in. I made her listen *before* she started helping me remove the gravel from my legs, in case her shock caused her to accidentally stab me.

Devon was silent for a moment after I'd finished. "You're in deeper shit than that time you rolled a natural one on a stealth check and tripped every alarm in the bad guys' castle."

"Thanks." I winced when she applied a pair of tweezers to pull a shard of gravel from my leg. "Was Judith acting oddly?"

"No more than usual," she said. "That girl can't tie her own shoelaces without asking the Order's permission. She's not in on this, whatever it is."

"How do you know?" Fear and frustration warred inside me. "Someone sent me after the amulet because they wanted me dead, and I don't even know if it was the same person who sent me to take the amulet back where I got it from. Maybe they wanted to finish the job."

"Uh, *why?*" she said. "Not that I don't believe you, but we don't have the full picture."

"No kidding," I said. "The rogue vampires want me dead, too, and on top of that, I got bitch-slapped by one of the four Elemental Soldiers because the Death King thinks I stole one of his subjects' souls."

"Then how in hell did Brant end up involved?" she wanted to know.

"He's looking for the soul thief for his own reasons," I said. "I think he knew I'd be targeted, too. And once we shook off the vampires, the water mage who stole the amulet to begin with hopped through the node and ran off somewhere in this realm to get away from the Death King's soldiers."

"But he doesn't have the amulet. You do."

"Fat lot of good it is over on this side," I said. "I can't even return it to the wastelands without one of the Death King's own people blasting me with elemental magic."

"I really doubt returning it will get the enemy off your tail, Liv," she said. "Sorry to be the bearer of bad news."

My shoulders slumped. "Yeah. I know. The vampires have me marked as a troublemaker—which is also the Order's fault, I might add."

"Damn right," said Dex.

I jumped to my feet, heedless of the pain in my legs. "What the fuck?"

"I'm insulted," said Dex. "I'm a who, not a what the fuck."

"You're not supposed to be here!" I said. "You're a spirit. You can't survive in this realm."

Dex twisted in mid-air. "Funny. Looks like I'm surviving to me. You're the one who dragged me through the node."

"So it's my fault?" Something seriously screwy was going on. Spirits weren't meant to be able to survive on this side of the nodes. There wasn't enough magic.

Granted, our house lay on top of a node, but he shouldn't have been able to follow me all this way from the Parallel.

"Yes, it's all your fault." Dex flew overhead, bringing a warm breeze along with him. "Not that I'm complaining. This place is neat."

Devon swore. "He'd better not break anything."

"He can't touch anything, it's fine."

An orc miniature fell off the table. Maybe not.

What the hell is going on?

10

It took a good ten minutes for Dex to get the euphoria over his sudden freedom out of his system. He zipped around knocking things over until Devon threatened to trap him in a jar like the phantom. Once the gravel was out of my legs and I'd used a cantrip to seal the wounds and dull the pain, I set about making sandwiches for both of us.

"Want me to toast those for you?" Dex blew a flame onto the plate, and I turned on him with a scowl.

"Look, it's been a long, shitty day." I distributed the sandwiches between plates. "I don't know why you're here, but to be perfectly honest, it's not even in the top five weirdest things I've seen today."

"Then I'll have to try harder." He flew over Devon's head, rattling the jar in which she kept her dice. "Can I join your game? I bet I can beat Brant."

"That's not how it works." Devon walked over and picked up a plate. "You're a ghost, right?"

"Ghost?" said Dex. "Never seen a sprite before?"

"No, I don't spend my time in the Parallel," Devon responded. "I prefer my limbs to stay attached to my body."

"You're already more sensible than this one." He flew over my head, backflipping in mid-air. "I like your style."

"Ghost or sprite, your kind don't normally hang around people." Devon took a huge bite of her sandwich. "What drew you to her?"

I took my plate to the sofa, swatting Dex away with my free hand. "I saved his life. I told you that, didn't I?"

"Yes, but if sprites could follow anyone through the nodes, we'd see them around more often." She chewed methodically. "I guess they don't always survive the crossing."

Dex zipped over to me. "I'm very much alive, thank you."

"Yes, I know, but it might not be as easy to return you as it was for you to come here."

He stuck his tongue out. "Maybe I don't want to go back."

"You can't stay," I said flatly. "We're the only practitioners on this street. So guess who'll get blamed if one of the Order's people spots you flying around?"

Dex didn't really understand the Order. Small wonder, when I was the only representative of theirs he'd met, and I wasn't exactly a poster example of their best and brightest.

"You worry too much."

"Want them to lock you up in a lab and study you?" I chewed on my mouthful, ignoring Dex's dramatic expression of shock. "Seriously. I don't know how I brought you over here, but in case you missed the memo, we're in enough trouble without you adding to it."

Dex had not got the memo. He zipped around like a maniac while I finished eating and tried to figure out how in hell to return him to the Parallel without running afoul of the Death King's latest horde of soldiers. On the other hand, perhaps I could make use of his presence here. For instance, his tracking skills came in handy whenever we paired up on missions.

"Can you fly away from the node?" I asked him.

"I followed you all the way to your house," he said. "That means yes."

I brushed crumbs off my knees and rose to my feet to return my plate to the sink. "Can you sniff out practitioners?"

"I thought you wanted me to avoid drawing attention."

I ran the tap. "From the Order, yes. But there's a certain water mage I want to have words with."

"Water mage?" echoed Dex. "You mean that thief somehow survived?"

"Not only that, he escaped through a node somewhere in the city." I washed my plate, dried it, and stuck it on the draining board. "If you'd listened instead of zipping around like a hummingbird on crack, you'd know."

"Are you sure?" said Devon. "He'll put out your sprite's fire like a hosepipe."

Dex pouted. "I got the best of him once before."

"I'll only ask you to track him down if you promise to stay inconspicuous," I warned.

Devon made a sceptical noise. "Based on what I've seen so far, that sprite would fail every stealth check."

"Was that an insult?" said Dex. "That was an insult, wasn't it?"

I turned to Devon. "Got any better ideas? That water mage got right into the Death King's territory and stole from him without being detected. He'll know who's pulling the strings, and as an added bonus, it's harder for him to evade detection when he can't use his magic. He only came here because it was that or perish in the Death King's dungeon."

"Pulling the strings?" echoed Dex. "We're talking about the thief who wants to steal people's souls for reasons unknown, right?"

"Not for reasons unknown." Devon gave me an assessing look. "Brant knows the reasons, doesn't he?"

"He's adamant that it's all speculation." I returned to the sofa. "Look, I'm not supposed to be involved. For some reason, the Order wanted me off the table, and instead of docking my pay, they sent me to die instead."

"We don't know for sure what the Order wants," she said. "Except that amulet gone. Are you sure the water mage will tell you how to get back into the Court of the Dead? Because it's one hell of a risk if he won't."

"The Order—or at least some of them—want him behind bars as much as the Death King does," I said. "If he fails to cooperate, I can haul him in. They'd hardly be able to call me the villain if I bring them a wanted criminal."

But if they had an inkling that I'd so much as uttered the words *spirit magic*, I'd be slammed with another black mark at the very least. And if I handed over the amulet, I might well be delivering it into the hands of the enemy myself.

"Can I come with you to see the Order?" said Dex. "I've always wanted to meet them."

"Look, if they find out you're here, who do you think they'll blame?" I said. "The enemy already has me marked as a spirit mage. Which is ridiculous. I don't need the Order finding out as well."

If they didn't already. Devon gave me a sideways look, drumming her fingers on her knee. "Who told the soul thief about your past, exactly?"

I shrugged. "It's not a big secret. To anyone except for me, that is."

But I couldn't quell my suspicions that the Order's contradictory claims had another purpose. That not everyone had approved the original mission, I had no doubt, but what did Mr Cobb have to gain by sending me back to my death? I didn't know the guy. Or I thought I didn't.

"Big secrets?" said Dex. "I'm a great spy. Let me know who you want me to follow and I'll be good, I promise."

My mouth parted. The Order had my notes somewhere in their files. They'd know what information they'd stripped from me—and, potentially, the reason the soul thief thought me a danger to his plans. But if I'd ever known where they kept their classified information, I didn't now. On computerised records, no doubt. Dex might be an expert at break-ins, but he wasn't exactly savvy on all things technology. The Parallel had never quite caught up to this one even before the war.

My phone pinged with a message from Brant. *What's the plan?*

I looked up at Dex. "How would you like to help with a

little espionage? You'll have to be quiet and inconspicuous. No screwing around. That clear?"

"Of course," he said. "What, you're going to break into the Order?"

"I don't need to break in," I said. "I can just use the door. And I don't know about you, but I'd like to know why someone in the Order might be conspiring to steal liches' souls."

———

It wasn't a perfect plan, but short of sending Dex to scour the whole city in search of the water mage, the Order was my best bet. As I rode the bus into the city centre, I ended up having to shoo him out the window to stop him blowing hot air onto the other passengers.

"You're a menace," I said out of the corner of my mouth as I climbed off the bus. "I'm already seen as the resident weirdo. Aside from all the other weirdos who sit next to me, anyway."

Dex blew onto the back of my neck in answer. Ignoring him, I spotted Brant waiting for me. His jeans and plain coat made him blend into the scenery so thoroughly that you wouldn't have thought he was a mage with firepower at his fingertips.

The three of us made our way towards the Order's office. "I'm going to have to go in alone, I think. Dex, stick close to me."

Brant startled at the sight of the fire sprite. "How'd he get here?"

"He followed me," I said. "Don't ask me how."

His expression darkened. "He shouldn't be here."

"But he is, and he's going to help us," I said. "He's my best spy."

"You bet," said Dex. "Who am I looking for?"

"Mr Cobb," I said. "I told you. He's lurking in one of the offices at the back of the ground floor. But don't go in through his window, he'll be able to see you. Go through the doors instead."

Sprites might be semi-corporeal, but they could be seen in the right lighting, especially to sharp-eyed practitioners. I was relying on the Order personnel being as distracted as they usually were.

"I don't know about this," Brant said in an undertone. "Even if we did find evidence of foul play, who are you meant to report it to?"

"The other supervisors. I don't know." I scuffed my toe, frustrated. "I'm sick of being the person who knows the least, so let's start at the top."

In truth, I hadn't the faintest idea how to deal with the fact that my reputation as a spirit mage had made it into the Parallel's underworld, but let's be real: I was no match for the vampire rulers *or* the Death King. I needed the Order on my side. Which meant finding out who was a lost cause, and who was likely to support me.

"There's someone coming through the doors," said Dex. "Want me to knock them out and slip in?"

"No knocking people out!" I said. "Not if we can avoid it. We're going to stay inconspicuous. Go on, fly in. If you get spotted, it's on you, not me. Deal?"

Brant nodded. "I'll stay out here and keep an eye out. Be careful in there, Liv, okay?"

"I will." I hung back as the Order's employees exited the building, watching Dex zip up to the open doors and into the lobby. I held my breath, half-expecting to hear panicked shouts from inside, but none came. From this distance, I could see a number of Order staff walking around the lobby, oblivious to their visitor. I knew most of them by sight, but had trouble putting faces to names. Whether I'd had that trouble pre-memory spell, I hadn't a clue, but it made it bloody difficult to tell who might believe me and who might put me in chains.

As I prepared to follow Dex, I caught sight of a long-cloaked figure reflected in the windows, slipping down the opposite end of the street. I spun around, squinting at nothingness. Then the figure flickered back into existence before vanishing again.

The water mage. He was using an invisibility cantrip, and not a very good one—but it seemed I wasn't the only one who'd had the idea of visiting the Order. What the hell was he doing here?

I turned away from the Order's building and trod after him, wishing I still had my own invisibility cantrip. As he whipped around a corner, so did I, reaching for my pouch and pulling out a cantrip. Then I pounced, flinging a paralysing spell at him.

The blast knocked the guy clean off his feet, and his invisibility spell snapped off in a flash of light. He yelped and tried to cover his face, but the trap held his arms pinned to his sides. I climbed over him, blocking his escape.

"You again?" he spat. "Leave me alone."

"I've got something I think you want." I reached around my neck, revealing the amulet.

He tensed. "Give that here."

"Why, so you can hand it to your thieving friends over

in the Parallel?" I said. "I don't think so. But if you tell me how you got your hands on it and who you're working for, I'll consider letting the Order handle your punishment and not the Death King."

He fought the paralysing spell and tried to lunge at me, but I slammed a foot into his ribs. He yelped and slumped against the alley wall, all the fight going out of him. "What do you want?"

"Tell me the identity of who you're working for," I said. "And how you got into the Death King's realm without being detected."

"That information's worth more than my life."

"Can't be worth much, then." I kicked him again, and he gasped in pain. "Look, I can't say I enjoy kicking the shit out of you, but believe me, your amulet has got me into a world of trouble. I want it gone."

"Then give it to me." A faint blue glow lit up his arms. He was trying to use magic, but there wasn't any water within sight. Unless…

A rumbling came from below the earth. Oh, *Elements.*

With a deafening noise, the lids flew off the nearby sewers, sending torrents of water into the air like a series of miniature fountains. I jumped out of range of the nearest one, stowing the amulet back in my coat and running away from the surging water. The water mage broke into a run in the opposite direction. *Dammit, I won't let him get away that easily.*

I skidded to a halt when I saw someone striding the other way, marching towards the water mage like a human hurricane. I flung myself into an alley, not a moment too soon. A torrent of air roared past, slamming into the water mage and sending him flying a good six feet into the air. He smashed into the brick wall with a cry lost in the panicked shouting from the nearby streets. People would think there was a freak storm at work, which was better than anyone knowing the Death King's Air Element was here, walking around in broad daylight with their magic on full blast.

The water mage slumped into an unconscious heap in the filthy water he'd dredged up from below the street. I held myself out of sight, cursing my rotten luck. Dammit, *this* time I'd get that amulet into the Air Element's hands.

The Air Element had opted to go without the armoured uniform of the Death King's soldiers and instead wore plain trousers and a long coat. Probably for the best, considering the proximity of the ordinary shoppers who'd be wondering how the freak storm had stopped as suddenly as it'd started. The Air Element's mask was off, too, revealing pale, angular features and a shaved head, and while I'd defaulted to male when I'd seen the mage in armour, now I wasn't sure which pronouns to use. I'd have to ask. Assuming the mage was willing to have a conversation without blasting me off my feet this time, which was debatable.

"You got him?" The voice came out of empty air, and my whole body froze to the spot. A flickering image appeared beside the Air Element. A human-shaped figure, dark around the edges and cloaked in black. "Is that the thief?"

"Yes, I caught the thief," said the Air Element in a low voice. "You don't need to check up on me, master."

Master.

Fuck me. That was the Death King. Nobody else wore that dark armoured coat and mask. I hadn't known it was possible for him to be here on Earth—but then again, he kept his soul detached like the person whose amulet I held. Who knew what other tricks he could use?

"I have good reason to doubt the competence of my soldiers," the shadowy man said in soft, cold tones. "Does he have the amulet? Did anyone see him?"

"He never got to the Order." The Air Element crouched beside the body of the fallen water mage, searching his pockets. "No… he doesn't have the amulet, sir."

The Death King's voice was an impatient bite. "Then where is it? Don't let me regret giving you permission to cross the node. You know how the Order feels about us overstepping our boundaries."

"There's more than one thief," the Air Element said. "The water mage has accomplices."

I have your missing soul. Yet my mouth remained sealed shut, my body locked with more than just fear. The Death King's magic seeped through the street, insidious, deadly, as though his chilling essence had infiltrated my blood.

The Death King's flickering figure stilled. "If you're certain he does, then I'd advise you to find out where they're hiding. And don't return to me until you have that amulet."

"What do you want me to do with him, then?" queried the Air Element.

"Allow me." The Death King's shadowy figure moved forward, and a gasp caught in my throat as he *lifted* the water mage into the air. I'd thought liches didn't have physical bodies, that they'd cast them aside along with their souls—but he was carrying the water mage in his arms as though he was as solid as I was.

I stared open-mouthed. *What the hell?*

The Death King's gaze roved around, coming to a halt at the mouth of the alley where I hid, as though he knew I was standing there, unseen. Fear stabbed me in the chest like a series of knives.

Then he turned away, and both he and the water mage vanished, like smoke.

My body unlocked, trembling all over like a leaf caught in a blizzard. I'd heard rumours of what the Death King could do. He'd traded his soul for power, after all. But I'd never seen it in action before. Not like this. He'd dragged that water mage into the Parallel without any need for a node at all.

Maybe I was better off leaving the amulet lying in an alley somewhere instead of continuing to make the Death King believe I was working against him, but I knew better than to believe leaving the soul of a lich lying around wouldn't come back to bite me.

As I shook off my momentary shock, movement caught my eye in the mouth of the alley, and two uniformed Order employees approached the Air Element.

The Order. I never thought I'd be glad to see them. Let alone my arch-nemesis, Judith French. Her partner was a black male shifter, muscled like a lumberjack. He could probably have taken on the Air Element in a fight, minus the armour, anyway.

"What are you doing here?" he asked the Air Element.

"None of your concern."

"You're one of the Death King's Elements," Judith said, her tone somewhere between awed and contemptuous. "Was it you who flooded the streets?"

"No," said the Air Element. "I have no reason to make trouble for the Order."

"Then why are you here?" said the shifter. "Has your master started sending his underlings to stir up trouble on this side now? Don't think I haven't heard about his army marching around terrorising everyone in Arcadia."

"If you heard," said the Air Element, "you'd know something valuable was stolen from us."

Yes. I have it. I inched forward, but something held me back. Judith didn't need an excuse to sell me out, her companion didn't know me, and the Air Element would never take my side. If I decided to throw myself on the mercy of the Order, I'd need to find someone at a higher level who wouldn't arrest me on the spot. If such a person existed.

"Mr Cobb claims that's just your boss making excuses," said Judith. "He said you've been looking for a reason to take over the vampires' turf ever since they gained power."

"Really?" The Air Element looked between them. "If you'd take me to speak with this Mr Cobb in person, I'd gladly set the record straight."

Mr Cobb was the one who'd given me the amulet and ordered me to take it back into the Parallel. It didn't take a genius to figure out he wanted me dead, but it didn't sound like he was much of a fan of the Death King, either.

Is he working with the soul thief?

"Fine," said Judith. "Come with us."

The three of them walked out of sight. I remained still, my heart thudding against my ribcage. I would dearly have loved to have followed them to see what Mr Cobb had to say for himself, but I'd already burned out my invisibility cantrip. I needed to find Dex and Brant and get the hell out of here. I was responsible for Dex, considering I was the one who'd dragged him over here to begin with.

As for the Air Element, I was in real trouble if one of the Death King's people found out I worked for the Order. All they needed to do was ask them who they'd sent after an amulet lately, and the Order would give them my name. The only advantage I had was that as far as they knew, the thief and the person who currently held the soul amulet were one and the same. A common enemy. Not someone who'd stumbled into this by accident.

Once I was sure the coast was clear, I backed out of the alley and looked around for a likely escape route. The water mage had flooded the nearby streets, but he wouldn't be coming back. The Death King had him in his clutches now.

An echoing shout rang from nearby. Kicking into a run, I pelted out of the warren of streets and past the bus stop. More scuffling sounds ensued from the tunnel where I'd found the hidden node, and I glimpsed a figure fall to the ground. *Brant.*

A tall, shadowy figure stood over him. The third vampire was back.

11

"Hey!" I shouted at the vampire. "Get away from him."

"There you are." He smiled, revealing his fangs. "I knew you'd come."

I felt in my pocket for a cantrip. He wasn't as strong or fast here, but Brant's fire magic was dampened on this side, too, and he wasn't moving. *Shit. Please say he's okay.*

"Go burn up, you pile of bones." Dex flew into the vampire's face, causing him to stumble backwards with a curse.

I took the opportunity to swipe the vampire's legs out from underneath him, sending him crashing into a heap. Even if I'd had a weapon to hand, I couldn't exactly stake the guy in a public place, but if I hopped through the node, maybe I could take him with me. It was that or let the Order haul both of us off to jail—not to mention Brant.

I grabbed Brant's arm, feeling for a pulse. He groaned and stirred, and relief swept over me, instantly tempered by alarm as the vampire rose to his feet. With a snarl, he lunged at me, tackling me onto my back.

Fire flickered past my head, and Dex flew into the vampire's eyes. He might not have much firepower, but vamps hated flames even more than they hated phantoms. A second, more powerful, flash of flame scorched the vampire's hair. Brant was awake. He looked a little dazed, but his firepower was still working. The vampire backed away from him, and I felt the rush of energy from the node, realising what he was about to do.

Brant realised it, too. He flung himself at the vampire, and I did likewise. In a group, we crashed through the node and rode the energy current into the Parallel.

I landed on top of Brant, who lay pinned beneath me, groaning. Blood plastered his hair to his scalp, and alarm blazed through me at the sight of the puncture wounds on his neck. The vampire lay sprawled nearby, along with…

"You ruined it!" Dex wailed. "I was just getting to know your delightful realm."

"You saw a tiny fraction of one city." I rolled off Brant and straight into the vampire's grasping hands. He was back at full power now. Oh, *hell.*

Dex flew at the vampire before his teeth could make contact, while I set off a paralysing cantrip. Magic surged from the node, bolstering the cantrip's power enough to send the vampire flying backwards. Brant's hands blazed with fire, and the vampire landed on his feet, inches away from the flames. Another blast of fire, and the vampire got the message and ran.

"Sensible guy," said Dex. "More than you two."

Brant groaned, rubbing his head. "Ow. I should have seen him coming, but I wasn't paying attention. I was too distracted wondering why you hadn't come back from the Order, Liv."

"Are you okay?" I said. "We've got to do something about those bites. We don't need that vampire bringing his friends along for a snack."

He leaned a hand against the nearest wall for balance. "I have cantrips in my place. It's not far from here."

I recognised the street now. I wished we'd taken out that vampire while we had the chance, but Brant was in no shape to fight and I wasn't much better. Especially with my newfound worries that the Air Element and Mr Cobb might be conspiring against me right this instant.

Brant led the way into his hideout and sat down, while I dug a healing cantrip out of the drawer and handed it to him. The wound on his head closed up, as did the puncture wounds on his neck.

"You aren't going to go all bitey, then," said Dex. "Good."

"Mages can't be turned into vamps," I told him. "Anyway, did you see anything interesting at the Order? You weren't spotted, were you?"

"If I was, you'd have worse than vampires on your tail," he said. "I was on my very best behaviour."

"What did you see, though?" I pressed. "Because while that vampire was attacking Brant, the Air Element got a personal invite to go in and talk to Mr Cobb."

Brant's brow furrowed. "Cobb? Who's he?"

"Supervisor." I revealed the amulet. "Also, the dickhead who sent me to return this thing to the swamp."

"You think he's the one who wants you bumped off?" His eyes narrowed dangerously. "Which one was he?"

"You won't have seen him," I said. "Dex might have. He

might be a senior supervisor, but he's a practitioner, not a mage, as far as I'm aware. Not sure what he has to gain by taking me out of the picture, but he isn't even in my department and he ordered me to take the amulet back. Said the request came from the upper room, but who knows?"

"So you think he's the traitor?" asked Brant. "Was he the person who sent you after the thief to begin with?"

I shook my head. "Nah, that was the retrieval unit. They tend to assign missions at random unless I did something to really piss them off." Or I thought they did. Now I didn't know what to think.

"Where did the Air Element even come from?" he said. "I saw the water and thought there was a mage around, but—"

"That was our thief," I explained. "He's currently rotting in the Death King's dungeon, I'd guess. He came back to the Order for some reason, but the Air Element caught him first."

"Wait, our esteemed thief escaped into your realm only to go back to the people who arrested him?" said Dex. "What was he thinking?"

"I don't know what he was thinking, because he's probably dead." I turned to Brant. "You said your theory was that he gambled away his soul, too, right? So for whatever reason, he didn't feel safe staying incognito. He went back to the Order, maybe to ask for their protection. Let's face it, he must have been desperate. I mean, he made enemies of the Death King *and* the soul thief, considering he lost what he was sent to steal."

"Maybe," he said. "Or, alternatively, someone at the Order is working with the soul thief."

"Mr Cobb." Certainty raced through my blood. "He's not powerful, but he's a senior supervisor with connections. Two of the Order employees took the Air Element to see him, and I'd really like to listen to that conversation."

"Damn, I wish I'd stayed," said Dex.

"You could have, you know," I said. "But you chose to come back."

"I chose to save your sorry arses." He blew hot air into my face. "Look, if this Cobb dude isn't much of a threat, you could just take him out as though he was a regular criminal."

"We can't do that to a senior Order member without repercussions," I said. "Especially back home. I'm gonna have to think about this one. He wants me dead, and he has the law on his side to boot. If I get this amulet off my hands, I can at least take away one of his excuses to punish me."

"You didn't pin the amulet on the water mage?" said Brant. "Wait, if the Air Element went to see the Order, who took care of our thief?"

"Very good question. You aren't going to believe this."

I told both of them about the Death King's sudden disembodied appearance and apparent use of illegal magic to take the water mage back to his territory.

"You *saw* him?" Brant paled. "That changes things. Did *he* not want to go to see the Order?"

"I think there's a more important question… *how* was he there?" I said. "He's a lich. He shouldn't have been able to cross over into this realm without turning to dust."

"We're talking about the most powerful guy in the Parallel, though," said Dex.

"In the Parallel," I repeated. "Not on Earth. We weren't even on top of a node, so how's it possible for him to cross over?"

"The guy has more tricks up his sleeve than a stage magician," said Brant. "Creepy bastard. Did he see you?"

"No, but he did this weird thing where he froze me to the spot without even knowing I was there." A shiver ran down my spine. "I was sure he sensed the amulet, too. And since he and his Air Element are the disembowel-first-ask-questions-later type, I think I need to pay a visit to his castle directly to set the record straight."

Brant shook his head. "If he or his people catch you with the amulet, they'll think you're handing yourself in."

"If you have better ideas on how to get this thing back into the right hands, I'm all ears," I said. "I'd have cornered the Air Element, but the Order got there first."

"There's another way into the Death King's castle," he said. "Use the nodes."

I frowned. "What, there's a node on the other side of the gate? Since when?"

"You can find one," he said. "You've always been able to sense them, haven't you?"

"Not when I can't see them," I said, puzzled by the emphatic hint to his words. "Of course I can sense the nodes. If I couldn't, I wouldn't be able to travel here at all. All practitioners can sense them."

"Yes, when they're standing on top of them." He looked me in the eyes. "You can do more than that, can't you? Really think about how you followed that water mage."

My mouth parted. He had a point. I'd almost drawn the node *into* myself as I'd thrown myself after him. I'd always been able to feel the nodes more strongly than most, but I put that down to the frequency with which I used them to travel between realms. Now I thought about it, they said the nodes were the main source of magic the spirit mages had drawn on when they'd created the Parallel.

"I brought Dex with me." The fire sprite had vanished, perhaps to give us some peace. "I didn't do it on purpose, but it's like the energy from the node just… dragged him along for the ride. How?"

"I don't know." His intense stare didn't waver. "I can guess, though. I know it's a lot, but… can you remember when you first learnt about the nodes?"

That, I could remember. It was one of our first lessons on magic at the academy, long before my two years of corrupted memories. "Sure. I remember learning that the nodes are sources of magical energy, which is why cantrips work better when used close to a node. I *don't* remember learning that they can be moved around at will."

"Except by spirit mages." His tone was uncharacteristically hesitant, and he didn't meet my eyes. "You once told me… I don't know if you remember, but you mentioned travelling the nodes was the first stage of spirit magic."

I faltered, hearing a voice echo in the back of my mind: *"Lesson one: travelling through the nodes is the first stage of spirit magic."*

I *had* heard it before.

"Anyone can travel through the nodes," I protested. "If they couldn't, nobody would be able to come here at all. Not to mention the original Elements wouldn't have been able to create this place to begin with."

But who'd been the original founders of the Parallel?

The spirit mages. They'd opened up the nodes and used their combined power to create a paradise designed for the magically inclined. A paradise, at least at first.

"Yes, anyone can travel via the nodes," he said, "but spirit mages can sense them in a way none of the rest of us are capable of. And you can use the same method to find the node on the Death King's territory and travel there without risking capture."

My throat went dry. "I don't know how. Look where using spirit magic got me last time. Spirit magic breeds corruption."

The image of the blood on my hands flashed into my mind and bile burned the back of my throat.

He shook his head. "I'm not gonna argue semantics with you, but before the war, spirit mages were considered as legitimate as the rest of us."

"Until they destroyed the Council of the Elements and themselves along with it."

"Well, yes," he said. "But the Order took your memories, not your magic. You still know how to travel the nodes, on a subconscious level. Whoever that mentor of yours was, he taught you well."

"He's dead," I said. "And I don't remember a single second of our training. It's useless to me. All it's done is paint a target on my head."

"And saved your life," he said. "I don't blame you for being afraid, but travelling via the nodes isn't breaking the law. And it might be the only way for you to circumvent the Death King's army and get to the man himself."

I wished I could believe him. Hell, maybe he was right, but that didn't mean I was any more equipped to sneak past the Death King's defences without risking capture. As for exposing the traitor in the Order... no way.

"There's someone coming." Dex appeared. "Someone who looks very much like a certain vampire."

I tensed, falling into a fighting stance, and Brant moved towards the door. A moment later, the door crashed open, revealing the vampire.

"So this is your little hidey-hole." He bared his teeth. "I'm going to enjoy taking you apart."

"Nice try." Brant's hands sparked with fire. "This is your last warning. You should have told your thief boss not to screw with either of us."

"Oh, he knows the girl survived," said the vampire. "He also knows what you're hiding. Give me the amulet."

Fire flared from Brant's hands, but the vampire vanished, reappearing behind me an instant later. Flames danced past my cheek, and I pivoted away from the vampire's even white teeth. I wasn't about to get bitten again.

"Brant, stop!" I said. "He's trying to trick you into setting the place aflame."

"It'll be worth it if he's in it," he said.

"Not if we're here, too." Brant couldn't be burned by his own flames, but the house was a different story. And me, for that matter.

Teeth snapped inches from my ear as I spun around, dodging the vampire by a hair's breadth. Brant hit him with a flaming fist. The vampire shrieked, his body ablaze. His hands flailed, but the scorching flames devoured every inch of him, his skin peeling from his bones like mouldy wallpaper. In seconds, nothing remained of him but a pile of ashes.

I released a breath. "What're the odds that he alerted his friends about our hideout's location?"

"Pretty high." Brant irritably kicked the vampire's ashes across the floor. "C'mon. We should leave."

We crept out into the street and made our way through the outskirts of the city towards the warehouses and the swampland beyond.

"We have to end this." I felt for the amulet tucked away in my cleavage. "Once this is off my hands, I can stop worrying about the enemy getting hold of it. It'll be the Death King's problem."

"Speaking of problems." He indicated the stretch of visible swampland behind the warehouses. "There's an army between us and there."

Sure enough, the swamp was alive with warrior wights. Some on horseback, others on foot, cadaverous figures with sharp blades in their hands. Behind them, meanwhile, were other shadowy beings. *Liches.* One of them must be the amulet's owner, but if I walked into their midst, they'd kill me before I could speak.

No. I had to get past the army, and it seemed the only way to do that was to hop through a node and come out somewhere closer to the castle.

I turned to Brant. "How confident are you in my untested abilities? I have no bloody clue what I'm doing."

"I have every confidence in you," he said. "If you get that thing back to its owner's hands, we'll be free to pursue the thief without fear of retribution from more than one side."

"Sure, and the Death King himself will sign up to join us." I rolled my eyes. "Dex, I need help."

"At your service." He gave a salute. "Want me to throw fire around and ruin someone's day?"

"No, I want you to tell me whereabouts that army comes to an end. Is there anyone standing closer to the Death King's castle, behind the gates?"

"Oh, sure, I'll just pop in there." He gave a snort. "I can't do that, Liv."

"What do you mean, you can't?" I said. "You can travel through walls."

"Not whatever the Death King's got around his castle, I can't," he said. "I tried once. It was like trying to fly through a brick wall."

Damn. Maybe he has some kind of spirit-proofed barrier. For someone who employed spirits himself, it was a reasonable enough explanation. "Can you just tell me where the army ends, then?"

"Yes, O master." He flitted away above the swamp, while I walked with Brant to the nearest node. The shimmering current of energy tugged at my heart, humming underneath my skin.

I turned to Brant. "It sounds like the Death King's prepared for intruders."

"There'll be a workaround," he said. "I'll stay here and wait for you."

Dex reappeared. "The army is all around the swamp-lands, but there's only two liches on each side of the gates. As for what's *behind* the gates, I couldn't see that well, but I think all four of his Elemental Soldiers are out here in the swamp again."

"All right." I drew in a breath. "I'm going to try to travel through to a node on the other side of the gate."

"You're what?" he squeaked. "What ridiculous idea has that mage of yours put into your head now?"

"Dex, this is serious."

"If you say so." He snorted. "I can't get near the place. It's like there's some kind of barrier in the way, keeping me out. Who's to say it won't do the same to you?"

"Only one way to find out." It stood to reason that the Death King would have some hardcore defences around his territory, but I had to get the amulet back to him somehow, and I was all out of other ideas.

"You're stronger than a sprite," Brant told me. "You won't have any trouble, trust me."

I opened and closed my mouth. "If you say so."

Every trick Dirk Alban had taught me was buried somewhere beneath the surface along with my memories. Too bad there was no reaching them. I just had my instincts, a few cantrips, and all the good fortune my lucky dice could bless me with.

Here goes nothing.

I stepped into the roaring current of energy, and then I jumped.

12

I flew through the node's current, fixing an image of the Death King's castle in my mind's eye, its spired roofs growing closer. Then I flew out of the node, the air buffeting me in all directions and the shape of the giant castle looming over my head. The structure looked positively prison-like from this angle, all turrets and towers and crenelated walkways. Dark grey in colour, it resembled a medieval fortress transplanted over here from the Middle Ages, while the gates stood behind me, sharp and uncompromising.

Nobody stood waiting to accost me. Dex was right. The lich guards must be on the outside of the gates, not the inside, while the army was mostly concentrated around the edges of the swamp. They knew the thief was in the city, but they couldn't possibly know I'd flown *through* the nodes and skipped over the swamp altogether.

I rotated on the spot, breathing hard. I'd made it past the army. Now I just needed to return the amulet.

Dex appeared at my side. "Time to storm the castle."

"I thought you were too scared to come near the place," I commented. "We're in. Now I need to find..."

I reached for the amulet, but no longer felt its weight around my neck. "You've gotta be kidding me."

"What?" said Dex.

"The amulet. It disappeared."

"Maybe it went back to its owner."

Somehow, I doubted we'd be that lucky. I scanned my surroundings, wondering when it had fallen... and then I realised I was floating several feet up in the air, above the swampy ground. No wonder the castle didn't seem quite as looming and tall as it did from a distance.

"Uh, Dex, is there anything different about me?"

"New haircut?"

"Seriously. Look at my hand." I extended my right arm, and it passed straight through Dex as though I was no more substantial than he was.

"Fuck me," he said. "I mean, don't. That's metaphysically impossible for both of us at the moment."

"Dex, I'm a ghost. A phantom."

"Most phantoms can't say one-syllable words."

No... but the Death King's defences had done something to me. When I'd hopped through the node, I must have left my body behind. I'd made it in, but the amulet hadn't.

"Bloody great." I sighed. "How do we get out of here, then?"

"Presumably, the same way we came in." Dex flew up into the air, admiring the towering shape of the castle. "Don't you want to take a look around? It's not like anyone can see us."

"Famous last words," I said quietly.

A shadowy figure emerged from the castle, passing straight through the oak doors as though they didn't exist. The breath punched from my lungs, and against my will, I found myself being dragged towards the ground as though pulled by an invisible force. Now the castle seemed to loom taller than ever, yet my eyes were fixed on the person drawing closer, clothed in shadowy armour.

The Death King closed the distance between us, silent and fearsome. His shadowy hood and dark mask were all but fused to his face, hiding his features, yet from this angle, the Death King looked more... present. Not the transparent shadow he'd been when I'd seen him talking to the Air Element back home. Still semi-corporeal in a way only liches were, but more solid than I was at the moment.

I'm dead. I'm so dead.

The Death King spoke. "Who are you?"

I found my voice. "Nobody."

"You're astral projecting," he said. "You're not one of mine. Who sent you?"

"I'm what?" I couldn't think of anything better to do than to feign ignorance. "I'm here to see the Death King, but I sort of expected to bring my body with me when I did it."

Astral projecting. A familiar voice whispered in my mind, *"The second stage of spirit magic is astral projection."*

"Did you really expect to gain access to my castle so easily?" He moved closer, his cloak whispering along the ground. "Nobody is allowed in here but my own kind. The only reason I am sparing you is because I'm curious as to how you learned to astral project and bring a fire sprite with you, too."

Dex startled, swooping into an exaggerated bow. "Oh, your Deathly Highness, we made a mistake. Terribly sorry."

"Yes, we are." I backed up. "But I'm willing to meet with you in the flesh. I have something you want."

"I don't negotiate with rogues." Behind him, several other figures emerged from the castle, all equally shadowy, albeit without the decorative armour or mask. Crap. Of course he hadn't sent his entire army out there into the swamp. Each of his fellow liches had an amulet like the one I'd unintentionally acquired, which meant they could get knocked down a thousand times and still get up again.

"Two intruders," said the Death King. "Take them out."

The liches floated towards me, insubstantial as mist yet cold as an arctic frost. Hands grasping, shadowy and skeletal, cloaks swirling like tattered curtains.

"Wait!" yelled Dex. "I'm just an innocent bystander."

If either of us had been solid, I'd have cuffed him on the head. "Hey! We're not here to harm your king. I'm on your side."

The Death King looked me directly in the eyes. "If you're telling the truth, I'd strongly advise that you run."

His companions advanced forward, each wearing black cloaks which moved like serpentine shadows. The Death King alone wore real armour, his own cloak more solid-looking, and embossed with the emblem of a skull. The twin of the mark on the amulet I'd unintentionally stolen.

No. It can't be.

Shadowy hands reached for me, sucking on the living

force within me like drawing the marrow from bone. If I let them touch me, I was worse than dead.

The node. Find the node.

I didn't need a body to travel through the nodes. Dex was proof of that. Pushing down my panic, I sought the bright rushing current of energy, piercing the swampland like a star in endless blackness. Dex flew closer, all but clinging to me, and the brief flare of energy was enough to restore some of my strength. I reached for the brightness, pulsing through the heart of the Parallel, and let the node draw me in, willing myself to travel back towards the point where I'd left my body behind. The node's embrace swallowed me up, and I emerged from the other side in a rush, spinning dizzily on the spot.

I'd made it outside the Death King's territory, but my body was nowhere in sight. The shimmering nodes stood out amidst my surroundings, bringing a rush of déjà-vu. I'd seen this before, once, though I couldn't recall when—and yet that wasn't the forefront thought in my mind.

I have the Death King's soul. Someone stole the soul of the most powerful man in the Parallel.

Worse, he'd seen me. Not *with* it, but I'd told him I had something he wanted, and now all his liches would know my face.

"Damn, Liv," said Dex. "What're you doing?"

"Finding my body, for a start." I peered down the street where we'd crossed over. "Brant's gone. Must have run."

Not that I blamed him. I'd drawn every lich within reach, and now they'd all be on the lookout for the rogue spirit mage who'd had the nerve to astral project onto the Death King's turf.

Did I learn to astral project when I trained with Dirk Alban? Before I lost my memories?

If so, then the memory was ingrained somewhere in my subconscious, and it must have been triggered when I'd tried to get into the Death King's territory. Instead of bouncing straight off his defences, I'd projected onto the other side.

"Hey, at least we found out you can leave your body," said Dex. "You're like me now."

"I'm not like you," I protested. "You're not human."

They said sprites were the remnants of the magic belonging to those whose lives had been lost in the war. The war, which was supposed to have wiped out all the spirit mages. And yet here I was, and I refused to die without finding out why Dirk Alban had sought to make me the exception to the rule.

I rotated on the spot, scanning for familiar territory. Brant couldn't have gone far. Now I recognised the way to his hideout, and flew in that direction, past warehouses and beaten down houses. Reaching the right one, I passed through the door, and the sight of my own body lying on the sofa bed sent a jolt of shock to my core.

Then my eyes flew open. I lay on my back, my gaze on the ceiling, my breaths coming quickly. Vaughn stood over me with an awed expression on his face. "Whoa, Liv. I thought you were dead."

"Not quite." Did he know what I'd done? It was bad enough that the Death King knew. "Where's Brant?"

"Looking for trouble," he responded. "The liches are out there patrolling the streets. Scary beasts."

I reached for my neck and felt for the reassuring weight of the amulet. Or not so reassuring. How had someone stolen the *Death King's* soul without him noticing? Granted, he'd been separated from it for centuries, for all I knew, but still.

The liches were ageless, and the Death King himself, most of all. When they separated their souls, they gained immortality in the process and became something far removed from the living beings they'd been beforehand. Everyone knew it, but I hadn't really thought about what it would mean. That loss of humanity. The utter disconnect from reason and sympathy. I'd been lucky to get out. Really lucky.

And now the Death King himself knew there was an illegal spirit mage here in the Parallel. He might not be on the same side as the thief, but that didn't mean he'd show me any mercy if he caught me. He'd take back his soul, and then take mine as a bonus.

I sat upright, shivering all over, when there came a knocking at the door. Vaughn paced towards it, and when Brant entered, the two exchanged a few words before Vaughn slipped into the street.

Brant strode to my side and swept me into a hug. "Congratulations."

Whatever I'd expected to hear, it wasn't that. "You what?"

"You made it in," he said. "I knew you could."

"Brant, my soul got ripped out of my body." I pulled back from him. "I nearly *died.*"

"Your soul wasn't ripped out," he said. "You tried to access the node, and I'm guessing the Death King's defences kicked off your powers."

"Yes, and he nearly killed me," I said. "What the hell are

you congratulating me for? Since when was it good news for me to wind up on the Death King's hit list?"

"You're a spirit mage," he said. "That proves my point. Your memories might be gone, but you still have all your skills."

"That's not the point." But he was right. I might have forgotten my skills, but my body and spirit hadn't. Like a muscle memory, they'd never been erased. "The Order will have my head for this, assuming the Death King doesn't get there first. He thinks I'm the thief, and I can't return the amulet if I can only get into his castle via astral projection, can I?"

More to the point, the amulet didn't belong to any old lich, but the King himself. No wonder he'd personally involved himself in getting it back.

"The amulet?" said Brant. "Ah. I should have realised you wouldn't be able to carry it through with you."

"Even though there's a soul trapped inside it," I added. "How does that work?"

"If I knew, I'd know how to save my own." He gave a half smile. "It's a lich thing, and I get the impression it's a one-way spell."

No kidding. They said their dark bargain was how the liches had survived the war, but if they'd ever had real bodies, they didn't anymore. I'd thought their amulets contained the entirety of their life essence, yet the Death King had still managed to astral project without his. Into the regular world, no less.

"Please don't separate your soul." I rose to my feet. My legs felt wobbly, disconnected, like I'd been asleep for a long time.

Brant caught my arm as I stumbled. "Whoa. You okay?"

I sank down onto the sofa bed again. "I just used spirit magic, for the first time in Elements know how long. I have no idea what the hell is going on, but now the Death King himself wants me dead and nobody is telling me the truth. I'm a long way from okay, Brant."

"I'm sorry." He pulled me against him, wrapping his strong arms around my shoulders. "Sorry I contributed. I had no idea, I really didn't."

I could believe that. He was as impulsive as a leaping flame, and here I was, hurling myself over the edge of a cliff with him again.

I wrenched away from his grip, ignoring his hurt expression. I wanted my own bed, my own house, and no liches trying to feast on my soul.

"Are the liches near the house?" I asked.

"Not close by," he said. "Most of them are in the swamplands."

"Looking for me." I gave a humourless smile. "Or whatever they saw of me. He knew I was astral projecting."

Brant extended a hand, then let it fall to his side, his mouth pinching with concern. "I swear I didn't know the Death King's defences would have that effect on you."

"But you were curious enough to use me as a lab rat," I said. "And you wonder why I have trust issues. Whatever happened to getting my memories back? Or was that a ploy to trick me into working with you again? Because you seem awfully keen on me using the same magic that got me slapped with a black mark once before."

"I just wanted you to get rid of the amulet," he said. "I already offered to take it off your hands—"

"And you think I'll let the Death King's army trample you?" The guy had zero caution. He'd get himself killed. He'd already all but lost his soul to the enemy.

I didn't want to lose him. The realisation scraped me to the core. He annoyed the shit out of me, he'd already taken off once, and yet... and yet I couldn't fathom the idea of turning my back and letting this so-called soul thief take away his soul.

"I never thought of you as a lab rat, Liv," he said softly.

"But you lied by omission." I clenched my shaking hands. "You knew I was a spirit mage, and only told me when it turned out someone wants me *dead* for it. Quite a few someones."

"Liv, I swear I didn't know it was this serious," he said. "I thought this thief guy was working with a few revenants and that's it. I got involved when my own soul was on the line, but I never expected..."

Someone to steal the soul of the most powerful man in the Parallel.

"So how do the souls fit into this?" I said. "What exactly is this thief planning on doing with the souls he acquires?"

Owning someone's soul meant owning their power, but surely the Death King wouldn't have made it that easy for someone to claim dominion over him.

Or would he?

Then it hit me. "The person doing this *is* one of the spirit mages. Right?"

Brant closed his eyes. "I swear, I didn't know. I thought they were extinct."

"Apart from me." I pushed upright, cursing my shaking limbs. Had spirit magic always had that much of a toll on me, or was it because it'd been so many years since I'd last used it? I was in no shape to fight. Let alone go head to head with a fellow spirit mage.

After all, he didn't want any old soul. He wanted the soul of the King of the Dead himself. He wanted to kick the Death King off his throne and obtain dominance... and I was the only person standing between him and achieving his goal.

13

No liches patrolled the streets when we went outside, to my relief. I could barely walk in a straight line, and I was in no fit state to traipse over to the Death King's swamp and beg for one of his faceless monsters to take the amulet off my hands.

Knowing its real value, though, I didn't dare leave it in anyone's hands except for its owner's. Anyone in this city, in this realm, might be working with the rogue spirit mage. And now I knew what I was up against, the enemy's interest in me made a horrible kind of sense. The enemy didn't just see me as an annoying obstacle, but a competitor with the kind of skills that could really mess up their plans.

Of course, the reality was that I had no skills but missing memories and instincts and little more. I stood as little a chance against them as I did against the Death King himself.

The person who'd stolen the amulet had been able to get past all his defences without resorting to astral projection. That brought theories I didn't like to contemplate, exhausted as I was, so I pushed them to the back of my mind and concentrated on getting to the node. Brant held my elbow as I walked, and I didn't have the strength to push him away.

Brant and I walked through the node and crossed over, emerging in the back room of the house. Devon wasn't around, but she'd still be working in the shop at this time and expecting me to come back on the bus. I'd lost track of the number of illegal crossings I'd committed by now, but I couldn't bring myself to give a shit.

Brant kissed me goodbye—a quick brush of his lips over mine—and walked through the door into the shop, leaving me too startled to voice an objection. After our clash earlier, kissing him had been the last thing on my mind, but his latest revelations painted a different picture of his reasons for keeping me in the dark. Elements help me, but I understood why he'd done it. That didn't mean I was any closer to figuring out what *I* wanted.

As the sound of the door closing echoed through from the shop, Devon emerged into the back room. "Liv, what's going on?"

I staggered over to the sofa and collapsed onto it. "You're not going to believe this."

Devon closed the door behind her. "You *did* go to the prom with Gap-Toothed Dave?"

"This isn't funny." I reached around my neck and held up the amulet with trembling fingers. "I have the Death King's soul."

She blinked. "I know. I mean, it's what we've been trying to get rid of for the last two days."

"I don't mean any old soul, I meant literally the soul of His Deathly Highness himself."

Another blink. Then her jaw dropped. "You're kidding. *How?*"

I held the amulet up to the light, which shone on the skull symbol, my swimming vision warping it into an even more grotesque shape. "If I knew that, I'd know how to get it back where it's supposed to be. I tried hopping through a node into the Death King's castle, but his security caused me to astral project instead."

Her attention turned from the amulet back to me again. "You did what?"

"Split from my body." I swallowed hard. "I don't know how. I guess it was because I couldn't get through the defences in a physical sense, so... my magic kicked in to compensate."

Devon was silent for a moment. I could almost hear the thoughts whirring in her head. "How did you get *back* to your body?"

"Instinct." I rested my head against the cushions, my eyes closing. "So I guess I'm a spirit mage."

"Tell me something I don't know."

"What?" I opened my eyes. "You are being way too casual about this."

"You got dinged for using illegal spirit magic," she said. "The Order wouldn't have zapped out your memories if that mentor of yours had just had you making him tea."

With difficulty, I shifted into an upright position so I could look at her. "Yes, I know I used spirit magic *then,* but that was all in the past."

"You can still use it," she said. "They say you never forget how to ride a bike, right?"

"I think hopping out of my body is a bit different," I said. "It explains why the soul thief thought I'd be a danger to his plans. I doubt even he would have guessed I'd accidentally steal the amulet, though. As for the Death King, the odds are high that he'll kill me before the soul thief has the chance to."

I filled her in on the other details. Devon started out fidgeting and ended with her gaze fixed intently on me. "I should have guessed there was more going on than a simple theft. I mean, there's a few hundred liches living on his territory. One amulet going missing oughtn't have warranted him sending out his entire army."

"Who stole the damned thing to begin with without him noticing?" I remarked. "I mean, he's been a lich long enough not to notice his soul's wandering around attached to someone else, but you'd think he'd be able to sense it..."

Like when he'd looked directly at my hiding place when he'd been astral projecting, for instance.

She gave me an assessing look. "Wait, does that mean he's watching us right now?"

"I hope not. I've been carrying that thing in my cleavage for the last day."

Devon howled with laughter. I didn't find it funny.

"You know how screwed we are now?" I said. "He thinks I'm trying to assassinate him."

"Nah, that's impossible," she said. "Pretty sure that thing's indestructible."

"Even Death Kings don't live forever." I turned the amulet over in my hands. "If we don't get it back to him, he'll kill all of us."

"Relax,' she said. "He rarely leaves the Parallel, and it's not like he knows our address."

"That doesn't mean he doesn't have contacts on the surface, though," I said. "Nor the soul thief, come to that. He hired someone to steal the soul of one of the most powerful people in the Parallel. He's not going to just give up and let the likes of me walk off with his prize. And what exactly happens when the Death King dies?"

She paled. "Motherfucking crap. Another war."

"Thank you for finally understanding why I'm scared."

"I'd be freaked out in your place," she said. "But really, there's something odd about how that amulet escaped his notice. I'm not sure that water mage was the person who stole it, to tell you the truth."

"He had an invisibility cantrip," I said. "I saw him using one when he was sneaking around near the Order."

"Why was he even there?" Her brow wrinkled. "You'd think he'd want to lie low."

"The Death King has him now." Chills raced down my arms. "But I reckon escaping the Parallel wouldn't put him out of reach of the soul thief, no matter how far he ran. He's marked for death. And so is Brant."

Devon tapped her foot. "I don't know if it's just me, but I'm starting to find it suspect that Brant knows more than you do about your own powers."

"Duh, so do you," I pointed out. "And Dex. And the Order. Hell, the milkman probably does, too. And the old lady who always tells me her medical issues on the forty-five bus."

Devon snorted. "Nah. We all know you were a spirit mage, but not the details. Brant, though, *he* knew you could use the nodes to get into the Death King's place."

"Because everyone can use the nodes," I said. "That's only the first stage of spirit magic. The second is astral projection. I don't know any of the others."

"Part of you does," she said. "And Brant, too."

He was no spirit mage, but he'd had good reason to research the subject, considering his own soul was on the line. "He's lived in the Parallel for years, he has contacts. Besides, I have no choice but to trust him considering how many other people are out to get me."

"I get that," she said. "I wasn't gonna tell you, but…"

"Tell me what?" My heart lurched. "Don't tell me the Order sent someone here again."

"You've got it." She pursed her lips. "They got a tip-off, supposedly, about someone exposing magic to regular humans. No concrete eyewitness accounts, but considering how few practitioners work independently…"

"That's not why they'd blame you." My hands fisted. "It's because they want another way to get at me. It did cross my mind, when someone attacked those people at the bus stop the other day. It didn't seem like they were trying to hurt anyone. More like they wanted to draw attention."

To me. No other practitioners had been present.

Devon pursed her lips. "Yeah. That."

"Who's giving them orders, then?" I asked. "Mr Cobb?"

"Judith didn't say," she said. "Don't hate me for this, but I think you should drop off the amulet with the Order and make it their problem instead."

"I thought you wanted me to put it back where it came from."

"That was before you ended up nose to nose with the *Death King,*" she said. "And before we found out it was his.

The Order and he are on close speaking terms with one another, I'm sure. They can get it into his hands."

"That's putting a lot more faith in the Order than I'd like," I commented. "For all I know, the Order knows the Death King's army is hunting for me, too, and they'll hand me over along with the amulet."

"Would he admit to the Order that he lost his soul?" she said. "I wouldn't, if I were him. The Order might be his allies, but he wouldn't want the whole world to know his vulnerabilities."

I opened and closed my mouth, recalling how he'd been able to use some of his powers even while astral projecting. Vulnerable was *not* a word I'd use in association with a faceless masked monster, but without his soul? Perhaps he was, however unlikely it seemed.

There was just one slight issue. "There's someone working against me within the Order itself, even if you disregard the Death King's people hunting me down. The person who sent me to get the amulet the first time and the person who told me to put it back are at cross-purposes, and there's no guarantee that whoever I give it to isn't just going to hand it straight to the soul thief."

I was almost certain Mr Cobb was as squeaky clean as a swamp monster, but with no proof of his guilt, I'd be the one to face the backlash.

"The Order or the Death King," she said. "Your choice."

"It's like being asked to choose between crossing a river of lava or trekking over a deadly mountain filled with dragons."

"Hey, I'm not the one who set up this scenario," said Devon. "What would your D&D character do?"

My tiefling rogue would have run like hell by now. She

knew how to pick her battles. I'd thought I did, too, but the notion of the Parallel potentially winding up in the midst of a second war made me go cold inside. The idea of Brant losing his soul, even more so.

Death or the Order. What a choice.

I swallowed against my dry throat. "The Death King."

———

Once Devon had closed up the shop for the evening, we set about devising a plan. With using the nodes off the table, that left one way into the Death King's castle… on the ground.

"I still think you might have been better off using another invisibility cantrip," she said.

"Normally I'd agree, but the liches can sense living people without seeing them, can't they?" I said. "I mean, they don't have eyes."

"If I knew how they sensed people, I'd know which approach to go with." She flipped a coin over in her hand —one of her spares, not yet imprinted with a spell. "Okay, a mimic cantrip. That might work."

"What, make me look like one of his people?" I considered this. "Perhaps not one of the Four Elemental Soldiers —I haven't seen them close up enough times to be able to accurately mimic one of them."

"Nah, that'd be way too complex for me to do in a single night," she said. "And wights can't talk, so you wouldn't get very far by pretending to be one of them. I think I should make you look like a lich. It's just a shadowy cloak, more or less, isn't it?"

"You can pull that off?" I asked.

"Easy." She flipped the coin again. "Want one for fire-boy, too?"

"Brant? Nah. He prefers to go in all guns blazing rather than slithering about in the shadows."

She snorted. "You've got that right."

He wouldn't be pleased at being left behind either, but I'd been lucky not to get either of us killed earlier. I had to return the amulet alone. "Are you okay with blowing off Judith and the others? You know you could get into serious trouble for helping me."

She gave a shrug. "Yeah, but I'd be in deeper shit if you hadn't helped me with my taxes."

"That's what I'm good for." I grinned. "Aside from entertaining you by rolling natural ones at the worst moments."

"You bet." She palmed the coin. "If it helps, I think you're crazy enough to pull this off. The soul thief, though, you're better off staying away from."

"I would if I knew who it was," I said. "Brant doesn't know either."

"You sure about that?"

"Of course I am." I looked away. "Yes, he did omit information and I'm pissed at him for that, but the thief had him on his hit list before he even found out I existed."

"You can't deny Brant has that whole overprotective macho shit going on, though," she said.

"When we first met, I knew pretty much nothing about the Parallel," I said. "I needed saving a lot, by necessity, but I think he liked doing the saving. He liked having someone to protect."

I'd made less of an objection than I might have done in other circumstances, because it was nice to have someone who liked the person I was now, not whoever lay between those years of broken memories. Now, though? I had to be the one to end this, and I hoped he understood that.

"You know him better than I do," she said. "At least he seems to respect you."

"He knows I can handle myself. Most of the time." He'd convinced me to use spirit magic, and I'd pulled it off. Okay, it hadn't exactly gone as planned, but he'd had nothing but confidence in my abilities, which made a refreshing change.

Yes, it would have been nice if he'd mentioned it earlier, but he'd known less than I did about spirit magic when we'd met and knowing wasn't the same as being able to use it safely in action. It was difficult to tell if any of my paranoia was justified after what felt like a lifetime of people tiptoeing around me as though I'd shatter if they held me too hard.

Devon's expression softened. "You're overthinking, I can tell. You head to bed, and I'll get on with the cantrip. I've had time to nap today. You haven't."

"I kind of had a power nap when I was knocked out of my body, if that counts."

"That's not the same," she said. "I'll handle the cantrip, and tomorrow, you'll sneak back into the castle and put the matter to rest. Or bury it in a coffin. Whatever."

It wouldn't be that simple, I knew, but with the Death King off my back, I'd be free to direct my efforts at the Order.

The Order, and the traitor in their ranks.

With Mr Cobb still commanding respect, it was too risky to mention the amulet in front of them, or even show my face. I'd been lucky not to be caught earlier.

Luckier than escaping the Death King, even. The Order would have to wait until later.

The Order or the Death King. The Order or Death.

Please say I made the right call.

———

Despite the churning mass of thoughts in my mind, I passed out cold the instant my head hit the pillow.

The next second, I found myself coming to wakefulness, floating above my bed and through the ceiling until I hovered above my house. The nodes were bright from this angle, vibrant pinpricks spreading throughout the city. I'd never seen them so vividly before, like pillars of cool light piercing the heavens.

Elements. Was I out of my body, or astral projecting again? A mere dream couldn't be this vivid, surely. In the streets below, drunken teenagers staggered around the park, Uber drivers idled at the side of the pavement waiting to pick up partygoers, and night blanketed the world, nobody paying me the slightest iota of attention.

Impulsively, I floated into the current of piercing energy in the middle of the house. The light swallowed me up, and I emerged from another node elsewhere in the city. One blink and I did the same again, until I floated in a halo of lights. Traversing the nodes was much easier without the Order watching my every move.

"You." The voice came from somewhere behind me, sending a cold wave of fear through my body. I skidded to a halt in mid-air, my mind reeling with shock. I knew that voice.

Slowly, I spun around. The Death King hovered in

front of me, a shadowy outline shaped like a person. I couldn't escape him even in my dreams, apparently.

Unless I wasn't dreaming. Unless I'd really floated halfway across the city and found him waiting on the other side. I looked down, unnerved to see only darkness where my feet should have been. "Why are you following me?"

"Because you stole something of mine," he said.

"Not on purpose," I said. "I got my hands on your soul by accident, but I'm going to put it back where it belongs, if you'll let me."

"Forgive me if I don't believe you." The shadowy form of the Death King moved closer. "I don't take kindly to people stealing my property."

Shivers danced down my spine. He sounded too close to be anything but real, but most dreams felt real, didn't they? My one slim advantage was that it was full dark, and I'd travelled miles away from my house. He shouldn't be able to find my body, or Devon, but that was a small comfort right now.

"I expect you don't," I said. "How are you here? In this realm?"

"And you?" he said, his voice barely a breath. "Tell me your name."

A wave of chills gripped me. "You know, I was willing to play along with this dream scenario thing for a minute there, but you're officially freaking me out. Goodbye."

I turned my back, sensing him watching me floating away. The node's embrace came as a sweet relief, sending me back towards home. As I fought my way back to wakefulness, I heard a familiar voice whispering in my head.

The first stage of spirit magic... travelling through the nodes.
The second... astral projecting.
And the third... the third...

My eyes flew open and I found myself back in bed, Dirk Alban's voice fading from my mind.

14

By morning, the mimic amulet was done, my dream was behind me, and I was ready to pretend to be a lich. Preferably with my soul remaining attached to my body.

Devon presented the cantrip to me with a flourish. "Way easier than last time. Granted, I just turned you into a floating cloak, so don't do any stripteases."

"Not on my agenda, believe me." I pulled a face. "Weird dreams about the Death King are bad enough without turning into nightmares."

"You were dreaming about him?" she asked.

"That, or he can astral project at me in my sleep." For all I knew, that was one of his talents. It was no more absurd than the notion of him astral projecting around the city while everyone else was asleep. Liches didn't need to sleep, being dead, so maybe that's how they entertained themselves. Who knew?

I twisted the cantrip in my hands. With a flash of light, I turned tall and shadowy. Devon looked up at me, which was weird as hell considering she was usually taller than I was.

"Good. The cloak's a bit long, but most liches are taller than you are."

"Maybe that's why I never got invited to join them," I said. "There's a height requirement."

There came a knock on the door. Devon sighed.

"Hang on." I twisted the cantrip as she walked to the door, but the shadowy cloak didn't disappear. The door opened, revealing Trix the elf.

"Oh, hey, Liv," he said. "You look different. I like the cloak. Bit dark for my tastes, though."

Another couple of twists and I managed to turn off the lich disguise before I used the cantrip up without even setting foot in the Parallel. "How did you know it was me?"

"I assumed Devon didn't invite an actual lich into the shop," he said.

I suppressed an eye-roll.

"Here's your charm." Devon held out a cantrip to the elf. "That'll be twenty-five pounds."

He handed her the money. "I wouldn't go to the Parallel today. There's trouble."

"Death King trouble?" I asked.

"Yeah… why?" He looked me over. "Is that why you're dressed like one of them?"

"Kind of," I said. "What's he doing, sending his army out to terrorise everyone in Arcadia again?"

"Yes, his people are prowling the streets," he said. "Looking for someone. Wouldn't want to be them."

"Nor would I."

Devon arched a brow at me. Trix, of course,

remained happily oblivious. "Will you be at D&D night this week?"

"Wouldn't miss it." Assuming I lived that long. "Trix, do me a favour? Stay away from the Parallel until this mess is sorted out."

I'd deal with this alone. As long as I didn't say the wrong thing, I'd be able to pass as a lich, get to the Death King… and hand over the amulet.

———

Unsurprisingly, Brant wasn't a fan of my plan. We'd met near the node and headed to his safe house to plan our next move, at which point he'd insisted going in alone was foolish at best.

"Last time, you nearly lost your soul," he said. "It's too risky."

"You were congratulating me yesterday," I said. "What's the problem?"

"The Death King is bringing out reinforcements," he said. "Not that I don't think you can pull off the act, but his army is on full alert. He wants that soul, and he's willing to do anything to get it back."

"All the more reason to get the amulet off my hands before the situation gets any worse."

"With my help." He opened the top drawer beside the sofa bed, revealing piles of smooth round coins. "I have more cantrips than you can carry yourself."

"Are you capable of going more than a minute without conjuring up a flame?" I queried. "Because it doesn't matter how well you disguise yourself. If you use your fire, you'll draw attention to both of us."

His jaw locked. "So I'm expected to watch you walk into the swamp alone?"

"More floating than walking," I said. "I'm going to be a lich. Check this out."

I flicked on the cantrip. At once, I turned into a tall shadowy figure. Brant's eyes widened as he found himself looking up at me. "Um… Liv? Are you in there?"

"Yes," I said. "This is my resting lich face."

Brant grinned. "Very scary."

"I try." I gave a twirl, and my feet tangled up in the cloak. Brant caught me by the arm. "I guess this is why the Death King doesn't throw dance parties."

His hand lingered on my arm for a moment, then he let go. "I'm still not sure about this."

"If I was ever a hundred percent certain before acting, I'd get nothing done at all."

I tried to be patient with him. He was just looking out for me. Maybe a little more than I wanted to, but that wouldn't last forever. Not when I made it clear I wasn't that girl who'd escaped the Order with her memories broken and her mind shattered.

I was ready to be someone else.

Maybe not a lich, though. I tripped twice more on my way to the door and ended up hiking up my shadowy cloak to keep it off the ground. I turned off the disguise to walk through the streets, since the Death King's forces had pulled back to his territory and people might get suspicious at the sight of a lone lich walking alongside a fire mage through the streets of Arcadia.

I stopped by the tree at the swamp's edge to pick up the weapons I'd left behind. It was a testament to how well the hollow inside of the tree was hidden that nobody had swiped them until now, though the liches had far more effective weapons at their fingertips. I grabbed two knives and concealed them beneath my coat along with my cantrips. Then I straightened upright. "All right, Dex, let's do this."

Dex didn't answer. I hadn't seen him since I'd come back to the Parallel, but maybe it was for the best that he stayed out of this one. After all, the Death King had spotted him when we'd accidentally travelled through the node together.

Brant nudged me. "I'd better go before someone sees me."

"Then I'm going in." I drew in a breath. "Wish me luck."

I turned on my disguise and walked towards the swamplands, holding my head high. I didn't know if that made a difference, but it made me feel marginally more confident about pulling this off. I wasn't about to try hopping through a node after last time, so I walked on foot, trying to ignore the way my cloak dragged in the marshy waters in an un-lich-like manner. Dark shapes appeared in the distance, making my shoulders tense, but they were only phantoms, drifting around without cause.

I passed the spot where the water mage's hut had collapsed, a scorched area of the swamplands where no traces remained of their visitor. The Death King's Fire Element had done that. I'd better not run into one of *them*.

"Dex," I whispered. "Where are you?"

Worry gnawed at me. Even if he'd feared for his own safety—which was a legitimate concern, considering the Death King's people didn't see having a physical body as a necessary requirement to inflict horrible torture on someone—it didn't seem right for him to vanish on me in a time of need. It made me feel vulnerable, alone, like I had when I'd drifted above the nodes and faced the Death King in last night's bizarre dream.

Closer to the gates, I spotted groups of skeletal wights walking among the shadowy forms of liches, as though they'd been invited to network at a Grim Reaper convention. None of them spoke to me, though some of the liches gave a cursory glance to acknowledge my presence. My gaze panned across the gates circling the Death King's castle. There didn't appear to be any other way in except on the ground, and it looked as though he'd positioned extra guards outside after yesterday. Two liches stood on each side of the gates, wielding sharp-looking scythes.

Had he assumed that after my accidental astral projection, I'd try to get in another way? Maybe. Unlike the wights, liches retained their intelligence, so fooling them wouldn't be easy. I moved among the shadowy figures, as casual as possible for a faceless being in a long dark cloak, catching snippets of conversation among the dead.

"He still thinks the thief will come back here," one lich murmured to another. "He thinks it's a human."

"A spirit mage," returned the second lich. "No regular human. A threat."

Fear trickled down my spine. It was all I could do to keep my steps steady, to maintain a cool exterior. Murmurs of wars, of the Death King's wrath, passed among the liches, with more enthusiasm than I cared for. They didn't seem afraid of their leader, but then again, they'd ripped their own souls from their bodies voluntarily. The notion of going to war excited them. *Why did I come here again?*

The gates remained closed, guarded by four scythe-wielding liches. I might look like one of them, but I'd never pass an in-depth interrogation. I'd need to find another way to get the amulet into their hands.

I began a casual stroll alongside the gates until they merged with the fence circling the castle. Maybe there was a back gate somewhere around the other side, one I hadn't seen yet. Fewer liches drifted around this area, and I picked up speed, counting on the spindly trees to hide me from sight. Liches could go wherever they liked, so there was no reason for anyone to accost me, in theory, but the army was mostly concentrated around the front of the castle gates.

A lich flitted out from behind a tree, heading straight for me. Quick as a flash, I darted out of sight, holding my breath and hoping the lich had mistaken me for a phantom.

The lich drifted past my hiding place, towards a very human figure heading the other way.

Hang on. I know him.

Even with his hood pulled up, I recognised Brant's earth mage friend. Vaughn walked furtively towards the lich, his head down and his cloak arranged to conceal his features. What was he doing here? I hadn't told him my plan. He shouldn't be on the Death King's territory.

Damn. He's working against us.

I held my body still, ears pricked. The lich leaned closer to Vaughn and said, "You know where the spirit mage is."

"I told you, I don't," he said. "She's too close to Brant. Has too many allies, too."

My throat went dry. *The scumbag.* Brant might not

know he was working against me, but he wasn't here. How had the earth mage got past the lich army without being caught? Something didn't add up. But it couldn't be more obvious that someone inside the Death King's ranks was working against their leader.

Vaughn glanced my way, and I squashed my fear, remembering I looked nothing like myself. The Death King needed to know one of his people was a traitor. He needed to know about Vaughn, too, come to that, and while I'd normally hesitate at taking on both of them at once, I had weapons and the element of surprise on my hands.

Roll for initiative...

I made my steps confident as I whipped out from behind the tree, dropping my voice. "What exactly are you two doing?"

Vaughn's expression said *oh, shit,* but he jerked his head at the lich. "Deal with that, or else *our* deal is off."

The lich advanced on me, his shadowy hands reaching out. "You aren't one of ours."

"Surprise, dickhead." I flung a paralysing cantrip at him. The lich might be indestructible, but he was more solid than he looked. As his body froze into position, Vaughn raised his hands, and the earth split down the middle, quaking beneath my feet until my teeth rattled in my skull. With difficulty, I eased out another cantrip and flicked the switch.

A cantrip bloomed in my hands, creating a beacon of light which speared the overcast sky. Let's see the Death King overlook that.

"Get her out of here!" the lich hissed.

The ground shook beneath my feet, then a series of

cracks split through the swampy earth. The earth mage laughed, grasping my shoulders from behind as the torrent of earth swallowed us up and drew the pair of us into its embrace.

Oh, Elements. Of course that's how he'd got so close to the castle—by using his earth mage power to tunnel underground. If I let go of him, I'd be crushed to death beneath the collapsing soil, so I clung to him for balance as he steered me through a dark tunnel. After several tense minutes of silence, we emerged from a wall into a room so utterly pitch-black that I couldn't even see Vaughn beside me. Not until his grip tightened on my arm, dragging me across the earthen floor, and his fingers scraped against my neck. "I'll take that amulet."

I tackled him blindly, snatching at empty air. A heavy blow struck me in the chest, knocking the wind from my lungs. My back hit the ground, and the sound of a door slamming reverberated through my ears.

The lights brightened, revealing a darkened cell with a low ceiling. Vaughn stood on the other side of the barred door, a grim smile on his mouth. "I didn't expect to get the amulet from you without any trouble, but you delivered it into my hands. I'm grateful."

"I'll give you trouble," I spat. "Where the hell is Brant?"

"At home where he belongs," he said. "He's amazingly naive when it comes to his allies. Then again, I can say the same about you."

Raw anger exploded in my chest. "I always thought you were a scumbag. What's in it for you, then? Aren't you concerned the Death King will rip out your soul?"

"It's his own soul he needs to worry about, as well you know," he said.

"I don't think so." I reached for a cantrip. "You left me armed. Are you that confident I'll stay put?"

"Considering these cells are made to contain even an earth mage?" he said. "Yes, I am."

My cantrip fizzled out on contact with the jail door. Damn him. "If you'd wanted me to stay out of the way, then you could have just sent me home, not set me up to take the fall for your crimes."

"To be frank, you're too dangerous to leave to your own devices," he said. "I don't think you have an inkling of how valuable you are… though you can thank the Order for that."

"What the hell do you mean?" I leaned against the bars, hungry for answers, but he simply turned his back on me and walked out of the room. Leaving me in the darkness.

I'm in trouble now. The enemy, the soul thief… he knew about Dirk Alban. He knew I'd lost my memories. For all I knew, he'd been a part of my history, too. And yet it was Vaughn whose name I cursed as I felt around the edges of the cage for a way out. None came. The tunnel in the wall had sealed itself, and besides, only an earth mage could travel out that way. I was stuck.

"Dex," I whispered. "Now would be a really great time to show up."

He usually found his way to me of his own accord, but I'd travelled through the depths of the earth to get here and I hadn't the faintest idea what lay aboveground. It wasn't like he could fly along the same route to find me, unlike the nodes…

Hang on. The nodes. Could I sense them from here? Maybe. If I was a real spirit mage, I ought to be able to find them… and I also shouldn't need to be near a node to astral project.

I sat down on the cold floor and concentrated hard. At first, cold silence answered, but in the background lay an ever-present humming sound which indicated the magic present in the atmosphere here in the Parallel. Whatever the spirit mages had done to create this realm, they'd brought almost all of Earth's magic over here with them. Even here, I could sense it.

Tingles ran through my hands, then a burst of light sprang to the corner of my vision. West of here, there was a node. But I didn't have a clue what to do with that information, considering I couldn't get there unless I astral projected. Which I'd never done consciously before, much less while in an underground cell.

First time for everything. I remained still, focusing on the humming sensation until I could almost feel it beneath my skin, and imagined I stood in the middle of a node, its current running through my veins like wildfire. With one step, I slid out of my body as though immersing myself in cool water. Now that was more like it.

I floated through the locked door of the cell then upwards, through the shelf of earth above my head and into an unfamiliar street. So the earth mage had brought me out of the swamp altogether and into a hidden base beneath the city's streets. That ought to mean I could find the way in, but first, I needed backup.

"Where are you, Dex?" I muttered. He'd picked a fine time to disappear. Unless the liches had caught him, but surely I'd have seen a trace of him on the Death King's territory if they had. They could damage spirits as easily as living beings…

Wait. Dex and I had one thing in common: we could travel anywhere, in and out of the nodes. I floated above the warehouses and spotted a flash of fiery light nearby.

"Dex." I floated closer to the transparent fiery shape in the sky. "Hey—Dex."

He wheeled around in mid-air. "Liv? You're floating again."

"Yeah. It's me. I could really use some help." I glanced down. "My body's stuck underground somewhere. Vaughn captured me and locked me in a cell. Tell Brant, won't you? Tell him to come and find me."

"What in blazes and tides have you done?" He shook his head at me. "Tell him to come where?"

"There." I pointed vaguely down. "It's an underground lair, but there's got to be a way in from the surface. I'll find it—"

A chill shot through my limbs, and I lurched upright, back in my body again. The cell bars brushed against my arm as I caught my balance, and darkness blanketed the room. Not natural dark. A lich was outside my cell.

Oh, *hell.*

My blood froze, my body locking to the spot at the sight of the same lich who'd met with Vaughn earlier. I wouldn't have been able to see him at all if not for the cold malevolence radiating outwards from his presence.

"You picked the wrong side, mate," I told the darkness. "I'm guessing you're the one who stole the Death King's soul and smuggled it out of the castle?"

My heart drummed against my ribcage. Cold sweat slicked my forehead. *Now would be a really good time to show up, Brant.* Too bad Dex had to find him first, and then *he* had to find the way in here. All I could do was stall until then.

"If you assume you're going to survive this, Olivia, you're wrong." The lich's breath made the chill air even colder.

"So you're going to taunt me until I die?" I said. "Why are you people so obsessed with me?"

"You really don't remember a thing." The lich's voice whispered over the back of my neck. "You'll die along with our false King, in the darkness. Alone."

"Not alone." *Come on, Dex.* He couldn't be too far off, and Brant must know his mate's favoured haunts.

"I beg to differ." The lich's head tilted. "You called someone."

A few seconds later, shouting came from outside, followed by a burst of flames that lit up the whole room.

Brant. Thank the Elements.

Light flooded the cell, and Dex flew into the room, a bolt of fire aimed at my attacker. Brant, meanwhile, ran straight to the locked door of my cell. Dex zipped around the lich's face, diverting his attention as Brant worked on the lock.

"Brant, where's your traitorous rat of a friend?"

"I don't know." The door opened and he pulled me out, into his arms. "I'm sorry, Liv."

Coldness brushed against my spine, and the lich loomed over me, a cold shadow masking the light. Brant swore and released a burst of fire at the lich, and he glided back out of range of the flames. Brant grabbed my hand and pulled me after him out of the room. Using the light of the fire to see by, we ran out into a gloomy corridor.

"He's not dead," I told Brant. "Liches can get up after anything, even being set on fire."

"I'm more concerned with that shithead Vaughn," he said. "I should have known there was a reason he took such an interest in you. I'm glad your fire spirit friend found me."

"And there I thought you were avoiding me," I said to Dex, who pouted.

"I can't be expected to follow you on all your madcap schemes."

"But the amulet." I swore. "He has it. And that lich… he's working right under the Death King's nose, and I bet he's the one who smuggled the amulet out of his castle and gave it to that water mage. I have to warn him."

"One thing at a time," said Dex. "And I vote for getting out."

"Not without the amulet." Which meant facing off against the bastard of an earth mage who'd betrayed us all. "Where's he hiding?"

"Not down here," Brant said. "There's nothing in here but your cell."

"Ah, hell." The corridor came to an end in a narrow staircase that led up to the surface. The earth mage had gone, taking the amulet along with him.

15

Brant and I followed the staircase up to the surface and emerged into an alley among the warehouses. We looked around the area, but there were no signs left behind of our traitorous backstabbing friend or the amulet he'd stolen.

"He ran off," said Brant. "Didn't want to face me after what he did, no doubt."

"Hey, I'm the one he screwed over." I walked ahead of him, my fury spiking. "You need to pick your friends better. I guess he thought the soul thief made a better offer."

Brant shot me a concerned look, his mouth pinching. "I didn't know. It's lucky I *did* know where his underground hideouts in the city are."

"Let me guess," I said. "He's the one who told you he knew someone who could get my memories back. You told him my history."

He looked stricken. "Of course I didn't."

"Why'd you trust him?" I was lashing out at the nearest

target and I knew it, but my rage crested like a tidal wave, sweeping up everything in his path. "Were you so desperate to save your own soul that you willingly allied with someone as bad as that dickhead soul thief?"

"No, of course not," he insisted. "We've known one another for years. His soul is on the line, too, and he probably figured that handing over the amulet to the enemy was the only way to save his own skin."

My rage broke like the wave breaking onto the shore. "That's why you're so intent on me learning to use spirit magic again, aren't you? You're hoping that when it comes down to it, *I'll* save your soul."

He opened his mouth to argue, then stiffened, pointing mutely ahead. I rotated on my heel to see a large number of shadowy forms spreading throughout the streets. *Don't tell me the liches are out to play.* Of all the times not to have the amulet on me. Not that it would do any good if I did. The Death King's soldiers had seeped into the streets, some on horseback, some on foot, all on the lookout for the thief. They wouldn't spare anyone who got in their way, and they wouldn't stop to listen.

"We have to find a node," I breathed.

Running away was hardly ideal, but neither was being captured by an army of liches. Even if they brought me straight to the Death King, he'd never listen to me before ripping out my soul.

Backing down the alley, I made my way towards the nearest node. As I reached it, a lich crossed my path, and my breath stuck in my throat when the creature's sightless face looked right at me.

"You," said the lich, gliding across the ground. "You look familiar."

"Wrong person," I said. "I'm here on Order business. Just heading to the node."

I turned away, my heart thudding, and walked towards the node. As I did so, someone called out, "Olivia?"

I wheeled around, spotting Judith French and a female friend of hers I didn't know. "What are you doing here?"

"I could ask you the same question," said Judith. "Mr Cobb wants to see you."

"He does?"

He's the traitor. It has to be a trap. On the other hand, how else was I supposed to get past the liches and through the node without the Death King's army hauling me back to their master? If I went back to the Order, I might at least be able to plead my case before I was sentenced to death.

Brant put a hand on my arm. "Don't go with them."

"I doubt I have a choice," I said in an undertone. "It's them or the liches."

If I went with the Order's underlings, I'd at least have some measure of protection against them. Brant wasn't a suspect, so they wouldn't have reason to harm him.

Backing away from the lich, I made my way over to the node. Relief warred with guilt inside me. I couldn't do a thing for the amulet now, but that didn't change the fact that I'd let it fall into the hands of the enemy when I'd been intending to return it to its owner. Even if said owner was proving to be a major thorn in my side.

The two Order employees fell into step on either side of me, and we passed through the node, landing just down the street from the Order's headquarters. The thunder of heavy traffic filled the background as the ordinary people carried on with their lives, oblivious to the magical battleground beneath their feet. At times like this, I understood why the Elements had sought to establish their own magical community a literal world apart from the rest of humanity. I shuddered to think of what someone like the Death King would do if given power over ordinary people without an ounce of magic of their own to defend themselves with.

We entered the Order's main office without being challenged. Judith stopped walking, nodding towards the back row of offices. "Mr Cobb's waiting to talk to you."

All right. Now all I had to do was bluff my way through a confrontation with a suspected traitor without winding up arrested. No big deal. I'd accuse him of treachery if I didn't know it'd land me in deeper shit, but if he wanted to talk to me alone, maybe he'd give away something that might give me an edge over him.

I halted outside his office door, spotting a shadow against the wall which indicated he wasn't alone in the room. Someone else stood there, blocking the view of his desk, and it was too late to back off. The door swung inwards as the second person held it open for me to walk into the office.

The Death King.

I almost didn't recognise him at first. His hood was down, his mask off, and a human face looked at me, an oddly handsome one with angular cheekbones and rumpled dark hair. Had to be an illusion spell. Everyone knew the King of Death had no real face, and that he'd given up his body along with his mortality. He put on a show when he met with the Order, evidently. Or borrowed someone else's face—and hands, too. He was still holding the door open as I gaped at him, unable to believe my rotten luck. I hadn't reckoned on him being here, in the same room as the person I suspected of being the Order's insider.

For a moment, he looked as startled to see me as I did to see him. Then his usual indifference slipped back into place. "Olivia Cartwright. Are you coming in?"

Not like I had a choice. I slipped into the room, and the door slid closed behind me. My gaze went to Mr Cobb, who sat in the only chair, tilting his head at me. "I have to admit I didn't expect you to show your face here. Guilty conscience?"

I blinked a couple of times, thinking hard. "Guilty about what, exactly? You're the one who sent me to my death."

"The Death King here claims you stole from him," said Mr Cobb, as though I hadn't spoken. "He also claims you infiltrated his territory and attempted to fool your way past his guards."

"Because they kept attacking me," I said. "I wanted to return the amulet, which you told me to return yourself, I might add. You neglected to mention the person who stole it was conspiring with a thieving spirit mage."

"Spirit mage?" he echoed. "They're extinct."

You have got to be kidding me. I was living proof that wasn't true—but what the hell, maybe he didn't know. "I heard it from someone who wouldn't lie."

"That fire mage friend of yours?" said Mr Cobb. "The Death King here says he's been taken care of."

Ice slid down my spine. "What are you talking about? Brant didn't do anything wrong."

"You were somewhat difficult to pin down," said the Death King, his voice chilling despite his deceptively human face. "So much that I found myself compelled to come here to the Order's office in person."

He couldn't *actually* be here. He must be astral projecting and using an illusion on top of it, though that didn't explain how he'd managed to hold the door open. But that wasn't the important bit. The bastard had taken Brant. His liches must have snatched him the instant I'd gone through the node with Judith and her friend.

I took in a breath. "If you had any idea what was really going on, you'd be looking for the real traitor in the Order, not me."

"Excuse me?" said Mr Cobb. "Please enlighten me on what you mean."

"There's an insider right here," I told him. "Someone in a position of authority, I'd wager, and someone whose motives were at odds with whoever sent me to retrieve the possessions of a thief hiding in the swamp."

Mr Cobb arched a brow. "Really? What proof do you have of that?"

None, unfortunately. Mr Cobb had the law on his side, and the Death King had already assumed I was working with the soul thief. And now the Order had confirmed his suspicions. With the amulet gone, so was my last hope of clearing my name.

"Enough," said the Death King. "I will take care of her myself. See to it that I am not disturbed again."

I backed up towards Mr Cobb. He was no practitioner as far as I knew, so I had a shot at pinning him down—if I wanted to risk arrest at the Order's hands. The Death King blocked the door. There was no other way out.

Mr Cobb's hands gripped my shoulders. "I wouldn't

attack me, Miss Cartwright. Who do you think the upper room will believe of the pair of us?"

"Did you hear that?" I shouted at the Death King. "He's all but admitted to being the traitor—"

The Death King stepped in front of me with dizzying speed, and a familiar rushing sensation gripped my body. A current of energy, like a node, roared through my veins, and ferried me away into darkness.

———

I came to alertness on the other side, finding myself standing in the swamp, in front of the Death King's territory.

"I thought you'd take me directly into your castle," I said to the Death King.

"I'd prefer not to allow you to breach my defences again," he said. "Besides, I so rarely get to visit the Order."

"You seem confident I won't run." I reached into my pouch for a cantrip.

"Don't force me to hurt you again." His tone was cold as ice, yet he still wore that oddly human face. "It's a pity it turned out like this. You could have been one of us."

I narrowed my eyes. "I'd rather die. In the permanent sense, I mean. What the hell did you do with Brant?"

"The same as I'm going to do with you, of course," he said. "Come with me."

No use in running, so I walked with him through the swamplands towards the large looming shape of the castle. The liches on either side of the gates didn't challenge us. Why would they? I was captured now, and so was Brant. I didn't dare call for Dex. I couldn't drag anyone else into this.

My only hope was to convince the Death King himself that we were innocent. Which we weren't.

Fuck my life. If I hadn't lost the amulet, I'd at least have had something to bargain with, but I had nothing but my word of a traitor in his ranks, and I wouldn't have been able to pick the lich who'd attacked me out of a crowd. Every one of his liches looked the same. Shadowy, inhuman. Soulless in a literal sense.

The castle loomed ever closer, but the Death King led me to a smaller building made of the same impenetrable dark grey stone.

"That's your prison?" I studied the squat dark building. "And there I was thinking you executed your enemies rather than locking them away."

"It depends on the severity of their crime," he said. "I think I'll let you think on your errors before I invite you to speak with me again, Olivia."

He halted in front of a jet-black door set into the prison wall, which opened at the hands of two other liches. Alarm blared through me at the sight of the pitch-dark space ahead of me. Liches blocked every possible escape route. There was nowhere to go but forward.

The Death King extended a hand and pushed me into the darkness.

I stumbled forward, and cold hands caught me, steering me to the left. I heard a door slam, and a brief flash of light illuminated a narrow cell. On either side of me, barred walls revealed identical cells, lit only by a dim lantern hanging overhead. I swallowed hard, the chill already seeping into my skin. The Death King hadn't killed me outright—which was all I had going for me now. Nothing was inside the cell except for a bench to sit or lie on, and a dank hole in the corner which I assumed I was meant to use as a toilet. Maybe being turned into a lich would have been advantageous after all. Liches didn't need to worry about food or water or other human necessities.

Movement stirred on the other side of the barred wall. In the neighbouring cell, a hunched figure sat on his own bench, his gaze fixed on his feet. The water mage. It seemed the Death King hadn't killed him after all.

And he'd escaped jail once already.

Nothing for it. I approached the wall dividing our cells. "Hey."

"You." His head whipped to face me. "You're the bitch who chased me down and got me captured."

"You're the bastard who stole the Death King's soul."

He shot an alarmed look in the direction of the door. "Don't tell him that. I didn't know whose soul it was. I just wanted to save my own arse."

"Didn't work out so well for you, huh." I leaned closer to the bars. "Shouldn't have allied with the soul thief, should you?"

And yet it wasn't his face I saw when I pictured the enemy, but the falsely human face transplanted over the soul's owner. The Death King hadn't even wanted to listen to reason. He thought I was guilty by default, and he'd never intended to spare my life.

Where the hell is Brant? He must be somewhere in here, but I could only see the cells on either side of me, and the other was empty.

When the water mage didn't reply, I whispered, "You escaped once before."

"Got lucky." He looked up. "You're the one they were all searching the city for, aren't you? The spirit mage."

I pressed my mouth together. Maybe there was no point in denying it, given our captive state, but it seemed the rumours had reached even the darkest hole of the Death King's territory. "I'm the scapegoat. Have you seen a fire mage? He'd have been brought in here half an hour ago at most."

"I can't see anyone in here," he muttered. "It's too dark, and cold. We're going to die here. All of us."

"Only if you give up." I tensed at the sound of a door opening. *Have they come back for me already?*

The water mage began to tremble. "No. No…"

Several liches appeared outside his cell, their shadowy forms making the darkness even more potent. "Come with us."

"Please no," he whimpered. "I'm the victim here. I swear…"

I stumbled back, sinking onto the bench as the chill reached me even through the cell walls. The shadowy forms closed in, pushing the water mage out of his cell and drawing him with them into the gloomy swamp outside. The brief chink of light was dispelled as the door closed behind him.

Then I was alone.

Minutes passed, blurring into hours. Nobody else tried to speak to me. They seemed terrified into silence. Even Brant, if he was here, but I was starting to get the sinking feeling he'd never been given the chance to plead in his own defence. The Death King had taken him else-where. Or worse.

The Death King was as much of a monster as I'd always been led to believe. Perhaps it would be a mercy when the soul thief destroyed his amulet and took his place.

Nobody came to give us food or water, but the liches fetched another prisoner after a few hours. His screaming resounded in my ears long after they took him away. Every time the doors opened, I sat up expectantly, but the liches outright ignored my cell and left me in silence. Maybe my final punishment was to be left to die alone in the darkness. Like the criminal they thought I was.

A sob choked me, and I pressed my knuckles to my mouth. No. I wouldn't bend. Not now. If only my spirit magic was accessible in this place, but I wouldn't know how to begin tracking a node from here. Besides, the Death King would never have made it possible for anyone to escape, even a spirit mage.

I was dozing lightly on the bench when the door opened again. I didn't even look up this time, at least until I heard the solid noise of footsteps. A living person. Not a lich.

The footsteps came to a halt outside my cell. I squinted through the gloom and found the Air Element watching me. "You're not what I was expecting."

"Sorry to disappoint you." I pushed off the bench, shaking the stiffness from my limbs. "May I talk to your boss now? I deserve a chance to explain myself. And I'd really appreciate it if you let me know where my friend is."

"The fire mage?" The cell door clinked open. "You'll

present yourself to my master. If you can answer questions to his satisfaction, perhaps he'll let you see your friend."

He's alive. Brant is alive. Okay, he was in captivity, like me, but it was better than being dead.

The Air Element roughly grabbed my arm and dragged me out of the cell and to the door. The blinding sunlight stabbed me in the eyes, and it took several seconds for the world to reassert itself into the shape of the colossal castle standing alone in the swampland.

"What do I call you?" I asked the Air Element. "I mean, I assume you have a name, aside from Air Element."

The Air Element cut me a sharp look. "You may refer to me as Air Element, and I use they/them pronouns."

The warning bite to their tone implied they expected a derisive comment in response. "Air Element it is, then. Just so you know, you might want to invest in a nicer prison. Your master can afford that, surely."

No response came. The fear squeezing my chest grew tighter as the Air Element led me up a set of stone stairs and through a pair of oak doors. Faced with the forbidding splendour of the castle, I was aware of my dirty, dishevelled state. I'd also lost all my weapons, but I wouldn't stand a chance of fighting my way out of this place. The entrance hall was vast beyond measure, a high-ceilinged room marked by pillars made of what appeared to be human skulls. The Death King's taste in décor matched his fashion sense, it seemed.

"Did those skulls used to belong to trespassers?" I asked.

"Who else?" said the Air Element. "Go on. He's waiting for you."

The Death King no longer wore his false human face. He cut a terrifying figure standing there on a dais at the front of the hall, like a king addressing his subjects. Around him stood the three other soldiers. The Fire Element, pale and lean with hair the colour of bark. The Water Element, a black woman with curly dark hair and a curvaceous figure. The Earth Element, a tall Asian guy who looked barely out of his teens. And finally, the man himself, without the human mask he'd worn to visit the Order, cloaked in black and wreathed in shadows.

"You may leave," he told his soldiers. "As for you, Olivia…"

Shadowy ropes shot from his hands, wrenching my arms behind my back. Now I was in trouble.

16

I struggled against the shadowy bonds as the four Elemental Soldiers retreated from the hall, leaving me alone with their king.

"So here you are," said the Death King. "In the flesh. So to speak."

"I'd say the same for you, but... well." I arched a brow at his shadowy form. "I know who has your soul amulet."

"Yes, your fellow thieves have it," he said. "If you think that's news to me, then you're mistaken."

I blinked, disarmed by his lack of concern. "It's your soul. Aren't you worried someone will damage it or worse?"

"No," he said. "They can't do anything with it. You ought to be worried for yourself, however."

The shadows tightened around my wrists, and a chill spread through my limbs. I squirmed, fighting panic. "I told you, it was an accident. The Order sent me to retrieve the haul of a thief hiding in the swamp, and all I found in his lair was the amulet. It isn't like it had a nametag on it, so I hadn't a clue it was yours when I took it back to the retrieval unit. Then the day after, someone else at the Order gave me instructions to take the amulet back here and leave it where I found it. That same someone is probably the insider in the Order who's working for the enemy."

"Insider, you say?" He looked down at me, his gaze pitiless. "I've worked with the Order for years, and I find it hard to believe one of them would seek to break the peace agreement between our realms."

He worked with the Order. Of course he did. They were both as bad as each other.

"There's a lot you don't know about the Order." I swallowed hard. "Same with me. But I do know there's an earth mage who's working with the soul thief, Vaughn, and he's the one who has the amulet. He took it from me when I was on my way to bring it back. He and one of your liches."

"One of my liches," he repeated. "You're not helping your case, Olivia. My liches know their very existence depends on my goodwill."

"One of them is a traitor," I told him. "If you don't believe me, don't blame me when the pair of them knock you off your pedestal."

"It would help if you told me *who* the traitor is," he said. "Then I might be more inclined to believe you."

"All the liches look the same to me," I said. "How the hell would I know?"

"You expect me to believe one of my own would conspire against me, but you're completely innocent of any crimes?" he said.

"Not in the Order's eyes," I said. "I'm not allowed to

cross a node without filing paperwork, and I've broken that one a dozen times. But I'm not with the soul thief, and I didn't intentionally steal your soul amulet."

He watched me for a moment. "I see you're determined to be a nuisance, Olivia. I have been generous with you so far, and I would like very much to have my soul back without resorting to more… permanent methods."

I gritted my teeth, the shadows still holding my arms behind my back. "Like sending an army into the streets and terrorising everyone in the city?"

"I thought the vampires could use a lesson in humility," he said. "A long overdue one."

"You're aware some of *them* are working with the soul thief?" I said. "They're planning to collect the souls of elemental mages as well as yours, and I'm pretty sure their intention is to topple you from your throne."

He waved a dismissive hand. "It seems I'm mistaken in the level of knowledge you were allowed access to."

My mouth dropped open. "You *know* their plan?"

"Of course I know," he said. "Audacious though it might be for them to steal my soul, I don't need my amulet at my side to access my powers, and I certainly don't see the need to act as though my reign were in peril."

I had it wrong. He wasn't afraid of the soul thief at all. "He's a spirit mage. Does that make a difference?"

"I was told *you* were the spirit mage." He studied me, and shivers ran down my spine at the sensation as though his gaze pierced through me to my very soul.

"Whatever I am, I'm not the scheming mastermind you're looking for." I dropped my gaze, my shoulders aching, my throat parched. "What're you going to do, then? Rip out my soul and then turn my skull into one of your decorations?"

"Not quite." A moment passed. "I think my only option is to conscript you into my lich army. It's more than you deserve, and far more generous than I usually offer those who betray me. You won't want for anything, for liches have nothing to want."

Horror choked me. "Your Air Element told me you'd let me see Brant. He didn't do anything wrong. You can't—"

I recoiled as shadows washed through the hall, surrounding me on all sides. Liches, stripped of their souls. Any one of them might have been the traitor, but I'd never be able to tell which one it was.

The shadows parted, revealing a newcomer, and my breath stopped. The shadowy figure *almost* looked like Brant, but a more faded version, cloaked in black. Without any life in his eyes.

The Death King had stripped out his soul.

Cold fury rippled down my spine. "You despicable monster."

"You sound surprised," said the Death King. "I don't take kindly to being defied and lied to."

"I didn't lie!" My voice echoed throughout the hall. "I was set up. The Order wanted me to take the fall so you wouldn't guess Mr Cobb is working against you. He invited you to arrest me so that you'd see me as the villain and him as the hero, but he's the one who ordered me to get in the line of fire. He told me to bring the amulet onto your territory. Did you ask him how he knew I was guilty?"

He looked at me for a moment. "You think digging yourself into a hole is going to help you now?"

"Digging." Inspiration struck. "Tell you what, have a look around outside your fences and you'll see evidence that someone's been digging their way in and out of your territory using earth magic. The earth mage and the lich who's working against you have been meeting in secret. They have a base underneath Arcadia, near the warehouses."

He tilted his head at me. "Underground?"

"You heard me." My voice trembled with rage. "The earth mage held me hostage there and took the amulet, and then one of your liches tried to kill me. It's the truth."

"You're not making things any easier for yourself," he said. "Perhaps another week or two in the dark will suffice."

"Go ahead, if you want me to starve to death before I have the chance to turn lich."

"You will be provided for, despite your insolence." He gestured to two of his liches, who closed in on me. No matter how much I screamed at him, I might as well have lectured Death himself.

Whoever the soul thief is, he can't be worse than this guy.

Flanked by liches, I had little choice but to head back to my prison cell. This time they left me water and a tray of food, which I fell on with shaking hands. Nobody else occupied the cells on either side of mine, and as the silence persisted, I started to suspect I might lose my mind before too long.

I had too much time to think, yet no matter how hard I racked my brain, I couldn't recall the rest of Dirk Alban's lessons if my life depended on it. Maybe the Death King really would send his people to investigate the base the earth mage had taken me to, but I hadn't the faintest clue where the amulet's latest thief had taken it. Hell, maybe Mr Cobb had had it there in his office, the fucker.

Hours passed in silence. Then two liches brought me more water and another meal. The Death King had kept his word, but he probably didn't want me to die before he could turn me into a lich and force me to join his army. Everything he did was to further his own ends.

And to think I'd assumed he was any better than the thief who'd taken his soul.

Another day or two passed, not that there was much visible difference between night and day. I was lying on my bench, trying to get comfortable enough to sleep, when the door opened with a blinding flash of orange light and a yell of dismay cut through my stupor. The cell door slammed, yet the flash of light remained, casting shadows onto the floor of my cell.

I knew that light. "Dex, is that you?"

He flew up in front of me and swore at the top of his lungs. "So this is where you've been hiding out?"

"At least I have company now." They'd even thrown us into the same cell, probably to save on space. Dex took up almost no room, after all.

"Excuse me?" he said. "What part of this is ideal for either of us? I came here looking for you and got myself captured instead."

"Oh, Elements." I squinted at his fiery outline. "Can't you just fly through the wall?"

"It's spirit-proofed." He extended a hand to the bars and winced. "That's what I get for being so soft-hearted."

"If it's any consolation, I think giving the Death King

the benefit of the doubt is what got me into this mess," I said. "I should have just let the thief take his soul and be done with it."

"And consign yourself to death?" he said.

"He's going to turn me into a lich against my will," I said. "He already did it to Brant. That's worse than death. Being his personal servant. At least you're already a spirit. There's nothing he can do to you."

He gave me a dark look. "I'd rather not imagine, thanks. There's no other way out of here. I checked."

Unless Dex gained the ability to turn solid and use his firepower to melt the place down... but even that probably wouldn't work. The place was designed to hold the most powerful of mages. Even, perhaps, spirit mages like me.

At least I had someone to talk to now. Dex kept me entertained by flitting about making amusing shadows on the walls, but even his antics weren't enough to convince me we'd ever see the light of day again. Not as a living human, anyway.

"I'm not cut out to be one of the living dead." I lay back on my bench, staring into the darkness. "How am I supposed to play D&D?"

I didn't even *have* my lucky dice anymore. The Death King's people had taken them away along with everything else in my rucksack. Dicks.

"How do you think I feel?" he said. "I can't play either. Maybe we should start a club of disembodied adventurers."

"Devon would go for that." Though I'd be hard-pressed to think of a D&D character in a worse position than I was now. "I'm not the best DM. That's why it's absurd that the Death King thought *I* was the master-mind. As if."

Dex cackled. "Yeah, didn't you once lose control of your players and end up with them opening a portal to hell?"

I never should have told him that story. "That was one time. Besides, that's not the same as coming up with a scheme to steal the Death King's soul and actually succeeding at it."

That wretched water mage would be long dead by now, unless the lich traitor had smuggled him out of here. If only there was a way for me to find someone sympathetic who might do the same for me.

"He must be worried." Dex flipped over in mid-air, his little pointed face glowing in the darkness. "I mean, he's got to be concerned his soul might be used against him."

"He really didn't seem to be." I pushed into an upright position. "The Death King pretty much wrote the rule-book himself. Must've done, if he's still allowed to use spirit magic after the Order banned it from use."

There wasn't much the Order could do to command the King of the Dead, though it sounded like he checked in with them frequently all the same. Anger boiled in my chest at the memory of Mr Cobb's casual dismissal. And the Death King had looked at the two of us and deemed *me* the guilty one. The two of them were probably BFFs. For all I knew, the Death King himself was the spirit mage mastermind behind this nefarious plan.

"What are you talking about?" Dex said when I voiced this aloud. "Why would the Death King plot to overthrow himself?"

"I have no idea." I flopped back onto the bench. "Give

me a break. I'm tired and I've forgotten what the sun looks like."

"Like this." Dex's light brightened.

"Not quite." I covered my eyes as a blinding streak of whiteness pierced the gloom. "Okay, turn it down."

"It's not me."

I jumped upright to face the door, which stood widely open, framing the Air Element's armoured figure.

"Oh, it's you," I said, without enthusiasm. "Go on, then. Take me to my eternal fate as a warden of the night."

"You were right." They walked up to the door of my cell. "We found an underground hideout like you described. We also found evidence of earth magic on our territory."

"I'm sorry, what?" I blinked. "You actually listened to me?"

"My boss did," they said. "But I cannot believe your claim that a rogue spirit mage has my master's soul. The only spirit mage who's been seen in the city is yourself."

"Says who?" I said. "I never actually met the rogue. Perhaps they escaped through a node. Or they're operating from somewhere else. Anything's possible."

"Perhaps." Their gaze flickered from me to Dex. "You're proof of that, but you still haven't explained how you ended up with my master's soul in your possession."

"None of you gave me a chance, especially your master." I gave a dark chuckle. "I suppose it's too much to hope for you to be convinced he's a depraved beast who's exploiting you for his own gain."

"Exploiting?" they said. "We live like royalty, all four of us do, and we are compensated generously for protecting our master."

"Maybe you don't have a soul after all, then," I said. "You must know that no matter what crime I might have committed, Brant didn't deserve to have his soul ripped from his body."

"My master has his reasons for what he does," they said. "If your friend lost his soul, he must have done something to deserve it. I rather think the Death King has shown you mercy, considering the damage you've done."

"I tried to return the amulet and you blasted me into the air," I said heatedly. "I tried to track down your traitor and it got me locked up underground. My friend did *nothing* wrong, and your master permanently turned him into his own personal servant."

"You should be grateful he allowed him to live at all."

My fists clenched. "I'll give you grateful."

Out of the corner of my eye, I saw Dex move up to the door of the cell, unseen by the Air Element. The walls of the fortress might be spirit-proofed, but the door was open. I held my breath, determined to keep their eyes on my face.

"Enough." My cell door clicked open. "It's time for you to face my master."

Their iron grip enclosed my upper arm, dragging me through the jail and into the blinding light. Dex flew closer, hovering above my head.

"Distract them," I breathed.

Dex zipped over my head, and light flashed into the Air Element's eyes.

I dragged my arm from their grip, and then we were running for freedom. Dex flew at my side as the ground tore away beneath my feet, and even though I could barely see where I was going, I remained ahead of the soldier. After all, I'd always been a better runner than a fighter. They wore heavy armour, and it slowed them down.

Guilt stung me for leaving Brant behind, but he was beyond help now. I couldn't put his soul back into his body. I couldn't save him, but he'd want me to save myself. If nothing else, perhaps I could win enough time to get some actual proof to take to the Death King before it was too late for all of us.

The Air Element's magic slammed into me like a solid force, sending me flying forward. I let the momentum carry me, and Dex whooped.

"Thanks for the help!" he shouted at the Air Element.

I caught my balance, and spotted several liches approaching from near the gates ahead. Damn. I'd never reach the edge before they caught up.

On the other hand, there was a node on the inside, too. I picked up speed and changed directions, pelting towards the current of light piercing the sky. Then I willed its current to draw me in. *Come on...*

I ran headlong into the node, and its power flooded my veins, roaring to life inside me. I heard the Air Element yelling behind me, as the current carried me away.

17

The darkness resolved into the shape of the back room at home. I reeled back, catching my balance, the carpet impossibly soft beneath my feet.

Devon jumped to her feet from the sofa. "Holy shit, Liv."

I raised my head, shielding my eyes from the ceiling light. "Ow. Too bright."

Devon swore again. "I thought you were dead. You were gone for days, Liv."

I flopped onto the sofa, dislodging an Xbox controller. "I know. I nearly suffered a fate *worse* than death."

"And your friend came back too."

"My…" Not Brant. Brant was a lich, doomed never to take another breath. Pain and guilt clenched a hard fist over my heart, but I looked up and saw Dex zipping about. "I guess I did."

"I'm free!" Dex whooped, flying through the living room with jubilant cries.

I didn't have the energy to tell him to pipe down. Brant was still with the Death King, while I hadn't nearly enough allies left to marshal my own forces against him. Sure, the Air Element had told me their boss at least believed my claims about the earth mage visiting his territory, but at this point, it was too little, too late.

"Are you okay?" Devon leaned over me. "Liv, you look like death."

"Appropriate." I choked on a weak laugh which turned into a sob. Devon's arms came around me as tears began to leak from my eyes. She usually wasn't the hugging type, but she let me gasp out my story without letting go of me. Dex added his own interjections, including how he'd got caught himself.

"I thought that bastard of a thief caught you," she said. "The Death King... I had no idea he had you in his jail the whole time."

"Yeah, and Brant paid the price for it with his soul. Literally." I rubbed my eyes with the back of my arm, regretting it when I saw how filthy my sleeves were.

"Crap," she said. "I'll be the first to say I wasn't a huge fan of the guy, but Brant didn't deserve that."

My gut tightened. "I know. And get this—we got caught because the Death King was at the *Order*. With Mr Cobb."

"Cobb?" she said. "You still think he's working with the enemy?"

"I know he is," I said. "Not that the Death King believes a word of it. He sees the Order as his allies. He hasn't set eyes on the soul thief yet, but he rarely leaves his castle except via astral projection."

"That's how he got to the Order." She let go of me and

grabbed her phone from the coffee table. "All right. I'm ordering takeout, and you should probably shower and change before the other players show up."

"Wait, it's D&D night?" Had I really lost that much time?

"Or so my schedule says." She pushed to her feet. "I can't cancel it now. Besides, Trix and the others will be glad to see you're not dead."

I sighed. "I never thought I'd say this, but I can't. I have to—"

"You have to recuperate, and what better way to do that than by venturing into a dungeon in the comfort of your own home?" she said. "Don't argue with me on this. You're in no fit state to go back into the Parallel."

"I'm more worried about them finding me here." But the Death King wouldn't know my address… unless, that is, the Order had told him.

I'm so screwed.

After a shower and food, I felt almost human again. Dex flitted about asking annoying questions, which Devon tolerated with more than her usual level of patience. She must have missed me a lot.

"Your mum is seriously worried for you," she said. "I tried telling her you were busy at work, but given how long it's been—"

"Shit. I should call her." Even when I was running daily missions for the Order, I'd never been away for that long without checking in with my family. But I was far too tired to conjure up an excuse for my absence. "I don't want to draw the Order's attention to my family, though. Or the Death King. Especially him."

Fuck the Death King. Him and the undead horse he rode in on.

Guilt twisted inside me at the thought of Brant, stuck there serving the Death King like a glorified servant. The notion of going back and begging him to set Brant free made my skin crawl, but I didn't have any better ideas. The bastard had even taken my lucky dice.

Dex flew around knocking things over while we waited for the other players to show up. Devon and I soon wound up in an argument over whether or not to include my current misadventures in our campaign which only ceased when there came a knock on the door.

I tensed, following Devon to the door, but it was only Trix.

"You're alive!" he exclaimed. "You came back especially for D&D night."

"Not exactly." I beckoned him into the shop before anyone outside saw my face. "Have you been in the Parallel over the last few days?"

"Not very much, no," he said. "I don't like the liches. They make my skin crawl."

"You and me both." I heaved a shudder. "And Brant's stuck as one now."

"He is?" His eyes widened. "But I saw his friend, and he seemed fine."

"Friend?" I frowned. "You mean Vaughn. The earth mage."

"The bastard who betrayed you," Devon interjected. "Trix, Vaughn screwed Liv over. He stole the amulet from her and handed her over to the Death King."

Trix exclaimed something in the elven tongue. "Was that why he was meeting with a lich?"

"Yes… wait. You *saw* them?" That changed things. "The lich is a traitor to the Death King, but His Deathliness doesn't believe one of his people would turn on him. If you could help me find him—hell, just tracking down the earth mage would be enough. Whereabouts is he hiding these days?"

"He lives in South Street, opposite the warehouse," he said in solemn tones.

Wait… "You were watching him? Did he see you?"

"I don't think so."

Damn. Of course nobody paid the elves any attention.

"You're a genius," said Devon.

He blinked modestly. "I'm considered above average intelligence for an elf, yes."

I turned to Devon. "Should I give Vaughn's address to the Order? If I just *knew* who else at the Order might be working with the enemy, I'd know who to trust with this. Better than going back to the Death King again."

Odds were, he wouldn't give me the chance to explain myself next time. Then again, how long would it be before the Death King told the Order about my supposed transgressions and sent someone to pick me up again? He might not know where I lived, but the Order did.

Dex flew overhead. "There are people outside, and I don't think they're players."

"It's them." Devon paled. "The Order."

"Shit." I spun on the spot. "Dex—hide."

As he flew into the back room, I followed suit. Before I could close the door behind me, two Order employees burst into the shop.

"What are you doing?" Devon said. "We're closed for the night."

"We're here to arrest a fugitive."

Trix came to my rescue, to my astonishment. Putting on a dramatic wide-eyed face and stepping in the way of the door into the back room, he said, "What are you *doing* here? You're not part of our group."

"Who are you?" said one of the Order employees. "What crime have you committed?"

"Crime?" he said. "I'm not with the Order. I'm here to play Dungeons & Dragons."

"Enough of this." Mr Cobb strode to the forefront of the group, advancing on Devon. "If Olivia won't come out, I'll give her an incentive."

"Don't you fucking think about it."

As I ran into the shop, Mr Cobb released Devon, fixing me with a look of contempt. "So there's our fugitive. Did you really run from the Death King's prison and assume we wouldn't track you down?"

"No, but I hoped you'd let me take a nap first." I needed to convince the Order he was a traitor, but I'd rather do it in front of witnesses with equal authority to him, not people conditioned to obey his every command. His underlings would never take my side on this one.

Mr Cobb gave me a cold look. "The Death King is poised to fall. You might have stood a chance of surviving if you'd remained imprisoned."

Devon dropped to her knees. Mr Cobb glanced at her. "What do you think you're doing?"

"Looking for my keys," she said. "Don't mind me. You get on with your big speech."

"Your keys are in the door," said Judith.

"Never mind," said Devon. "I was looking for the last fuck I had to give, but it's gone."

A loud cantrip went off with a blast, knocking the intruders backwards and freezing them all on the spot.

"Damn, that's good." Even Mr Cobb had gone utterly still, his arms stuck to his sides. "Um… what're you going to do with them now? Tie them up in the back room?"

"Good question." Her gaze went to the door. "You can take us to *any* node on the other side?"

"Theoretically." If I was feeling particularly vindictive, I'd leave them stranded on the Death King's territory, but that was as likely to backfire on me as not. "This will only stall them, you know."

"Of course I do, but if we can take them straight to the evidence…"

"The earth mage's lair," I said. "There's a bunch of cages in there, too. And if the lich traitor comes back, we'll have him, too."

Even one fewer person in my way was a point in my favour.

Devon, Trix and I moved all three intruders into the back room and on top of the node. If the other players showed up while we were gone, we'd have a hell of a lot of explaining to do, but I figured we'd deal with the immediate issue first.

Grabbing Devon's hand on one side and Mr Cobb on the other, I pulled our group through the node and into the Parallel.

Devon landed on her feet at my side. "Damn, this place stinks worse than I remember."

We'd landed as close to the underground lair as I could get us, but at once, I knew I'd made a mistake. Several figures clustered around us, skeletal and hungry for magic. Blasted revenants.

Dex conjured up a flash of light, sending the revenants cringing backwards, but they remained hungrily focused on me. They fed on magic, and we'd just come out of a node with its energy still tingling in my veins. A veritable feast.

"Get back." I shoved one of the revenants, and to my own surprise, it stumbled back without my hand making contact. My skin still glowed with the node's light. Hang on…

A voice echoed in my mind: *The third stage of spirit magic is drawing the node's strength to bolster your own.*

Instinctively, I stepped back into the path of the node's energy. The energy rose to a peak, and I splayed my hands, blasting the revenants aside like skittles.

Behind me, Devon yelled. I pivoted, ducking out of the node's path, to find someone held a knife against her throat. Shaking off the remnants of the paralysing spell, Mr Cobb pressed a knife to my best friend's neck.

"Devon!" Trix stood frozen beside me, while Mr Cobb extended a free hand, holding out the amulet.

Revenants gathered at both ends of the street. They were with him, too.

"Enough games, Olivia." He held the Death King's soul in his casual grip, the chain dangling from his fingers. "You nearly ruined everything when you brought this into the Order's base the first time around, but it's finally time for me to claim it as mine."

A chill raced through my blood. He was the spirit mage, the mastermind. *He'd* started all this.

"So much for pretending to be on the right side of the law," I said. "Let Devon go."

"The laws of the Parallel are on my side," he said. "You should have run."

"I thought you wanted me dead." I clenched my hands at my sides. "This isn't dead. This is pissed off. Let her go."

Trix looked between us, his eyes wide with terror, not speaking.

"I did want you dead," Mr Cobb said. "Until I heard of your recent achievements, that is. You're remembering a lot of your training. Faster than I anticipated."

My heart gave a sickening dive. I'd suspected he must have some idea of my history, but *this* was something else entirely. "So you wanted me to be with the Death King when you overthrew him."

"It's better this way," he said. "Trust me."

"Nobody in their right mind would ever trust you," Devon said, struggling against his grip. "Screw you."

Mr Cobb glanced down at her. "I didn't want to harm any more people than I had to. You won't get hurt if you comply."

"No, thanks." She thrust an elbow backwards, spinning out of his grip and grabbing for a cantrip, but he seized her wrist first, the knife back in his hand. Being without magic didn't make him incapable of doing damage.

More revenants spilled into the alley, drawn to the power of the node. Blocking my escape route. Not that I'd run without Devon. Never.

Mr Cobb shook his head. "This has grown far too complicated for my liking. It was supposed to be a quiet coup, but the Death King knows too much."

"He's not afraid of you." Why it mattered that he knew, I didn't know, and yet I found myself saying the words anyway. "He doesn't even care that you're planning to claim his soul."

"Really." He looked me in the eyes. "Then it won't matter if I ask for your assistance, will it? If you decline, your friend will die, so I'd suggest you take this seriously."

"Assist you?" I said. "You can forget it. I'd sooner die."

Bastard. He and the liches were as bad as each other, yet it gave me no joy to see him holding the amulet containing the Death King's soul.

"It's your friend's life on the line, not yours," he said. "It might interest you to know that you alone have the potential to topple the Death King from his throne."

"What?" I said. "You've got to be joking. I can't beat the Death King, even if I wanted to. Which I don't."

"Even after he captured and tortured you?" he said.

"We both know that was your doing," I said. "Besides, there was no torture involved. Aside from a little neglect."

All I could think of to do was stall. His grip on Devon hadn't relinquished, while his revenant army thickened by the second. I should never have brought him through the node, but I hadn't known he'd shake off the effects of the cantrip so damn quickly. Maybe it was down to the amulet in his hands, which glowed in the light streaming from the current of energy at my back. He might not have any magic himself, but he held the Death King's life in his hands.

And yet he was offering it to me.

Devon groaned as the knife pierced her neck. Trix took a step forward, but the revenants had us surrounded. I didn't have any better ideas, so I reached out and my hand closed around the amulet. The cold pulsing beneath the surface took me by surprise. I tried to tug it from him, but my whole body froze.

"Don't try to fight me," he said. "I need you to finish the job, that is all."

Rough hands grabbed me from behind, and I let go of the amulet, my palm stiff with cold. Mr Cobb steered Devon through the path of revenants, leaving me with no choice but to follow him until we reached the stairs leading underground to the earth mage's hideout.

Trix's shouts echoed in the background, and a flash of light indicated Dex trying to burn his way through the liches to me, but soon enough, the darkness closed in overhead. Mr Cobb pushed Devon into the cage, where she spat at his feet. Revenants filled every inch of the hideout, and Mr Cobb turned to me, the amulet's chain dangling from his hand.

How was it possible for him to be the spirit mage? He had no strong gift for magic, and I'd have known if he was like me. He must have put out those rumours on purpose, to disguise the fact that he wasn't even based in the Parallel. But then, how had he learned spirit magic existed?

There was only one possible answer to that question.

"You knew Dirk Alban." I said quietly.

"Knew him? I trained with him." A smile curled his

mouth. There was something mocking, bitter, in his expression. "Yet I suffered worse than you did for my transgression. They only took your memories."

Oh, Elements. He *had* been a spirit mage... before the Order had caught him. *They kept him around, though. Why?*

"They didn't take yours," I said. "You remember me."

His mouth twisted with hate. "I'd rather have no memories than no magic. They took away what was mine and forced me to lower myself to begging them for a second chance. It was fortunate that they were unaware that Alban taught me far more than a few simple tricks. He taught me that I deserved to take what was owed to me, and that it was worth playing the long game in order to get there."

"You think the world owes you a favour?" I scoffed. "*That's* why you're trying to depose the Death King and incite chaos in the Parallel?"

"You wouldn't understand."

"I understand just fine," I said. "You people have screwed me over, majorly. All this for a dead guy's soul."

"That amulet is more than a soul," he said. "It's my salvation."

"Then why the fuck do you need me?" I spat.

"I require the assistance of a spirit mage to transfer the Death King's life essence to myself," he said. "I confess I thought you incapable when you first brought the amulet to me, but now I've seen what you can do, I'm glad I chose to spare your life."

"I told you, I can't do spirit magic," I said. "I have no memory of any of my lessons. And besides, I don't think you deserve it."

"If threatening your friends isn't enough," he said,

"then consider the amulet. I imagine you wanted it off your hands either way, didn't you? If you aid me, I'll clear your name and you can go back to your old life. The Order doesn't have to know."

"The Order doesn't know you're a traitor," I said. "I imagine it ticked you off when another of your fellow Order members asked me to bring in the thief and swiped the amulet in the first place."

"It all worked out in the end," he said. "Do you think I would be a much worse leader than the Death King? Has he ever treated you with humanity and compassion?"

"He's not human," I answered. "You supposedly are, but I'll be honest, I'd be more than happy to see you destroy one another."

"Enough chatter." He grabbed my hand and pressed it to the amulet once more. "Go on."

Cold pulsed beneath my palm. I could feel *something* there, but I didn't know what to do with it. "I might have no memories, but I think I'd remember if I'd ever ripped out someone's soul before."

That was the realm of the liches, not humans. Not even spirit mages could rip out other people's souls. Or so I'd thought.

"Dirk Alban studied the liches extensively," Mr Cobb said. "He was training you when we were both caught. I know he told you what he knew."

"Telling me and teaching me isn't the same thing." My palm began to go numb with cold. "I really don't know what I'm doing. Any of us could get hurt. Including you. Hell, especially you. You're human. I'm..."

A spirit mage.

Cold fury leapt into his eyes. His grip on my wrist turned bone-crushing. "Do. It."

"She can't!" yelled Devon, sounding panicked. "Look, I'm the last person who knows about spirit magic, but she can't put someone else's soul in your body."

"I'm aware." Mr Cobb held up another amulet. "That's why I need this. Transfer the Death King's soul to this vessel and it'll be bound to me."

Oh, Elements. That might actually work. If I were a real spirit mage, anyway. And if it did, then his powers would be on a level with the Death King. Higher, because the man himself would be dead. Or as dead as an undead person could be, anyway. *Think, Liv.*

Maybe I could fake it. Even when he'd trained with Dirk Alban, he'd probably never actually seen anyone place a person's soul into an amulet before. They didn't go for that kind of thing in the Order.

"The first stage of spirit magic is travelling via the nodes," he said. "The second is astral projection."

I heard the echo of Dirk Alban's voice beneath his, and cold fear rooted me to the spot.

He continued. "The third stage is drawing the node's strength to bolster your own."

My breaths came too quickly. In vain, I searched for a node, but the chilling presence of the amulet drowned out everything else.

Mr Cobb looked me with eyes brimming with hate, and then he spoke Dirk Alban's words. "*The fourth? Moving the soul to another source.*"

The amulet grew colder, seeming to fuse to my palm. Then a blurred figure rose from its cold surface, a human male with pale, pale eyes…

The Death King? That couldn't be him, and yet, his sharp-edged features looked familiar to me. Maybe it was the person he'd been, before he'd split his soul, Elements knew how many years ago.

Mr Cobb leaned in, his mouth curling into an eager smile. "You see him, don't you?"

He saw *me,* too, his face startlingly human for a disembodied soul belonging to a dead king. I gave the floating figure a pleading look, but there was nothing he could do. I literally held his life in my hand.

Mr Cobb slid the second amulet into my other hand and pushed my palm towards the other. At once, the two amulets locked onto one another like magnets, and the soul in my palm began to disappear. As the skull amulet dimmed in colour, the other one grew brighter.

Shit. I tightened my grip on the first amulet, willing the soul to move back where it belonged, but I didn't know how to.

The pale figure hovered above the second amulet, whose glow brightened—and then the Death King's form vanished into it as though sucked below the surface of the glowing metal.

"It is done." Mr Cobb took the second amulet from my limp hand. "I'm glad I chose to spare your life after all, Olivia."

Nausea choked my throat. "The Death King is still alive. You can't command him, not even with his soul in your hand."

If that were true, I'd have been able to get the Death King to listen to me while I'd been carrying his soul on my person and we never would have ended up in this mess.

"The one who owns the Death King's soul is recognised as the master of the entire Court of the Dead." He turned the amulet over in his palm, then looped the chain around his neck. "This amulet is as strong as the original vessel, and now it is in my hands, the wights will flock to my side, and the liches will soon recognise me as their master, too. They're simple creatures. Even that lover of yours."

Brant. I'd—ridiculously—hoped he was safe from the soul thief behind the gates of the Court of the Dead, but even the Death King himself might be incapacitated by now. Who knew what effects moving his soul into a new vessel would have on his lich form?

Mr Cobb jerked his head at the first amulet, clenched in my hand. "You're welcome to keep that as a memento. If I were you, I'd want to celebrate the fine use of spirit magic you just displayed. But then again, you didn't really know what you were doing, did you?"

I said nothing. My words were gone, my grip on the amulet nothing more than autopilot, my soul frozen in horror at what my magic had done. No wonder the Order had erased my memories of my lessons if that's what Dirk Alban had been teaching me to do.

Yet my ignorance had cost me, like it always would.

Mr Cobb walked away, leaving me alone in the darkness with the amulet which had once housed the Death King's soul.

It's too late.

He was gone.

Devon groaned from inside the cage. "Please don't tell me he has the Death King's soul now."

"I won't." A sob caught in my throat. "Would you

believe it? I had the power to do *that*, and the Order robbed me of my memories so anyone could use it against me."

Not Mr Cobb. He hadn't been involved in their decision, and he was furious I'd kept my powers and he hadn't. Furious enough to nurse a grudge against me for years until he'd found a way to lay hands on some real power.

My one consolation was that having the Death King's magic at his fingertips didn't mean he was able to use it. The Death King kept his secrets close to his heart, and while Mr Cobb's memories were fully intact, he'd implied Dirk Alban had trained me further than him.

The bastard. Now Mr Cobb was off to declare war on the Death King, and for all I knew, the entire army would take his side. My hand clenched on the other amulet. No life pulsed against my hand now. The soul amulet was dead.

The revenants had gone, along with their master, so I opened the cage door and helped Devon climb out. She was shivering, blood streaming from her neck where the knife had cut her. I needed to get her out of here before I thought about my next move.

Devon leaned heavily on me as we climbed the stairs to the surface. The revenants had vanished from the alley, too—along with Trix. But someone else stood waiting for us, dressed in armour and a cloak embossed with the Death King's symbol.

The Air Element.

"If you want this back, then go ahead and take it." I held out the amulet. "Mr Cobb won. He moved the Death King's soul to a new vessel."

"I heard the disturbance," they said. "The amulet…"

"His soul isn't in there anymore," I said. "We've lost."

Their eyes were angry slits. "Not as long as I'm breathing, we haven't. Pull yourself together."

Guess I shouldn't have expected sympathy. "What's it to you? I'm no concern of yours. There's no point in locking me up again when you'll soon be without an army or a territory to rule over. Your new master might decide he doesn't need Elemental Soldiers to protect him and cast you all out."

"I have only one master, and not that pretender," they said.

"He's going to claim the Death King's army," I said. "Seems to me like you'll soon be out of work. Unless you're less loyal than you pretend to be."

"The traitor is wrong, but when he realises that, there'll be hell to pay." They paused. "I need you to come with me. Not as a prisoner, but as an ally."

"You want me to come back?" I forced a laugh. "You locked me up and turned Brant into a permanent lich. Go fuck yourself."

"Have it your way, then."

They walked away, leaving me alone with Devon. "C'mon. I'm getting you out of here."

19

We walked back to the node and crossed into the living room once again. The rest of the D&D group hadn't shown up yet, thank god, but Devon's phone was ringing on the table. I ignored it, helping Devon to a seat on the sofa. Then I ran into the shop in search of a cantrip to heal her bleeding neck.

The shop was a mess, to no surprise. Cobb's underlings hadn't cared how much damage they left behind. I ran through the shop and scanned the shelves until I found a cantrip that would staunch the bleeding. I'd left Dex behind in the Parallel, but he was better off staying out of this one.

I returned to the living room with the cantrip in my hand. The wound wasn't as bad as I feared, but Devon was chalk white under the bloodstains. "Chill, Liv, I'm fine. It's not a deep cut."

The phone rang again. If it was a customer, they could

wait. "Damn, it's probably the Order. I wonder if Mr Cobb asked their permission before storming our shop."

The ringing continued. Devon groaned. "Make that godawful racket shut up."

I scooped up the phone. *Fine.* If it was the Order, I'd tear them a new one.

"What?" I growled into the phone.

"Hello, Liv," Mum said brightly.

Oh, hell. So much for avoiding the inevitable. "Hey. Sorry I didn't call—"

"Oh, good, there you are," she said. "That nice young man is here, and says he wants to speak to you. He's quite insistent on it. I tried your phone, but I couldn't get through to you."

"What young man?" I frowned. "Brant?"

That couldn't be right. Brant was a lich, conscripted into the Death King's army.

"The... he calls himself a death king?" She laughed. "He must be in your Dungeons group."

The Death King. *He'd* gone after my family. "No," I said. "Don't move. I mean—can you hold on for a second?"

"I'll give him the phone."

I did not want to talk to the bloody Death King on the phone with my mother potentially in danger right next to him. Did he know his soul had switched vessels? Even if he did, he plainly didn't need it to astral project into my family's home. Mum lived a bus ride away from my house, and while I might have been able to use the nodes to get there, I didn't dare risk it. Mr Cobb might have got what he wanted from me, but that didn't mean he wouldn't come back to tidy up the loose ends if I barged into the middle of his plan again.

But there was another way I could reach her.

I tapped into the node, astral projecting out of my body and soaring headlong into the current. Fixing the image of the right street in my mind, I soared out of the other end of the node, turned left, and floated through the door into Mum's house.

Inside the hall, Mum startled at the sight of me. "Liv… what are you doing? How are you here?"

She reached out a hand, which passed right through me. Oh, hell. Why hadn't I thought of a cover story? Right, because my immortal enemy was here in my mother's house.

"Sorry," I said. "I wanted to be sure you were safe. Where's the Death King?"

"In the living room." She looked through me. "What is this? Are you a hologram?"

Thank the Elements. Or rather, thank the Star Wars movies. Mum wasn't as big a nerd as I was, but at least I had an understandable way to explain this which wouldn't make her think I was dead.

"Close enough." I turned to the door leading into the living room. "I have to talk to him. I'm sorry he showed up without asking."

"Don't be sorry. He was perfectly polite."

I bet he was. I floated through the door into the living room, where the Death King stood with the phone in his hand. He wore his human face, of course, otherwise Mum would never have let him into the house.

"There you are," said the Death King.

"What the hell do you think you're doing?" I exploded.

"My mum knows nothing about this. If you hurt her like you did to Brant—"

"She cooperated with me, so there was no need to," he said. "I had to get hold of you somehow, and I don't have your address."

"Why not ask the Order?" I said.

"I'm aware that my position on the Order, particularly with regard to a certain member, was misinformed."

"Mr Cobb," I said. "I don't care how behind you are on realising the bleeding obvious. Get the hell away from my family, you fucking cadaver."

His brow arched. He sure as hell *looked* human, for someone wearing a mask. No wonder my mum had become enamoured with him in an instant. "Where is Barrett Cobb?"

"He forced me to move your soul to another vessel in order for him to take control of your army. I'd pretend I'm sorry you're going to lose your title, but I'm really not. You can both rot in hell for all I care."

"Thank you for clarifying the matter," he said. "We will meet face to face to discuss this further."

"What?" I said. "You aren't coming to my home. My friend is injured, and the Order trashed the place. Are you astral projecting from your castle?"

"Where else?" he said. "Find me there."

"Only if you promise you won't arrest me again," I said. "Or hurt anyone else I care about. And you'd better leave my family out of this."

"Is that all?" he said. "I'd say you're in no position to make demands, but I will acquiesce to your wishes and leave your family alone. If you tell me your address, there'll be no further need for me to pay any unexpected visits."

If he and I had been solid, I might well have thrown something at him. Death King or not. He had some nerve trying to get into my good graces after how he'd treated me so far.

The Death King gave me a long look before vanishing from sight. Hands shaking, I rotated on the spot when Mum entered the living room again.

"Honey, what's going on?" Mum said. "Are you in trouble?"

"I'm okay," I lied. "I've got this, but the guy who just showed up here isn't… isn't what he seems to be."

Ridiculous as it seemed, however, I found myself fervently glad that it hadn't been the Order who'd paid her a visit. How in hell was this my life now?

Mum picked up the phone. "Should I call someone?"

"No—don't bother." I drew in a breath. "I'd better go."

Mum tried to hug me, but her arms passed through my transparent form. "I hope you aren't in trouble."

My throat tightened. "Not for long, I hope."

Assuming the Death King won this. If not, things would get a lot more dire for everyone involved.

I floated out the door in search of the node. I tracked down the glowing spot in the road, passed through it and back to my body.

"What happened?" Devon leaned over me as I opened my eyes. "You spaced out."

"The apocalypse is nigh," I told her. "The Death King believes me. He knows Mr Cobb is a traitor and that he stole his soul."

"Shit," she said. "He didn't threaten you?"

"No, he seemed to think he could handle the situation," I said. "He didn't need to show his face in front of my family, though. That was a low blow."

"Which family?"

"Mum and Elise," I said. "Just Mum, actually. I think Elise was out, which is probably for the best, considering the astral projection trick I used to get in there."

She blinked. "Wait, did he use astral projection, too?"

"Must have, but he had his human face on so she wouldn't run screaming."

"I didn't know he even had a human face," she said.

"Probably stole it from one of his victims." I gave a humourless laugh. "I can't believe I'm relying on that dickhead after all the trouble he caused me."

"So he's actually going to help you?" she said. "He thinks of you as an ally?"

"Well, I called him a fucking cadaver, so that's up for debate," I said. "But I think so."

Devon snorted. "At this point, I'd take him over the guy who put a knife to my throat."

"He did lock me up in a dungeon."

"I'm not denying he's a shithead. Just the lesser of two shitheads, that's all."

Which was probably the best we'd get at this point. "Yeah. I know."

Elements help us. I was going to have to place my trust in the Death King and save his life, or else leave everyone I loved to suffer a worse fate.

20

I'd start with saving Brant. Which meant getting on the Air Element's good side again. A tall order, but they'd been willing to compromise earlier. If the Death King believed me, if he thought the situation could be salvaged, then perhaps he could reverse what he did to Brant.

That was my bargaining chip. Elements knew I had nothing else to lose.

Once I was sure Devon was okay, I stocked up on cantrips and hopped through the node. I landed on a stretch of swampland close to the bushes I'd hidden in last week. Then I walked up to the two liches on guard outside the gates. "I have a meeting with the Death King. He invited me."

To my surprise, they stepped aside without arguing. Guess he must have told them not to challenge me. Too little, too late, but one fewer obstacle was fine by me.

I entered the castle without being challenged, either. The place seemed oddly quiet, which struck me as ominous. Had Cobb already recruited all the liches onto his own team? Or had they deserted their boss of their own accord now he'd lost his soul?

Despite the relative quiet, I found the Death King standing at the back of the main hall, as tall and menacing as ever, and not at all as though someone else carried the source of his power.

"My mother wouldn't have let you into the house if you'd come dressed like that," I told him.

"I'd never have guessed," he said. "As I promised, I will speak to you face to face about how we are to handle this vexing situation."

"You mean how Mr Cobb used me to transfer your magic over to him," I said. "Personally, I'd have gone and reported him to the Order if I didn't think he might be there himself, waiting to have his people arrest me."

"I doubt the Order cares, regardless," he said, "unless you have proof, of course."

At least he and I were on the same page as far as the Order was concerned. "I have a proposition for you, then."

"Oh?" he said. "Let me guess… you wish to trade your assistance for your little friend's soul."

"You had no right to take his soul in the first place," I told him. "He did nothing to you."

"I beg to differ," he said. "The two of you caused my people considerable trouble."

"That's no reason to permanently turn him into one of your personal soldiers!" I said. "If it can't be reversed, the deal's off."

"I wasn't aware we'd made a deal yet." He tilted his head. "Yes, it can be reversed. As you should know, having handled a soul yourself."

"Yours." I looked him over. "How are you still functioning? Are you so far gone that you can't even sense it when someone steals your soul and claims it as their own?"

"I always forget how limited your human perspective is," he said. "I suppose I can't fault your ignorance, at least, but I would dearly love to know what you think qualifies as 'far gone.'"

I was starting to regret needling him. "I meant that when you first took out your soul, hundreds of years ago or whatever, you might have been almost human. Now, you're a long way from that. But that's beside the point. You said you'd help me."

His whole bearing had changed as I spoke, and while I couldn't see his face, anger tightened the air around him. Maybe I'd pushed too far this time.

"Yes, though I'm having second thoughts on the matter," he said. "It's possible for anyone's soul to temporarily be transferred to another vessel without long-term consequences. As for turning someone into a lich, however, nobody except me can do that."

Reading between the lines, he was implying that if I ticked him off, he'd never let me have Brant back. "Good to know. What about your own soul? Because I held it in my hands, which was bizarre, I might add."

"That's not the same," he said. "You transferred it from one vessel to another. Removing it from a person's body for the first time is another matter entirely, and not one I have time to educate you on. Suffice to say, if I get my hands on the amulet in which my soul now resides, it will be simple for me to transfer it back into its original vessel."

"You're assuming I'll give it back." *Shut it, Liv.* I couldn't seem to stop poking at him, perhaps due to the fact that I'd bypassed fear a long time ago. Besides, I held his amulet in my pocket, for all the good it did.

The Death King studied me for a moment. "I will pretend you agreed to cooperate with me. You will start by informing me of the identities of everyone working with this rogue from the Order."

"One of your liches, for a start," I said. "I know the address of the earth mage who he's working with, too, but the enemy took my friend away before he could take me there."

Trix. I hoped he'd managed to get away from the revenants, because there wasn't anything I could do for him here.

He gave me another assessing look. "You still claim there's a traitor in my ranks. I have seen no evidence of any wrongdoing myself, though perhaps they aren't as united as they seem."

"Yeah, well, the liches all look the exact same," I said. "But I'm telling the truth. Your traitor has been paying visits to the earth mage, Vaughn. He lives in South Street, opposite the warehouse, if it helps."

"I see," he said. "If that's the case, you'll find him. I'll deal with the spirit mage myself."

"Excuse me?" I said. "You can't give me orders. You're not *my* master."

"This is a partnership," he said.

"Even if it was, that doesn't give you the right to boss me around," I told him. "If your liches have turned traitor, they'll be out in the streets along with the revenants.

Which means if I go out there, I'll be surrounded. There's way too many for me to fight alone."

"Then take one of my people with you." He looked over my shoulder. "Ryan seems well-acquainted with you."

"Who the bloody hell is Ryan?"

The Air Element walked in. That answered that question, then. Their gaze flickered from the Death King to me. "We will go into the city together."

I didn't move. "Brant knows the city better than I do. He also has a score to settle with the earth mage, and he can help us bring him to justice."

"Fine." The Death King raised a hand. "Come here."

He indicated the liches swarming around the edges of the room. Shadowy figures filled the spaces between the tall pillars of skulls, and one of them floated over, resolving into the shape of a man with blue eyes and broad shoulders.

Tears burned my eyes. "Oh, Brant, I'm so sorry."

"Don't be," he said. "I'm the one who came after the liches when they took you."

"You can catch up later," said the Death King, an irritable undercurrent to his voice. "Once my soul is back where it belongs."

"You said it can be reversed." I indicated Brant. "I want him back to normal. I won't make a deal with you otherwise."

"Fine," said the Death King. "Ryan, take her to the hall of souls."

The Air Element marched away without speaking, leaving me to follow with Brant floating alongside me.

"Are you okay?" I asked him. "I'm so glad it can be reversed. I was scared I lost you."

"Me too, believe me," he said. "It really wasn't that bad, though, compared to what they did to you."

"He didn't take away your free will?" I asked. "Or make you fight in his army?"

"I mean, I couldn't exactly leave," he said. "I thought you were still captive here, and besides, he wouldn't have let me go outside."

"This way," said the Air Element. "All the souls are in here."

They walked through a pair of doors into another hall. Row upon row of shelves filled the space inside like a giant museum, containing amulets and other trinkets. None were marked or had a name on them.

I scanned the rows of endless shelves. "How'd the thief get to the Death King's soul? Where was it?"

"If you're planning the same, it'll end badly for you," said the Air Element—or Ryan, the Death King had called them.

"If I planned to steal any souls, I'd already have done it." I scowled. "When will you people get it into your heads that I'm not interested in thwarting your little kingdom? I'm not even that interested in spirit magic, for crying out loud. Been there, done that, got the mental scars."

The Air Element frowned at me. "What do you mean?"

I remained silent for a moment, debating. Then I figured I had nothing to lose by telling them.

"The Order ripped out two years of my memories when they found out I was learning spirit magic," I said. "I was a student at their academy at the time. And no, I don't remember the specifics, but my mentor died for it, and the Order decreed that I should take on the full brunt of the punishment myself."

Ryan looked at me with an unreadable expression on their face. Guess I should have known better than to expect sympathy from one of the Death King's people.

"There's a lot of reasons I turned my back on the Order," they said. "They barely treated me like a person, and their ridiculous restrictions on magic use made staying on Earth unreasonable. I never understood how even regular practitioners could stand all the rules and regulations."

"We have no choice," I said. "We can't all be part of the Death King's personal team of soldiers. Most of us are just trying to stay alive. And you know, even if this comes to an end with everyone's souls in the right place, I've broken the law again and the Order won't care about excuses. Since I'm not underage this time, they'll probably sentence me to a lifetime in prison."

The Air Element turned my way with a frown. "If that's the case, you'd be better served staying here."

I forced a laugh. "There's nothing for me here, either. Pretty much everyone in the Parallel wants me dead."

"Not my master," they said. "Not now we all know the truth."

"Yeah, if that's an invitation to join your army of liches, I think I'll pass," I said. "For multiple reasons, chief of which is that Brant's soul is currently lost somewhere in this hall."

"It's not lost." They halted at an alcove. "All the new souls are here."

"The other prisoners, too?" I scanned the row of

shelves. "How does your master know they won't betray him if he turns them into liches?"

"Who told you he turned them into liches?" They paused beside the shelf. "If the person is unquestionably a traitor, they are punished in a different manner."

"Like what?" The question escaped automatically, though I wasn't sure I wanted to know.

They swept a careless hand at the walls, which were lined with human skulls. "Decoration."

That figured. Just when I'd started to understand the Death King's position, another reminder came along that these people were happy to let the world see them as monsters.

Ryan pulled an amulet off the nearest shelf and held it out to me, and a rush of familiarity surged when my fingertips brushed the surface. Brant's soul felt different than the Death King's, warmer. Made sense, given that Brant was a fire mage. The flames kindled in my hands as I took the amulet, and his figure appeared floating above my palms.

A faint whispering noise prompted me to turn around. Brant's lich had followed me, and now he floated at my side, his form shadowy and semi-transparent. I opened my mouth to say I didn't know how to help him, but I did, somehow. I held up the amulet, and he hovered closer, bowing his head.

I reached out and looped the amulet around his neck. As I did so, his form began to turn solid again. His eyes became sharper, his outline less shadowy.

"I don't know what I'm doing," I whispered.

"I trust you," he said.

Tears stung my eyes. Drawing in a breath, I splayed my

hands and gently pushed his soul to return to his living form. Slowly, his soul slid back into his body, filling out the edges, his feet touching the earth. His eyes became clearer, less foggy, and the shadows receded until all that remained was Brant. Alive, as though he'd never been otherwise.

He pulled the amulet off, and I exclaimed in alarm—but he didn't fade or disappear. The amulet was empty. Brant's soul was back where it belonged.

"Thank the Elements," I breathed.

Brant wrapped his arms around me and hugged me. Then he pressed his mouth to mine, and for an instant, everything was okay.

21

My next step was to get the Order on my side.
Easier said than done. After all, in their eyes, Mr Cobb was still a highly regarded supervisor. I wondered if he still had a black mark on his record from all those years back, or if they'd wiped it squeaky-clean when they'd taken his magic. He must have had connections in order to keep a position at all, in fact, but that was the Order for you. They preferred to keep their enemies closer than their friends, and they'd even kept *me* in their ranks when I hadn't had half the influence Cobb did. I'd bet he'd played up his innocence for all it was worth when they'd caught him, and if the only crime he'd committed was *learning* magic, they'd have considered him a nonentity of a threat compared to Dirk Alban.

Brant insisted on going with me. Ryan, too, though I refused point-blank to let either of them enter the Order's base. I still didn't know what'd happened to those underlings who'd been with Mr Cobb, nor how much they'd witnessed of his public betrayal. They'd still been frozen by Devon's cantrip, but they must have seen some of it.

Still, Mr Cobb would doubtless no longer care about making a public scene. He didn't care if the Order knew what he was, not now he had the power he'd wanted for so long. It'd been a decade since Dirk Alban's death. Nothing the Order gave him since then would have made up for what he'd lost.

I hopped through the node and landed outside their headquarters alone, my heart drumming with nerves.

Here goes nothing.

Going to the retrieval unit wouldn't do me any good, so I made for Mr Cobb's office instead, my body tensing with each step. A large part of me was certain I'd find the man himself there, ready to declare me a traitor, but another supervisor sat in his place, accompanied by two guards. All three were shifters, a somewhat unusual choice, and I recognised one of the two guards as the guy who'd been with Judith when the two of them had confronted the Air Element outside.

As for the supervisor, I recognised him from my early days as an Order employee. While he hadn't been on the committee that had convicted me, that didn't mean he had my back. His nametag marked him as Roderick Shepherd.

The shifter rose to his feet. "Olivia Cartwright?"

"That's me," I said. "I'm here to report a supervising officer for treason and for illegal use of spirit magic."

This was one hell of a gamble. If the Order found out it was me who'd ripped out the Death King's soul, then I'd be screwed for real this time. But there was no way I could get him jailed single-handedly. Most of the Order's representatives believed he was one of them. He could walk in here with the Death King's soul without anyone knowing the truth.

My one ace in the hole was that thanks to the Death King's soul, he *was* a spirit mage. That meant they'd be unable to deny his treachery if they saw the amulet he carried. That is, if they believed me without seeing him for themselves.

The shifter's brows lifted. "Who, exactly?"

I could see from his body language that he was seconds from ordering his guards to grab me. *Well, it was worth a shot.* "Mr Cobb. He handed me over to the Death King for a crime I never committed, and while I was locked up, he stole the Death King's soul for his own use. You can ask the man himself if you don't believe me."

One of the guards stepped closer to me. "You're confessing to your involvement in Barrett Cobb's disappearance?"

I nearly laughed. "Not hardly. He stole the Death King's soul. Two of your people were with him when he took my friend hostage in an attempt to get him on our side. They're still in the Parallel where he left them."

"Mr Cobb is a valued member of our team," he growled. "The council will not accept these allegations."

"Look at his record," I said. "He was a spirit mage, before the Order stripped him of his powers. He then schemed to get his hands on the Death King's soul because he believed it would return the magic you took from him. Which one of the two of us has a better motive?"

"You have black marks on your own record," said the supervisor. "Why should I believe you?"

"Because I don't remember a thing," I said. "My memories were erased, but Mr Cobb's weren't. He still remembers what it was like to use spirit magic, and it's driven him mad. I couldn't reason with him."

The Death King chose that moment to stride into the office, his human face twisted into an expression of annoyance.

"Death King." The shifter's face went ashen. "To what do I owe the pleasure of this visit?"

"It gives me no pleasure," he said dispassionately. "Olivia here was sent into my jail on false accusations at the hands of one of your staff members. That same person has stolen something of mine."

"I thought *she* stole from you," he said, jerking his head at me.

"A misunderstanding," said the Death King. "I intend to take back what was stolen by your supervising officer, but I would like to request you send a team to accompany me. I believe it's in your rules that you must take him in yourselves."

A chill ran through the room as the shifter guards exchanged glances. For once, the Death King's aura didn't hit me as strongly. After all, he was on my side this time. As for the Order? For all I knew, Mr Cobb would turn on his fellow Order members now he had what he wanted, and I could tell the same thought had crossed the others' minds, too.

"We will come," said the shifter supervisor. "I'll get a team together as requested."

The Death King vanished, leaving behind a long pause in which nobody looked directly at me.

"Olivia, you will wait for us outside," said the supervisor.

I heard him move around giving orders as I left the office, disbelief sifting through my thoughts. *The Death King stood up for me?*

Of course he had. He wanted his soul back, and he was even willing to work with the likes of me in order to get it.

Ten minutes later, a team of thirty Order members had assembled in the lobby. Most of them had some combat training, but that didn't change the fact that we were hopelessly outclassed when it came to fighting off the entirety of the Death King's army. Not to mention I couldn't openly use spirit magic in front of them. I had to make Mr Cobb seem like the villain in all ways. While the Order employees who'd seen the fight in Devon's shop should also have seen him put a knife to Devon's throat, they must still be in the Parallel.

When our group landed on the other side, I found Brant waiting for me as planned. Beside him, Ryan paced up and down the street. Dex appeared in the corner of my eye, but I couldn't even speak to him without risking drawing suspicion. Befriending sprites wasn't against the Order's rules, but from the wary looks some of them gave me, and the mutters they thought I couldn't hear, they thought I'd take Mr Cobb's side, given the chance.

I ignored them, walking up to join Brant. "These Order employees are coming with us to fight against Cobb and apprehend him."

"About time," said Ryan, scowling at the assembled group. "We've wasted enough of it."

Reading between the lines, Ryan and Brant had not exactly hit it off. No surprises there.

"I know where Vaughn is," Brant added. "Just say the

word and I'll have him by the throat." An undercurrent of anger ran through his voice.

"Yeah, I have a few words I'd like to say to him." I turned to Roderick Shepherd. "A couple of your people are somewhere in the city. You're welcome to look for them, or you can come with Brant and me to find the traitor's allies."

Whispers broke out among the Order members, but they didn't argue. The presence of Ryan in full armour scowling at them probably helped. Vaughn was in real trouble now. *Good luck running from two pissed-off mages.*

We followed Brant's lead towards a house set slightly apart from its neighbours. An air of neglect hung around the place, but that was nothing new. Was the earth mage hiding underground? At a guess… yes, he was. I turned to Brant. "Does he have a basement, by any chance?"

"Yes." His hands clenched. "I'm going to kill him."

"Might want to avoid letting the Order see," I commented. "They're not fussed about who they arrest."

"I don't think any of them are going to survive this," he said. "I saw what those liches can do to a person. Even if they're the Order's best, they'll die."

I halted mid-step. "You can't mean that."

"I know why they banned spirit magic," he said. "I understand it, even. On their own, the liches obey their master, but if a spirit mage takes them over…"

"So the Death King could have wiped the Order off the map at any time," I surmised. "Good to know."

"No, he couldn't," Brant said. "Because he and his liches have no power on Earth. The Order does. Mr Cobb belongs to both worlds, though, and he can use his leverage as Death King to bring the Order to its knees."

Please say it's not true. Earth wasn't prepared for a spirit war. Hell, the Parallel wasn't. It'd barely survived the last one, and the remnants of its violence still haunted Arcadia's streets. The Death King had been the closest to a spirit mage left in either realm—or so I'd thought.

Yet Dirk Alban had seen potential in me. He'd seen it in Cobb, too, and if I killed him, I could say goodbye to ever finding out the truth. But as little as I liked the Death King, I'd rather have him than the alternative.

I felt the liches before I saw them, cold and shadowy, drifting through the streets. Coming this way.

"Shit," I whispered. "I think he's already convinced them he's the Death King. They've switched to his side."

The Order's people had probably never fought against liches before. They wouldn't know what to expect. Worse, the only way to destroy them was to find their individual soul amulets—all of which were in the Death King's own hall of souls, far out of reach.

There was one option remaining. I had to use spirit magic—yet even then, I was no match for an army. *Think, Liv.*

Ryan stepped in, their hands alighting with air magic. A blast of energy slammed headlong into the closest liches. At the same moment, the earth trembled beneath our feet.

"Earth mage!" I shouted at the others. "He's laid a trap."

They got the message and moved out of range of the quaking earth. The earth mage was somewhere below our feet, and from the stubborn expression on Brant's face, he had no intention of letting him off easily.

I walked closer to Ryan. "Can you stop them? The liches?"

"I can only stall them," they said. "They obey my orders, up to a point, but their loyalties are confused thanks to the false king. If he shows up, they'll turn on me, too."

Crap. "Then I'll face him myself. Get the amulet off him. Vaughn will know where he is, I guarantee it."

As Ryan barred the liches' path, we advanced on the house once again. Brant walked ahead, fury simmering in his eyes. "I'll get the shithead."

I grabbed his arm for balance when the ground gave another heave. "I wonder if Mr Cobb is hiding down there, too?"

Dex flew up to me. "What're you doing with *them?*" He indicated the Order's team, who'd spread out behind the Air Element.

"Getting them to do what they do best, and throw the book at their traitorous supervisor," I said. "Assuming the liches don't get to them first."

"They aren't the only ones," he said. "The liches are fighting each other in the streets. I've never seen anything like it."

"Where's Mr Cobb? Does he have Trix with him?"

"That tricky elf of yours gave him the slip somewhere underground."

"Finally, some good news," I said. "How'd you stay hidden?"

"Oh, nobody notices me." Even the Order members didn't seem to have spotted Dex, though they were distracted by the liches and the Air Element's attempt to keep them away from us.

Brant kicked open the door to the house, revealing a

hallway which was mercifully lich-free. Inside, a trapdoor stood open, leading down into darkness.

As we climbed down, the sound of fighting rose to meet us. I blinked in confusion, then my eyes adjusted as Brant's fire lit up the way ahead. A sizeable basement lay beneath the house, and a large number of brawling revenants blocked the way. No wonder the earth mage hadn't come to the surface. The revenants had entirely blocked the way out, and they seemed too intent on tearing one another up to notice our appearance.

"What in the world is wrong with them?" said Brant.

"Maybe they're confused, too, about this whole leadership changeover thing," I said. "The false Death King's probably trying to convince the ruling vampires to join his team."

He'd kicked off a turf war, and we'd unintentionally landed in the middle of it.

Brant conjured a flame to his hand. "Not sure about that. Check out your friend."

Trix stood in the middle of the chaos, and when he saw me, he waved cheerily at me as though we were passing one another at the supermarket. "I thought you'd appreciate me distracting them. I used my magic to confuse them into attacking one another."

"And the earth mage?" I said. "We're looking for him."

"Oh, he's here." He casually lifted a foot, where the earth mage was pinned down.

"You." Vaughn raised his head. "You're supposed to be dead."

"Surprise," Brant said, through gritted teeth. "You traitorous bastard."

Fire blasted from his hand, burning a path through the

revenants. Vaughn ducked for cover, shooting headfirst into the earth. Trix groaned. "I had him!"

Vaughn emerged from the floor beneath my feet, but I pivoted aside before he could grab me and take me hostage again. I kicked him in the face, feeling a satisfying crunch beneath my heel. He groaned, blood streaming from his nose. "Hey. Hang on—"

"You tried to get us killed." Brant's fireball sent him scrambling for cover, but the earthquake continued, knocking revenants left and right. He'd lost control of his magic, and if we weren't careful, the whole house would come crashing down.

"Get to the surface," I told Brant. "I'll meet you there, but this place won't last long the way he's going."

"Then I'll finish him fast." His second fireball turned several revenants to ashes and sent Vaughn backing against the wall. The earth mage looked between us, genuine fear in his eyes.

Brant grabbed the scruff of his neck. "What are you playing at? Trying to knock down your own hideout?"

He spat out blood. "The city will be rebuilt from the ground up when our true leader takes his throne."

Brant raised Vaughn's head and smashed it into the wall. "No chance."

The wall trembled, and Brant staggered as the earth behind him began to fracture. Vaughn smiled, his face a bloody mess. "I'll take you down with me, Brant, you'll see if I don't."

Brant looked at me. "This is our fight. I won't ask you to get involved."

"Like hell," I said, incensed. "I'm not losing you again."

"How touching," said Vaughn. "You sicken me, you

know that? All that power at your fingertips, and yet you choose to toe the line rather than doing anything with it."

"Someone else said something similar to me once," I told him. "It didn't end well for anyone involved."

Brant was right, though—it was Mr Cobb I needed to find, before he finished off the Death King and claimed the rest of his army.

"I'll handle him," Brant said. "He doesn't have the amulet."

No... the false Death King did. "He's not underground. Where is he?"

Brant slammed Vaughn's head into the wall again. "Where is he? Where is your master?"

He grimaced. "He's at home, of course... his new home."

The Death King's castle.

He'd already gone there to claim his throne.

22

I ran for the steps back to the surface. Brant and Vaughn's shouts echoed behind me, interspersed with tremors that wrenched at the ground beneath my feet, but I couldn't worry about Brant now. I had to warn the others.

I ran out of the house and found Ryan directing liches out of the streets and away from the fleeing Order members. It seemed at least some of them still took orders from him, as long as the false Death King wasn't around.

"Mr Cobb is already at the castle," I told them. "He went to declare war on your master directly."

Ryan swore. "I should have known he'd try to give us the slip. We'll go there right away."

As we turned to leave, one of the Order guards accosted me. "Where are you going?"

"The Death King's territory," I said. "Mr Cobb has gone there to take his throne and his army in one go, unless we stop him."

"What's going on in there?" A shifter indicated the

house, which trembled as though a great beast stirred beneath the earth.

"Vampire turf war," I told them. "A diversion, to keep us from the Death King's territory. If you want to stop Mr Cobb, you'd better come with me."

I didn't wait for a response. Ryan took the lead, their air magic lending them speed the rest of us couldn't hope to match. Dex flew over my head, occasionally diverting a lich or two off our trail. While Ryan could command obedience for now, I suspected that would all change when we reached the swamp.

The Order guards fell in behind us as Ryan and I made for the outskirts of the swampland. Mist curled above the ground, while dark shapes swirled around a figure standing alone on the marshy ground.

Mr Cobb stood in the midst of the liches, an expectant look on his face.

With a curse, Ryan raised their hands and blasted Mr Cobb with air magic. He didn't bother to dodge. He just held up the soul amulet, and the attack slammed into an invisible shield. My teeth rattled in my skull as the air vibrated around us, but Mr Cobb remained unharmed.

"You can't lay a hand on me," he said. "None of you can. Your king is dead, and I am your new master."

He can't be.

A furious cry escaped Ryan, and they fired another blast of magic at the spirit mage. Ryan's magic was stronger, but they couldn't get through Mr Cobb's shield. The Order representatives fanned out across the swampland.

"Ryan," I said. "You help the Order deal with the liches. I'll handle him."

The liches, at least, could be stalled by the Air Element's magic, but as long as Mr Cobb held the Death King's soul, none of the Death King's soldiers would be able to raise a hand against him.

But I would.

"You will, will you?" Mr Cobb held up the amulet, which hung from a chain around his neck, then let it fall against his chest. Energy hummed around him like an invisible force-field. He was using the Death King's life energy to give him power.

I have to get it out of his hands. Whatever he'd done to get the liches to obey him relied on him keeping the amulet in his hands. He was borrowing the power through a conduit—and for all I knew, maybe I could do the same. After all, several feet away from him lay the node in the centre of the swampland, a current of power connecting both realms. Even through my panic, I felt its power humming beneath the surface.

"Do you really want to challenge me, Olivia?" he said.

"Yes, I do," I said. "I'm giving you one chance to hand over the amulet. If you do, the Death King might spare your life."

"The Death King is dead," he said. "These liches serve me now. You could join me, Olivia. I'm still willing to give you another chance."

"I'd rather eat dirt," I said. "You're using a dead man's soul to gain power."

"You care so strongly for the man who terrorised you?"

"No, the Death King was never my master," I said. "I think he's an utter dick, actually, on account of how he locked me in jail and turned Brant into a lich. But you're worse."

I called on power straight from the node, no longer caring if the others saw me use spirit magic. It was him or me, and I intended to win.

Energy roared from my hands, straight at the soul thief. He pivoted, tucking the amulet into his coat, and shot a blast of power from his own palms. I ducked and rolled, avoiding his attack.

"You can't beat me, Olivia." Energy surged from his hands, vibrant as the glowing current of a node. "My knowledge far surpasses yours, however powerful you might be."

He wasn't wrong. His memories of spirit magic were fully intact, after all. I might have remembered enough to save my life, but perhaps it wouldn't be enough to beat a master. Especially one holding onto a soul as ancient and terrifying as the Death King's.

Worse, more liches floated towards us, drawn by their master's aura. Dark shadowy shapes surrounded me on all sides, and Mr Cobb gave a thin-lipped smile. "Kill them."

A horrible scream came from behind me as the liches closed in on the Order's forces. Two went down, falling like puppets with their strings cut as the life was wrenched from their bodies. I cursed, aiming another attack at Mr Cobb, but a lich got in the way. Energy blasted from my palms, sending the lich flying into the air. The node glowed, too, and shock punched through me when I realised Cobb was utterly ignoring it.

I might not remember my lessons, but I was fairly sure that losing his magic meant Cobb had also lost the ability to sense the nodes. Even holding the Death King's soul hadn't restored that power. His magic was concentrated inside the amulet, and he couldn't bolster it with energy from elsewhere.

I began circling him, firing off blasts of energy as I did so, and keeping one eye on the node. Mr Cobb's gaze followed me, probably wondering what in hell I was playing at, but I didn't have any better ideas. The closer I drew, the more the node's power roared in my blood, and I wondered how I'd ever forgotten how to use it. Magic punched through my fingers, and the liches who grabbed for me flew in all directions, unable to touch me.

The third stage. Drawing on a node to bolster my own strength.

I raised my hand and directed a wave of spirit magic at Mr Cobb. The shock on his face sent a bolt of satisfaction through me, but it swiftly turned into a goading smirk.

I faltered, seeing a nearby Order employee watching me. Mr Cobb wanted me to suffer for the crime he believed I'd committed. My grip on the node slipped, and the liches closed in once more. I might be able to attack them, but they couldn't die, not as long as their souls were bound to their own amulets. And I'd tire out eventually.

Cold shadowy hands brushed against me from behind, and a piercing chill banished the buzzing in my veins. Two liches closed in, one on either side of me, and a horrible yawning emptiness pierced me, as though they were reaching for my very soul. Mr Cobb's mouth twisted with hate and bitterness intermixed with triumph. "Goodbye, Olivia."

Fire flared across my vision, and the liches released me, recoiling away from the flames.

Brant. He also came with Dex, who blasted sparks into

the liches' eyes from above and flew around them like an angry wasp. I retreated to safer ground, next to Brant.

"Glad to see you," I breathed.

"Likewise." Fire blasted from his hands, forcing Mr Cobb to conceal himself behind his liches. The bastard might have made himself immune to the Death King's Elemental Soldiers, but any other mage could harm him.

Brant and I moved to stand back to back. "Your fire can hurt Cobb," I told him. "He can only be harmed by people who don't support the Death King."

"Then I guess I'll have to continue being opposed to his reign of terror." A torrent of flame blasted from his palms, and Mr Cobb let his liches take the fall, a calculating expression forming on his face.

Don't you dare hurt him.

Mr Cobb deflected the next wave of flames with ease, and my heart sank. The Death King's powers were far beyond mine and Brant's. I remembered four lessons, that was all.

Out of ideas, I ran for the node again, but Mr Cobb swept in. He raised a hand, and my body ground to a halt, freezing on the spot the way it had when the Death King had unleashed his power on me.

"Useful tool, this." He held up the amulet. "I think I'll let you watch me kill your friends before I use it to finish you off."

Bodies already littered the swampland—Order guards, stripped of their souls. Ryan stood surrounded by liches, strong enough to hold them off, but they couldn't fight an army single-handedly. Order guards fell, crumpling as the life bled from them. Mr Cobb didn't care about killing his fellow Order members, and as long as he held me in his grip, I was powerless.

"Stop right there!" Currents of water swirled into view, and several liches vanished beneath a tidal wave directed by an armoured woman with a blue-lined coat. Her hair was braided down her back, her dark blue coat marked with the Death King's symbol.

At her side walked a soldier with flames dancing between his palms, while another rode on horseback, the earth cracking beneath his steed's skeletal feet. Liches fell into the cracks, struggling to regain their balance. The other three Elements had come to join the first in fighting against Mr Cobb. *They don't recognise him as their leader.* Unlike the liches, they had the freedom to make that choice, and they'd chosen to stand by their true master.

My heart lifted despite myself as the four Elements engaged the lich army, leaving Mr Cobb and I alone.

"Why not join me, Olivia?" said Mr Cobb. "You'd be better off at my side than with the Order."

"Never," I shot at him. "You killed them. Slaughtered them in cold blood. I'd rather join the Death King than you."

"I *am* the Death King," he said. "Or I will be, once I win the last of his servants to my side."

The four Elemental Soldiers' attacks had the liches retreating, but none could harm Mr Cobb, who remained as indestructible as ever. My body, meanwhile, remained frozen to the spot. Powerless to escape.

I reached for the node, willing its energy to come to me. There had to be a way to break out of his spell.

Astral projecting. It wasn't ideal, but maybe... maybe

there was a chance the Death King had survived, and I could reach him. If I left my body behind, that is.

I flew out of my body, arcing above the ground, and spotted Dex flying above the liches, throwing fireballs in them.

He gave me a wave. "Oh, we're flying away, are we?"

"No, we're going to find out how to stop that dick-head," I said. "How do I get that amulet out of his hand when I can't move and he can't be affected by anyone who recognises him as their master?"

"I can try," he said. "Can you give me a boost?"

"Can I what?"

He flew towards me in a whirl of flames. "I reckon I can take him. Or at least slow him down."

"How—what do you want me to do?" Now I was thoroughly confused.

"Do what you did when you brought me with you through the node," he said. "Get back into your body first. Before he sees you."

I sailed back into my body, and Dex floated in front of me. As I did so, I drew on the node's power, willing it to flow through me and into the fire sprite.

Energy surged from the node into me, right through Dex. The fire sprite launched forward and slammed into Mr Cobb with the force of a bullet. Mr Cobb staggered, and his spell broke. I lunged at him, tackling him to the ground and grabbing for the amulet around his neck.

"Deal with him," Mr Cobb snarled, fighting my grip. I grasped the amulet and tugged it over his head, and the Death King's soul appeared floating above it before vanishing again. My fingers grasped the chain, but Mr Cobb tugged back.

Dex screamed.

My grip on the amulet broke, and I looked up in time to see one of the liches seize the fire sprite. In a wrenching movement, Dex's body blazed all over—then he burst into flames, turning to ashes that scattered on the breeze.

23

A roar of fire swallowed my scream. Dex didn't even have time to cry out before his fragile form broke apart into splintered fragments. Time slowed to a crawl, each second painfully crystallised, before the node's power roared into my fingertips once again.

Instinct took over. The fragments that had once been Dex coalesced into a swirling mass in the midst of the node's power rippling from my hand. My magic caressed the ashes, kindling them into a flame. Willing Dex to return to life.

Dex's humanoid transparent figure reappeared in the same spot in which he'd vanished. "Ow, that hurt."

Mr Cobb's expression was raw shock, and despite my own disbelief, I knew an opportunity when I saw one. While Mr Cobb's attention was on Dex, I lunged for the amulet.

My hand closed around the cool metal, tugging it free from Mr Cobb's hand. He snarled and grabbed for it, but before he could yank it out of my grip, Dex flew into his eyes. He swore explosively, batting at the fire sprite and cursing when the flames singed his hands. The amulet came free, flying in an arc over the swampland.

I dove after it, kicking Mr Cobb as I did so. He grabbed at my legs, but Brant flung a handful of flames over my shoulder. Cobb swore and threw himself flat on the ground.

"Get him!" I shouted in the general direction of the four Elemental Soldiers. "He can't defend himself without this!"

My hand closed around the cold shape of the amulet. The liches instantly zeroed in on me, but when I rose to my feet, they stopped in their tracks.

"Stop fighting the Order," I told the liches. "Attack him. Keep him away from the castle."

Mr Cobb ran at me with a roar of fury, but the liches converged on him in a dark mass, no longer bound to his will. As for me, I gripped the amulet in my hand, and I ran towards the castle, hoping that I wasn't too late.

Magic roared to my fingertips, straight from the node, and the amulet's sudden glow nearly made me trip over in shock. The Death King's transparent form appeared hovering above the surface. My speed quickened, my feet skimming the ground as I ran. Was he loaning me his power?

Whatever the case, the liches weren't challenging me, Brant and the rest of the Order's people held back Mr Cobb, and I kept running until I passed through the gates leading to the castle. I put on a burst of speed, my nerves jangling, my lungs screaming at me. *I have to make it. I have to.*

Taking the stone steps two at a time, I pelted up to the castle entrance and into the main hall. My feet pounded on the stone floor as I ran up to the dais, where the Death King waited.

He was still alive, I knew at once, but fading, almost entirely transparent.

I held up the amulet. "Looking for this?"

"You." Even his voice was quieter than usual. "I need you to return my soul to its original vessel."

I dug my hand in my pocket and pulled out the now-vacant skull amulet, holding it side by side with the new one. "Can't you jump from one to another?"

"That's not how it works," he said. "A spirit mage must make the transfer. That's why... when the spirit war ended..."

"You were all stuck as liches." I'd thought they'd made that choice, but perhaps it wasn't a choice after all. "You couldn't reverse what happened to Brant, but I could."

No wonder spirit mages were such a valuable commodity. Liches could create other liches, but they couldn't reverse the process on their own. When the spirit mages had died out, the liches had been trapped in their current form. Yet with their resurgence...

"Go on," he said. "We can discuss the nuances of spirit magic later."

The Death King trusted me to put his soul back into place? It seemed surreal, but I had no time to dwell on the bizarre turn my life had taken. If I'd been a different person, I might have considered disposing of both amulets, but if there was anyone I trusted to bring an end to this conflict, it was the Death King. Rather him than Mr Cobb, anyway.

Holding the amulets side by side, I waited for the Death King's figure to appear floating above the new vessel. I willed it to move into my hand, which still buzzed with the power of the node.

For a few panicked seconds, I was afraid it hadn't worked. The glowing soul in my grip looked so insubstantial, it hardly seemed like it had ever belonged to a person. I held my breath, my hands trembling, and when I was sure the soul was disconnected from the amulet, I took the second one in my hand.

In the same instant, the castle door slammed open and Mr Cobb limped inside, his expression livid. "You ruined everything!"

I threw the disused amulet at him, and with my other hand, I completed the transfer, pushing the Death King's soul back into its original vessel.

The Death King flew at Mr Cobb and hit him with the force of a speeding train. The two of them might have been an equal match before, but now the Death King was at full power. He could tear out Cobb's soul and rip it into ribbons.

Mr Cobb staggered to his feet and tried to run, but the Death King raised both hands, causing his body to rise like a puppet on strings. He began to scream, as though torn from within by unimaginable pain.

"Stop!" I said. "He has to face justice from the Order. Otherwise, I'm the one they'll punish in his place."

The Death King cut me a sideways look. "He deserves worse than anything the Order can do to him."

"Worse than having his magic taken away and his memories?" I asked. "Regardless of what you think, the Order will be looking for a target to blame. And if he's dead or driven into madness, he can't testify. Leave him alive."

He raised a hand and Mr Cobb's body flew backwards, slamming against the wall. He went limp, his head lolling.

Then the Death King looked at me, his gaze starkly inhuman. "If you insist."

24

It wasn't that simple. My life never is.

The trial was scheduled less than twenty-four hours after the battle, and I was invited to testify against Mr Cobb. I'd never been in the Order's courtroom before, but prickles of déjà-vu hit me between the shoulder blades the instant I walked out of the elevator into the high-ceilinged, wide atrium up on the third floor. My heart climbed into my throat, and it was all I could do to keep breathing.

I might not remember, but I'd been convicted in this very room. I must have been.

Then my gaze fell on Mr Cobb, who sat palely in his seat, flanked by several uniformed security personnel. He looked dazed, as though the impact of losing the Death King's soul was finally starting to sink in, and he didn't even seem to notice me enter the room.

Yet as I took my own seat, dread gripped me as though I was the one on trial. The other Order members' judgemental stares were even worse than usual, as were the whispers they thought I couldn't hear. The Order hadn't faced a battle in the Parallel in a while, and they'd certainly never expected a suspected traitor to be the one to lead them into the fight against one of their own. While the liches couldn't exactly be trialled for murder, rumour had it that the higher-ups weren't pleased by the crimes the Death King's people had committed while under Cobb's control. So, in the absence of anyone else to blame, they directed their attention onto me.

"We are here for the trial of Barrett Cobb," said the judge, a tall black man dressed in sombre attire. "He stands accused of treason against the Order of the Elements and against the ruler of the Court of Death. The first to testify against him will be Olivia Cartwright."

An outbreak of muttering followed at the sound of my name. I swallowed hard, rising to my feet.

"Mr Cobb," I said, holding up the now-empty amulet. "I accuse you of treason against the Order of the Elements and against the crown of the Death King. You hired people to steal the Death King's soul amulet, after which you claimed his soul and his magic for your own use. Then, you attacked and killed multiple Order members and nearly brought about another war in the Parallel."

He finally looked at me, his expression taut with rage. "You accuse me of treason? You knew Dirk Alban. You benefited from his studies, and you used those skills against the Death King."

My heart drummed as the whispers picked up, and raw panic closed my throat. One wrong word from one person and I'd be condemned along with him.

"Olivia committed no crimes," said the judge. "By the order of the Death King, she is to be pardoned for any magic she used while under duress.

He what? The Death King had got me off the hook? Even though I'd stolen his soul. Then lost it. And then saved him from certain doom. Okay, at this point, I hadn't the faintest clue what to expect from him. But this?

"Can the Death King confirm it?" asked someone.

"Yes," said a cold, resonant voice.

Several gasps rose from the crowd as the Death King himself entered the atrium. All eyes followed his passage, right up until he stopped at my side. Then he faced the audience, and from the gasps that ensued, he wasn't wearing his human disguise this time.

"Go on," he said. "Get on with the trial."

I nearly laughed, mostly at how absurd the situation was. The Death King, interfering in Order affairs. I'd have expected him to keep his distance, but perhaps he'd come here for his own form of revenge on Mr Cobb. Who even knew at this point?

"I think that's proof enough of this man's treachery," said one of the senior supervisors.

The others seemed to agree. It was possibly the shortest trial in the history of the Order, but despite the fresh outbreak of mutters and whispers that followed Mr Cobb's removal from the room, nobody voiced any objections. Most seemed too distracted by the Death King's unexpected presence.

The lift doors closed, taking Mr Cobb away—and with him, my only shot at unearthing the rest of the secrets buried in my memories. For now, at least. With my freedom close to being restored, I'd be a fool to put it in jeopardy again.

Gradually, the others filed out of the atrium. The Death King, however, didn't move—and neither did I. He didn't speak either, so I took that as an invitation to lean closer to him and whisper, "Thanks."

He didn't respond. The others continued to leave, even the members of the upper room, until it was just me and the Death King. When he remained silent, I turned to leave, too.

"Olivia."

I halted. "Yes?"

"I would like to make you an offer," said the Death King. "Join my four Elemental Soldiers as our fifth member."

"The Spirit Element." I tried the sound in my mouth. "Yeah, no thanks. I don't remember any lessons in spirit magic. I'm less than a novice."

"I could help you." His tone sounded almost… normal, and it hit me that he'd switched to his human face at some point. When had that happened?

Disbelief rose inside me. "Help me? You locked me in your jail and nearly had me killed."

He shook his head. "I have already explained that I regret the misunderstanding—"

"What you did to Brant was a hell of a lot more than a simple misunderstanding," I said. "Also, might I remind you that the Order forbids its members from using spirit magic in any capacity? I'd rather not lose any more memories, thanks. Or be stripped of my magic, like Mr Cobb."

Not that I'd be making a habit of using it, regardless. I had zero desire for my own soul to end up stored in an amulet, passed around like a toy. I wouldn't be powerless again, and I wouldn't submit to the King of Death after how he'd treated me.

"The Order isn't the place for someone like you," he said. "They fear spirit magic."

"And with good reason," I said. "Look at what it did to the Parallel during the spirit war. It's the reason your liches ended up trapped, too, isn't it?"

He was silent for a long moment. "The liches made their decision, and we stand by it. I would like you to do the same, especially if you're going to continue to befriend spirits and openly use your magic."

Dex? Did he know that I'd brought him back from death?

"I'll take it under advisement," I told him. "I never said I forgave the Order for what they did, but I can either play by their rules or never set foot in the Parallel again. If I join you, then I'll never see my friends on Earth again, either. The Order would probably put a warrant out against me, besides. I'm already on probation."

"I can erase your record," he said. "I can remove all black marks from your file so that your choice is not affected by the Order's decisions."

"You can't get my memories back, can you?" I was only half joking. I wasn't joining him, one way or another.

"No," he said. "That's not in the domain of spirit magic, I'm afraid."

"Worth a shot." I shrugged.

"So you won't consider my offer?"

"Nah, I don't want to live in the realm of the dead, thanks," I said. "This is my home. Earth."

With my friends. Even Brant, who had not been invited to the trial. He'd be waiting for me outside, yet part of me wanted to stay here stubbornly until the Death King left before I did.

Then again, that wasn't a fair contest. He could literally wait until the ends of the earth, after all.

"So be it." He extended a hand, holding out a muddy backpack. *My* backpack, which his people had ripped off me when I was in jail. My hand closed around the strap on autopilot, and he let go of it, striding around me.

While I was staring into the empty courtroom, lost for words, he vanished from sight. Heartbeat quickening, I opened the bag. The contents had seen better days, but on top of a pile of muddy clothes lay my lucky dice.

"What's he playing at?" I whispered, not expecting an answer. It was weird enough that he'd offered me a job, when I'd assumed that he'd never want to set eyes on me again. Even weirder was the fact that he'd actually shown up here today. He could have left the Order to convict Mr Cobb alone and cut me out of his life forever.

Was he afraid that I'd tell the Order that without his soul, he was powerless? That anyone who held his amulet could use his magic? If I were him, I'd want to ensure the official reports didn't contain any evidence of my weaknesses. It was nice to imagine he'd also wanted to ensure the Order wouldn't punish me, but I doubted so. His own misguided assumption that Mr Cobb was in the right had cost both of us, after all.

I entered the empty elevator and pressed the button for the ground floor. The doors slid closed, and I released a breath, some of the tension seeping out of me. I was alive. I'd refused a job offer from the Death King and walked away intact. My friends would be safe. And the Order… they'd spared me from any punishment. My record might not be squeaky-clean, but I wouldn't be spending an eternity in a cell.

Sure, there were a fair few people at the Order who'd like to see me locked up, and maybe more who'd like to exploit my newly rediscovered spirit magic. Including the Death King. He'd hinted he knew what I'd done to save Dex, and doubtless there was more he could teach me, but at the cost of never being able to come back here to Earth. Maybe my two worlds would eventually clash again, but I'd lived to face another day.

Oh, and I had my lucky dice back. That was always a bonus.

———

The D20 rolled to a stop, and I punched the air. "Natural twenty."

Devon grinned. "Your attack knocks the wight into a thousand pieces of bone."

"Nice," said Trix.

Devon presided over our D&D game with eager enthusiasm. While she'd sworn not to tell the rest of the group all the details of my eventful week, she and I had had an involved prep session rolling up stats for an evil Lich Lord who captured souls. Petty, maybe, but it wasn't like the Death King would have any idea.

Trix had reprised his position as the dwarven fighter who led our team into as many traps as he got us out of.

Red, a computer scientist in real life, played an elven cleric on a quest to prove her worth to her magically proficient family. She was the healer of the group, a necessity with a bunch of ragamuffins like us. At her side sat Craig He, who also worked in the Order's retrieval unit on the admin side, played a wizard gunslinger gnome on a quest for knowledge. His sister, Carla, played a half-elf warlock who'd made a deal with an interdimensional demon and sometimes randomly started reciting her grocery list in demon tongues. This proved helpful in battles, as you can imagine.

Everything was proceeding as usual, yet Brant hadn't shown his face. He'd come to visit me a couple of times since the trial, to tell me his earth mage friend had been assumed dead at the Death King's hands. Since he'd only been a temporary player who'd taken on the role of an NPC who'd joined the party temporarily, Devon pushed ahead with the game regardless.

The doorbell rang—*INCOMING!*

"That'll be our food," said Devon, rising to her feet.

I did, too, and walked behind her into the shop. Cold air blew in when Devon opened the door.

Brant stood on the doorstep. "Sorry, I got held up in the Parallel. Some vampires decided to ransack my house."

I hugged him. "Glad you could make it."

"As if I'd miss it," he said. "You started without me?"

"Devon insisted." I planted a kiss on his mouth. "She won't mind if we take a couple of minutes out."

"She looks like she might."

I released him and glanced over my shoulder, where

Devon was giving me a signalling look. "Yeah, we have a new part of the campaign lined up with an epic villain."

"Oh?" He closed the door behind him. "I'm guessing some of our adventures made it into the game?"

"You bet." I led the way into the back room and picked up the lovingly painted miniature of the evil Lich Lord. "I have a new character I think you'll all want to meet."

ABOUT THE AUTHOR

Emma is the New York Times and USA Today Bestselling author of the Changeling Chronicles urban fantasy series.

Emma spent her childhood creating imaginary worlds to compensate for a disappointingly average reality, so it was probably inevitable that she ended up writing fantasy novels. When she's not immersed in her own fictional universes, Emma can be found with her head in a book or wandering around the world in search of adventure.

Find out more about Emma's books at www.emmaladams.com.